*In an ancient Azteque temple,
a grotesque and . . .
heartless crime . . .*

Lord Darcy took out his flint and steel, and Master Sean his fire-wand, and they went around the room, lighting the lamps.

"My lord, I think you'd better come over here," Master Sean called. "I believe I have found the Prince's cloak."

Lord Darcy hurried over to where Master Sean stood. There, stretched between two pillars, lay the wool cloak. On it was resting the body of a man. From the waist up he was bare. There was a gaping hole in his chest where his heart had been . . .

"It's wonderful being back in Randall Garrett's universe again. More! More!"
—Christopher Stasheff, author of the WARLOCK series

RANDALL GARRETT'S LORD DARCY

— IN —

A STUDY IN SORCERY

BY MICHAEL KURLAND

ACE BOOKS, NEW YORK

This book is an Ace
original edition, and has never
been previously published.

A STUDY IN SORCERY

An Ace Book / published by arrangement with
the author

PRINTING HISTORY
Ace edition / June 1989

ISBN: 0-441-79092-5

Ace Books are published by The Berkley Publishing Group,
200 Madison Avenue, New York, New York 10016.
The name "ACE" and the "A" logo
are trademarks belonging to Charter Communications, Inc.

PRINTED IN THE UNITED STATES OF AMERICA

10 9 8 7 6 5 4 3 2 1

A STUDY
IN SORCERY

1

FOR PERHAPS THE thousandth time Colonel Hesparsyn cursed Lord Chiklquetl the Most High; but, as always, he did it silently. It would be horribly improper for a representative of John IV, King and Emperor, to offend an envoy of a foreign power. And it would be foolhardy for *anybody* to insult the *Mexicatl Teohuatzin,* the High Magician and Chief Under-Priest of the Azteque Empire.

The treaty party was, once again, stopped dead in its tracks. Once again Lord Chiklquetl was out of his palanquin and kneeling on the ground, his thick hardwood staff with its massive gold frog-shaped head thrust into the ground before him, his forehead pressed to the brown earth, listening with his inner ear to the messages of Tlaltecuhtli, God of the Earth. Once again the special platform carrying the Eternal Flame for the rededication ceremony was grounded by the twelve slaves on whose shoulders it rested, and the ten special Priests of the Flame were on the ground before it, performing the intricate Ritual of Tsaltsaluetol, God of Fire, to keep the Flame happy while it waited.

They were progressing slowly, with many stops, up the valley of the Pethmotho-kah-goh, the "Grandmother of Rivers"; the

1

local name for the great river that drained most of the New England continent into the Gulf of Mechicoe. At this rate, Colonel Hesparsyn thought, the treaty party and its accursed Eternal Flame would not make it to New Borkum until July. And Duke Charles would blame him. The Imperial Legion was supposed to get things done, regardless of odds, irrespective of difficulties, despite hardships. Their motto was "The Legion *Does*." But how to get an overcautious Azteque Chief Magician to keep to schedule when they didn't use the same clocks or the same calendar, he didn't know. The Azteques refused to ride horses, although they would use them as pack animals, and they couldn't use the wheel, which they regarded as sacred, and he couldn't start them moving or hurry them or do much but attempt to guard them as they moved grandly and slowly along.

Colonel Hesparsyn raised his hand, palm forward, and lowered it, and Company B of the Duke's Own dismounted. Get your men off their horses as often as possible; better for man and animal. Hesparsyn stayed on his mount for the moment, to get a better view of what was happening among the Azteque priesthood gathered in the center of his little caravan. At his signal, four mounted scouts moved off in four directions to keep an eye on their surroundings.

Lord Chiklquetl stood and raised his arms to the sun. Then he gestured behind him. The slaves lowered the other three palanquins to the ground, and three more high-ranking Azteque priest-magicians got out and gathered around their High Magician. Colonel Hesparsyn was not invited to join in their deliberations. They sniffed the ground, peered up to the sky, and did a complex little dance around the six-foot frog staff. The bloated golden frog atop the staff was clutching a large pink gem crystal between its tiny paws. While his priests danced, Lord Chiklquetl carefully placed a highly burnished copper shield on the frog's head. Blue smoke billowed in thick steady puffs from the frog's mouth and ears.

The double file of junior-grade priest-magicians flanking the palanquins stood stiff as statues in their red- and blue-trimmed white mantles, waiting for orders from their chief. They each carried a carefully rolled leather battle-pouch holding the complex stuff of which battle magic is made.

The files of warriors that surrounded the priestly contingent, their polished brass breastplates and shields gleaming in the afternoon sun, stayed on the alert, peering fiercely about them as they waited in place. Every warrior wore a bronze shortsword, hardened by the secrets of the priest-magicians to the equal of any steel blade; two out of three had six-foot brass-tipped fighting spears, while every third warrior carried a matchlock musket with a wide belled mouth, filled with black powder and three pounds of copper shot, each peanut-sized shot cast in the shape of one of the many Azteque gods of war and imbued with a potent spell.

For the Azteques, life appeared to be a very serious matter. In the four months Colonel Hesparsyn had been with them, he could not remember having seen an adult Azteque smile. Life for those tribes surrounding the Azteques could also be singularly devoid of humor. Although they had given up blood sacrifice a century ago, the Azteques still took slaves. And while being a slave to the Azteques, Colonel Hesparsyn reflected, was no longer like being a steer in a slaughterhouse, it was not significantly better than being an ox before the plow.

And there were always the recurring rumors that in some distant corners of their Empire the Azteque priests still practiced the blood sacrifice to Huitsilopochtli, ripping the hearts out of young slaves—and an occasional volunteer—to assure that the sun would rise tomorrow, and the grain would grow, and the Azteques would remain Lords of Creation, as they had been for the past eight hundred years.

Colonel Hesparsyn dismounted and led his horse to the rear of the column, signaling to his Company Magic Officer, Lieutenant MacPhearling, to join him. "What do you think?" he asked MacPhearling. "What's going on with them?"

The young Lieutenant, who held a journeyman rating in the Magician's Guild along with his military commission, turned to watch the gesticulating group of senior Azteque priests. "They're looking for the enemy," he said, calmly.

"What enemy?" Colonel Hesparsyn demanded.

"They are determined to find one," his Magic Officer said, running a finger along his carefully trimmed mustache. "I would say that most of the tribes whose territory we're passing through are more or less the Azteque's enemies."

The Colonel shook his head. "That's certainly so," he agreed. "But they seem to be overcautious to my way of thinking. For a people with such a sanguinary history—bloody destruction of hundreds of thousands of captives over hundreds of years—they certainly have grown cautious since they gave up blood sacrifice."

The copper shield quivered and shook and, with a high-pitched whistling sound, left the gold frog's head and rose slowly into the air, gathering speed as it went. It ascended in a perfectly straight line above the frog staff to a height of several hundred feet.

"You misunderstand the Azteque, sir," Lieutenant MacPhearling told his commander as they stared up at the copper oval, which glimmered a reddish rainbow in the rays of the late afternoon sun. "They are not being cautious through fear of the enemy. Indeed, I would not say they were being cautious at all. As you must realize, slowing down or stopping a march through enemy territory is not the way to avoid being attacked."

"That is certainly so," the Colonel agreed. "Just what I was thinking. I'd say they are wanting to be attacked. And here we are in the middle, as usual."

"Yes, sir," the Lieutenant said. "That's what it seems like. It's just an impression, you understand, sir, but to my mind they've been looking increasingly vexed as the days pass and no local tribe has pounced on them from the hills."

"Just so," Colonel Hesparsyn said, keeping his eyes on the small, bright object far over his head. The faint but clear whistle emanating from it rose and fell slightly like the warble of some steam-operated bird. Judging from the pattern of changing colors, it was spinning in place at the rate of roughly one revolution every five or six seconds. "That thing up there—it's some sort of scryer, is it not?" he asked his Magic Officer.

"Well—" The Lieutenant paused thoughtfully, trying to decide the level of magical definition that his commander was seeking. "Yes," he said after the moment's reflection. "In a rough, offhand way, I'd say so. That is, it's providing one of those priests—I should think Lord Chiklquetl himself—with an overhead view of the surroundings. The image is contained in the crystal between the frog's paws."

"I wonder what he sees," Colonel Hesparsyn said. "You have your spells out, do you get any impression of—anything?"

"No, sir," the Magic Officer said. "But you realize that, in that regard, I have an interesting problem. Most of the spells we use to protect the troop against surprise attack are set to register hostile intent. And they do that, very well."

"So?" the Colonel said. "It's not usual to attack someone without first generating some hostile intent—or so I should think."

"That's so, sir, as you say—usually. But in this case none of the local tribes have any hostile intent against *us,* if I may say so. We're on very good terms with the Tunica, the Choctaw, the Quapaw, and the Osage. But I fear they will go through us, if they have to, to get to the Azteques."

"Then why, would you say, haven't we yet been attacked?"

"I'd say they're gathering, sir. I think we will be, and sometime soon."

The Colonel nodded. "That's what the scouts think," he said. "We've passed through several of the hunting and camping areas where we would expect to find one tribe or another at this time of year, and yet we haven't seen a single native encampment. It's not natural. And to my mind, what's not natural is artificial."

"Then you agree, sir?"

"Yes, Lieutenant MacPhearling, we're going to get it. And, as you say, sometime soon. More than that, Lieutenant, they've been forewarned. The local tribes are gathering to hit us a good one; and they knew we were coming."

"Forewarned?"

"Certainly. That's the only story to be read from the absence of a single hunting party along our route."

"We have seen a few hunters."

"And they've seen us. Scouts to mark our route. Lieutenant, you'd better get ready whatever magic you have in that bag of yours, because I think we're going to be needing it before too long. It's an interesting problem we have before us."

"What's that, sir?"

"We are charged with the mission of protecting this treaty party, are we not? And they're about to be attacked, I believe, by a group of tribes friendly to the Angevin Empire. Tribes who have somehow been both warned of the Azteque party's presence on their land, and provoked into doing something about it."

The whistling slowly lowered in pitch, and the copper shield spiraled gently to the ground, where one of the under-priests ran out to retrieve it. Lord Chiklquetl spread his arms and chanted a high-pitched, rapid iteration of syllables that was soon picked up by the other high priests, and then the junior-grade priests, until it filled the air with the shrill, irritating noise.

All at once the chanting stopped as if it were cut off with a switch. Lord Chiklquetl spoke a few words to one of his under-priests, who turned and relayed the message, in a clear, reverberant voice, to the Azteque assemblage. The warriors crossed their legs and sat where they had stood. One of the under-priests trotted back to where Colonel Hesparsyn was standing. "We stay here," he said, in his guttural approximation of Anglic, "for the night."

The Colonel shrugged. He had tried arguing this one before. Where Lord Chiklquetl wanted to stop, they stopped.

The slaves put down their packs and began unloading the pack horses. In ten minutes the cooking fires would be going, the big pots of maize would be suspended over them, and preparations for the night's encampment would be well underway.

Colonel Hesparsyn called his Company Sergeant over. "That's it for the day's travel, Sergeant Tavis," he said, "Settle the men down and start dinner. Post double pickets all night, and put it in the standing orders that I want to be informed immediately if anything happens. *Anything.*"

"Yes, sir," Sergeant Tavis said, "right away, sir." He saluted and trotted off.

"Tell me, Lieutenant," Colonel Hesparsyn asked his Magic Officer, "who has the stronger magic, or the better spells, or however you would put it; us or them?"

"You mean the Azteques, sir?" the Lieutenant asked. "It can't be answered that easily. Lord Chiklquetl is certainly more proficient than I am; I'm only a journeyman. But their magic is based upon such different premises, we'd have to go head-to-head to find out. That is, one of our Masters would. In the long run our magic is superior, as was proven in the Battle of the Three Prisoners two hundred years ago. Sommerson and Master Methuane and the King's Hundred stopped the Azteque battle magicians cold. It was that which caused the Azteque priests to give up human sacrifice: They saw that we got better results without it. And in practical magic, results are all. But comparisons are difficult, sir."

"What's the difference?" Colonel Hesparsyn asked. "I thought magic was magic."

"At home it is, sir," Lieutenant MacPhearling explained. "But here they started from a different place. Their primary god was

Huitsilopochtli, a Sun god. And one of their primary duties was to keep him fed. Which, as he only ate human blood, caused some rather strange—bizarre even, from our point of view—customs to develop. Their whole magic, you see, is based upon blood sacrifice."

"I thought they didn't do that anymore."

"They don't sacrifice people any longer, at least not in public, but they do sacrifice blood. Their own blood. And blood is a very powerful symbol."

"Symbol, hell!" Colonel Hesparsyn said. "You mean they cut themselves up?"

Lieutenant MacPhearling nodded. "They draw blood from their own ears, cheeks, shoulders, chest, and thighs. It's part of the ritual for most of their more important spells and sorceries."

"Sounds like black magic to me," Colonel Hesparsyn said, staring off at the cluster of Azteque high priests.

"Magic, you will remember, is largely a matter of intent," his Magic Officer told him. "In the Angevin Empire such magic would be of the blackest black. The sort that destroys the magician as well as his object. But here the history is different, the background is different, and the intent is different. I don't know for certain what would encompass black magic here. And you know, Colonel, I don't think I want to find out."

Company B of the Duke's Own settled down for the night, a little behind and to the left of the Azteque encampment. The two didn't mix at all. Not that the Azteque warriors objected to an Angevin trooper being among them, not at all. They appeared not to notice it. And being ignored is a hard way to strike up an acquaintance. Hesparsyn's men, who were trained and encouraged to make friends with the natives wherever they were, had shown small interest in befriending any of the company of Azteques, who were as alike and self-contained as peas in a pod. Fierce, stubborn, unyielding peas in a bloody pod, Colonel Hesparsyn thought.

The Colonel sat at the small, portable travel desk in his small, portable command tent and composed his daily report by the bright light of his small, portable alcohol lamp. The lamp's mantle had been treated magically to glow pure white in the alcohol flame. It burned out twice as fast, but gave three times the light of untreated mantles.

Hesparsyn had just written, "and, therefore, I strongly suspect the possibility of hostile action from the local tribes, although we have thus far seen no signs of them," when an arrow thunked into the desk top, four inches from his hand.

The Colonel leapt to his feet, pulling his Legion-issue MacGregor .36 from its holster, and raced outside. Dusk had passed into night, and the only light came from the stars and the three small campfires used by his men. There was no way to see anything beyond. Hesparsyn stood there for a minute, looking and listening; but all was silent beyond the campfires.

The guard outside his tent was standing at easy attention. "I take it you didn't see anything?" Hesparsyn asked him.

"Like what, sir?" the guard asked.

"Never mind," Colonel Hesparsyn said. "Pass the word for Lieutenant MacPhearling and for the Top Sergeant." He turned to look back at his command tent, and realized what a fine target it made, with the intense white light from the magicked alcohol lamp spilling out of the open flap. The tent canvas itself was treated not to allow any light to filter through, so Hesparsyn would just have to remember to keep the flap closed in the future.

Lieutenant MacPhearling came running along the row of sleeping tents, struggling to button his trowsers as he ran. As he reached the command tent, Sergeant Tavis appeared from the other side and walked calmly to the entrance, looking as though he were dressed for parade.

"Sir!" Sergeant Tavis snapped, coming to attention and saluting at the tent flap.

"What is it, Colonel?" Lieutenant MacPhearling asked, pulling himself to something resembling attention and managing a hasty salute.

Colonel Hesparsyn returned the salutes and beckoned to the two men. "Here," he said. "Look what I just, ah, received."

They stepped inside the tent and Colonel Hesparsyn pointed to the foreign object protruding from his travel desk.

Sergeant Tavis reached over and pulled it out. "It's Quapaw, sir," he said. "A Quapaw message arrow."

"It was shot into my desk," Colonel Hesparsyn said. "Four inches to the right, and it would have pierced my hand. We must find some way of discouraging them from sending messages in a like manner in the future. Lieutenant MacPhearling, is the avoidance spell around the camp not working?"

"It is working well, sir," the Magic Officer said. "My guess would be that this arrow was shot from beyond the effective range of the spell."

"I see," the Colonel said. "Can we not extend the effective range of the spell until it is beyond the effective range of Quapaw arrows?"

"No, sir," Lieutenant MacPhearling said. "Not easily. Not for an overnight encampment. Not with only one journeyman magician as Company Magic Officer, we can't."

"I see," Colonel Hesparsyn said. "Sergeant, would you unroll the message from around the arrow and let me take a look at it?"

The Sergeant broke the threads holding the message in place and unrolled it. It was a sheet of thin paper, that looked to be of European manufacture, in the standard six-by-eight-inch letter size. Sergeant Tavis straightened it by rubbing it against the side of the desk, and handed it to Colonel Hesparsyn.

"A printed letterhead," Colonel Hesparsyn noted. He read:

HE-WHO-LAUGHS-LAST, M.A., O.A.E.
CHIEF OF THE RULING COUNCIL
OSAGE TRIBE

to The Honorable Colonel-Commander Hesparsyn
   Company B of the Duke's Own New England Regiment
   The Angevin Imperial Legion
I bring you greeting.

We intend to attack the accursed Azteque horde at some moment in the immediate future.

As we bear you and your magnificent company of legionaries no ill will, we strongly suggest that you leave the area so that we are not required to kill or injure any of you.

If you choose not to, we will understand, but it is on your heads.

No Azteque warrior will again take prisoners from our peoples, for as long as the grass grows and the water flows. We have sworn it.

In hopes that this finds you in good health, I remain yours,
                             Laughs-Last

"What do you think about that?" Colonel Hesparsyn asked, passing it to his Magic Officer.

"Well-educated chap, I'd say," Lieutenant MacPhearling replied.

2

THE GUARD PATROLLING Fort St. Michael's upper battlements paused to study the tall, lonely figure who stood watching the bay. By the man's robes, the guard knew him to be a priest. By his careworn face, the guard judged him to be in his early sixties. In this the guard was mistaken. Father Adamsus was in his fifty-second year and—considering some of the hardships he had endured—in remarkably good health.

One cannot, however, deal with Those whom Father Adamsus had confronted without having the experience leave its mark. Father Adamsus was an exorcist.

In his fifteen years on this lonely path he had faced many Intelligences, many Entities and Powers. Some of these had been victims themselves, tools in thrall to a human sorcerer's twisted Talent. Others had also been tools, but not, Father Adamsus knew, of anything human or angelic. Such creatures served their Master well, each in its own malevolent fashion. Father Adamsus had fought these evil beings many times in the shadowland of ritual sorcery and each time had vanquished them, banishing them from the person or place where they had been uninvited and unwelcome tenants.

He had not—indeed could not have—destroyed them; a mortal cannot destroy the immortal. Had he ever failed to vanquish them, however, he knew all too well that the Law did not operate in reverse. They might well have destroyed him.

And death, of course, would be only the beginning.

Father Adamsus leaned against the crenelated battlement wall of the South Tower, feeling the cold of the stone seep through his robes, and looked again out across the great bay. It was almost barren of ships, which was perhaps not surprising given the violent March weather, and a faint mist moved above the water in rapid swirls. Still, from this vantage point at the southern tip of long, thin Saytchem Island, one could easily see the small island far out in the bay, and the massive structure which covered its entire surface.

This was an ancient Azteque pyramid of staggering dimensions; Father Adamsus had seen only one that was larger, at Tenochti-tlan, the great city in the Duchy of Mechicoe, historic capital of the Azteque Empire. He had been there four years ago, as part of the royal ambassadorial retinue of His Majesty, John IV, by the Grace of God, King and Emperor of England, France, Scotland, Ireland, New England, and New France; *Fidel Defensor*; and present occupant of the eight-hundred-year-old Plantagenet throne.

During that visit to Tenochtitlan, Father Adamsus had stood at the base of that great pyramid as others of the ambassador's party had blithely ascended the great stone stairs. None of the others, of course, were sensitives, which was probably for the best, as they were all career politicians and courtiers. The priest, however, was a sensitive of the first rank, a basic requirement for an exorcist. Thus, he could see a world far different from that seen by the normally sighted.

And he saw *blood*.

The pyramid had appeared to him a crimson abattoir, a giant staircase awash with carnage. The image had been a phantom overlay on the "real" world, and had it been only visual he might have endured it; but he had heard the screams, he had smelt the . . . burning . . . and he had sensed, as though it were his own, the terror and agony of centuries of sacrificial victims.

It had taken all his concentration to get through the simple shielding ritual, and even then, the impressions had not entirely vanished but had seemed to continue, like a conflict vaguely heard through the stone walls of a fortress.

His own stupidity had caused it, Father Adamsus had realized in annoyance. He knew that no human sacrifice had taken place at the pyramid for over two centuries, since the Azteque priests—partly of their own volition and partly under the benevolent guidance of the Angevin Empire's legionnaires and its Catholic missionaries—had given up their bloodier gods in favor of a more pacifistic pantheon. He knew too that three generations of priests had blessed the site and conducted purifying rituals. Still, one cannot always scrub the stain of blood from stone; sometimes the stone must be ground down. Sometimes it must be reduced to powder and scattered to the winds.

Little hope of that happening in this case, thought Father Adamsus. He stared out at the massive pyramid on the small island on the right-hand side of the harbor. It was a solid pile of granite topped by twin temples. One of those temples, the larger one, was consecrated to the bloodiest god yet invented in the long human history of bloody gods. The pyramid had lain in disuse for five centuries, since the fullest expansion of the Azteque Empire had begun its inevitable contraction to its natural boundaries.

Now, however, it was to be used again.

Probably no more than a few hundred miles away now, a treaty party was heading toward Nova Eboracum, the Royal Colony at the center of the settlement in the south-central part of Saytchem Island. In this party, Father Adamsus knew, was Lord Chiklquetl, the High Priest of the Azteques. As part of the treaty-signing ceremonies, an Eternal Flame would be kindled in the pyramid's other temple, the one dedicated to Tsaltsaluetol, a more peaceful god than his companion on the island. The Eternal Flame would be lighted with a flame from the pyramid in Tenochtitlan, carried from there by the High Priest. *And I would dearly love to know who thought of THAT little touch,* thought Father Adamsus with very unpriestly anger; certainly it wasn't a priest or any licensed member of the Sorcerers' Guild, who would have as soon suggested spit-roasting a joint of meat next door to a munitions room.

But it will be done, which means that Lord John and I must to go out to Pyramid Island tomorrow and cleanse that pile of stone; make it into nothing more than the empty, long-deserted stone structure it seems to be. If we can.

Father Adamsus was by no means certain that this could be accomplished; he had said as much to the Archbishop not twenty-four hours earlier. "This is not a simple cleansing, Your Grace," he had pointed out. "Such a technique is effective in purifying a structure that has been used for evil purposes, even if that evil has extended over a long period of time.

"But *that*"— Father Adamsus had pointed a finger out into the lowering mist beyond the great mullioned window set into the south wall of St. Brigid's Cathedral —"that thing out there was not simply a vessel which once held an unhealthy drink. It was *made* for evil. Every stone was set upon the one beneath it, with that thought and that purpose. The main temple was originally consecrated—if I may use that holy word in such a diabolic sense—to Huitsilopochtli; who was—and is, in some areas of Mechicoe today—a god of war, murder, and hatred. I am an exorcist, and a priest, and will do as I have been directed. It is my duty, however, to point out that the Rite of Exorcism removes a Being from a place to which it has no right. It is not intended to throw a god out of his own house."

"Are you saying," Archbishop Patrique had inquired, "that you can't do it?" His Grace forbore from mentioning that Father Adamsus had overstated the case in at least one particular; no one—not even the Holy Father—could *order* an exorcist to his task. In the exercise of religious—or secular—authority, one might risk another man's life, but never his immortal soul.

Now, standing on the parapet at Fort St. Michael, Father Adamsus recalled his reply. *No*, he had said, *not that I can't do it, with the help of Lord John. Only that in this case, it might not be enough. Whatever malevolent Being lurks in there will be driven out. But we shall have to stay alert for a long time. You see, Your Grace, it just might come home again.*

Rapid footsteps approached, a sharp staccato sound echoing off the stone. "Reverend Father?"

It was the guard. A young man not yet twenty, he wore the green-and-azure uniform of the Duke's Guard, and owed his allegiance to His Grace Charles, Duke of Arc, Imperial Governor of New England.

"Yes? What is it, my son?"

"A message just came over the speaking-tube, Reverend Father. There's a teleson call for you, from the Residence."

Father Adamsus could hear the capitalized *R* plainly, and knew that it could refer to only one residence—the palace of Duke Charles. "You'll have to lead the way. I'm not as familiar with Fort St. Michael as I'd like to be."

"Of course, Reverend Father. Just one minute."

After whistling down the brass speaking-tube for the guardhouse to send up a replacement, and receiving permission to leave his post before the replacement arrived, the young guard led Father Adamsus down through a maze of corridors and stairways, past torches flickering in sconces—only the Palace had gas lighting, as yet—and woven hangings, which did little to lessen the March chill.

As they made their way, Father Adamsus found himself brooding about the teleson. He had hoped he could be alone with his thoughts for a while longer, and had come down to Fort St. Michael at least in part for that reason. On reflection, he realized that a strategic outpost such as the Fort, with its view—and its guns—commanding a sweep of the bay and the narrows leading to the ocean beyond, would undoubtedly have the device. Instant communication with the Palace would not be a luxury but a necessity.

For many years telesons had been something of a rarity. The devices, which consisted of two cuplike shapes attached to a small wooden box, operated on principles not entirely clear even to the best theoretical thaumaturgists. Once the proper spell had been put on the crystals within the teleson, anyone could use it; you simply held one of the cups to your ear and spoke into the other one.

The spell for activating a pair of telesons, however, was not only intricate and difficult but had a tendency to wear out over a period of time. The expense had made the device affordable only for a privileged few.

But recently a new version of the device had been perfected by Sir Thomas Leseaux, Th.D., the Chief Theoretical Sorcerer in all the Angevin Empire. Sir Thomas had replaced the paired crystals with thin disks, almost membranous in consistency. A simple melding of a Relevancy Spell with a standard Sympathy Ritual would cause two disks connected by any length of symbolic copper wire to vibrate in unison, no matter how far apart they might be (as long as the wire did not pass through or over running water; no spell will operate with such a barrier). One spoke into the speaking tube of one teleson, and this caused the disk to vibrate; the disk in the earpiece of the other teleson vibrated in precisely the same fashion, reproducing the sounds clearly if not absolutely faithfully. Preparation of the telesons was simple for any skilled artificer, and even a journeyman sorcerer could master the elegantly simple activation ritual Sir Thomas had devised.

And they all will, thought Father Adamsus gloomily as he trudged along. Well, you couldn't stop progress, so they said. Before long, telesons would be everywhere, and most people would find them a wonderful convenience. It would be difficult to explain to such people that so convenient a device might have drawbacks, that the loss might offset the gain.

Sorcery, thought Father Adamsus, *is moving ahead too fast. Why can't we think about these things a little more before we do them?*

Presently the two men arrived at a paneled oak door just opposite the Gate Room. As nearly as Father Adamsus could tell, their journey had taken them to a point less than a hundred feet from their starting point. That starting point was, however, now directly overhead.

The door guard opened it for Father Adamsus, and the priest peered into a small windowless room. His guide hastened into the Gate Room opposite, and brought forth a spirit lantern, placing it in a wall bracket in the room. By its steady flame, Father Adamsus saw a small unadorned chair and table. On the table rested the teleson: a polished wooden box with what looked like a black caffe cup to speak into and a black wineglass to hold to one's ear. A small silver bell was provided to attract the attention of the person possessing the companion teleson.

Its own little room, Father Adamsus thought, *how nice.*

He picked up the teleson and spoke into it. "This is Father Adamsus." Many times he had used the devices, particularly during his long years in England and France; but he could never escape a slight feeling of foolishness at speaking aloud into a caffe cup.

"Lord John Quetzal here, Reverend Father." Lord John spoke perfect Anglic without any detectable Mechicain accent; he had been schooled in it from his youth in his native duchy, and had perfected it in London during the years he spent studying for his Master's in Sorcery.

Father Adamsus smiled wryly. "How did you know I was here, Your Lordship?"

"I deduced it."

"Really?" Father Adamsus was both curious and amused by the answer. "And just how did you deduce it?"

"Simple, really." Lord John was enjoying himself. "When I stopped by your apartment in the palace and found you gone, I noted that you had taken your heaviest cloak. It's chilly out, but not *that* chilly simply for travel, particularly as the priestly changeover from winter woolen to spring cotton is still six weeks off in this parish. So clearly you planned to be outdoors for some time. I checked with the seneschal and learned that you'd left without leaving any word of your destination. Most uncharacteristic of you; obviously you wanted to be alone."

"Hmm, yes," Father Adamsus agreed. "That's very good, so far."

"Well. You wanted to be by yourself, no doubt to think about our—project—tomorrow, and you expected to be outside in a place where it might be colder than usual. There are a few good possibilities, but only one of them has a view of the temple of Huitsilopochtli. *Quod erat demonstrandum.*"

Father Adamsus laughed, for the first time that day. "When I first met you in London, I remember you were a fresh young journeyman sorcerer with a burning ambition to become a Master Forensic Sorcerer like Master Sean O Lochlainn. Now that you have achieved that goal, it would seem that you're planning to become a master of deduction as well, like Master Sean's associate, Lord Darcy."

Lord John Quetzal laughed in turn. "Good heavens, Father, please don't ever say that to Lord Darcy, or Master Sean either for that matter. I have a long way to go before I even begin to match Master Sean in his forensic skills. I wouldn't want him to think I have pretensions of adequacy as a forensic sorcerer. And as for Lord Darcy, Heaven alone knows where he gets his miraculous deductive power. It certainly isn't magic, at least none that I've ever been taught."

"Your secret is safe with me, Your Lordship. Now I'll do a bit of deducing of my own. Something's up, and it must be fairly troublesome. You'd not have disturbed me otherwise, knowing I wished for a bit of solitude."

"Indeed, Reverend Father. If you'll forgive my interrupting you, I would like to see you before we retire tonight. I shall await you in my chambers. We've got problems. *More* problems."

"I'll start back now," Father Adamsus said.

• • •

Lord John Quetzal slowly paced the floor of his apartment in the west wing of the Palace. It was not an expression of impatience, for master sorcerers tend not to indulge in unproductive emotions. He simply found that he thought better when he was moving, and at the moment he had a good deal of thinking to do.

Having been raised in the surroundings of a ducal palace, and then having undergone most of his magical training in London— where the doings of King and Parliament were the lifeblood of society, both high and low—Lord John was resigned to the way politics permeated all activities above a certain level. Too, since the treaty signing was nothing if not political, one could expect more than the usual bureaucratic interference with one's work.

But why *this*? What earthly (or other, he thought wryly) purpose could be served by having a royal envoy standing around watching while he and Father Adamsus did their difficult and demanding work? The Count was not a sorcerer; indeed he had no magical training at all. Further, he was not a sensitive. So—he couldn't help, couldn't really sense anything; he would just be in the way, and possibly in danger if there was anything nasty in the residual psychic forces up there. And there would be hardly anything for the Count to see, and precious little that he would understand of what happened. Why was it necessary for him to be present? What did whoever was sending him think that he *might* see?

Lord John paused for a moment, staring at himself in the huge gilt-frame mirror that took up half the space of one of the sitting room walls. He had already dressed for dinner, in the two-piece blue and silver garment that was the dress suit of the master sorcerer. The colors were a striking contrast to the dark reddish-brown of his face. Beneath the shock of black hair the almost-as-dark eyes contemplated their reflection without enthusiasm.

There was, Lord John had to admit to himself, nothing really *wrong* with the Count de Maisvin. That went without saying, else the man would hardly have been an imperial envoy. To work directly for His Sovereign Majesty John IV was an honor, and a trust, given to few.

True, de Maisvin did have a strange air about him, a sense of watchfulness, and yet of distance and remoteness—but with the responsibilities he had to bear, this was hardly surprising. Lord

John had met him only briefly, at a reception earlier in the day, and his immediate impression of the Count was of someone thoughtful, dedicated, and serious.

Lord John stopped pacing.

There *was* something wrong here. Something his subconscious was trying to tell him. But it was probably not about the Count. He had no logical reason to suppose that de Maisvin would be any trouble at all tomorrow, not from his reading of the man. As for the presence of an outsider at a ritual, that had been a healthy part of Lord John's conditions of training, for one rarely if ever has the luxury of solitude for ritual work while investigating a crime. It would be more of a problem for Father Adamsus, who could not afford to be distracted while performing the actual exorcism.

But the Count, as a King's man, must be both highly intelligent and highly motivated; he should be amenable to reason. Especially when it was pointed out that what might be distracting to Father Adamsus could prove fatal to those around him. Between them tonight, he and Father Adamsus would make ritual provisions to reduce any chance of danger to the Count—or themselves—limiting de Maisvin's presence to a mere annoyance.

So what is bothering me? Could it be—?

There was a rapping at the open door, and Lord John looked up to see Father Adamsus.

"You made excellent time, Father."

Father Adamsus shrugged off his heavy woolen cape and draped it over a chair near the fireplace. "The master of the guard was kind enough to lend me a horse. Had I used the carriage, with the condition the roads are in, I'd have arrived barely in time to leave again."

Lord John frowned. "Isn't that road paved? I thought—"

"I keep forgetting you've not been here very long. Yes, the Great Way *is* paved, but it only extends from the north end of Saytchem to the Palace and into Nova Eboracum—or, as the locals call it, New Borkum—proper. Just south of town it turns into what is in the summer the dustiest road in the Empire, and at the moment a very shallow canal with a slight crusting of ice."

The Mechicain sorcerer laughed. "You sound like you're in no better a mood that I am. We really don't seem to be looking forward to our job tomorrow, do we?"

Father Adamsus regarded him narrowly for a moment. "No,"

he said after a pause, "we don't. You, for your own private reasons, and I for mine."

"Father—"

The priest held up a hand. "Understand; I don't mean that critically at all. I know part of what's been bothering you—you keep getting caught up in the fact that it was your own ancestors who built those pyramids, who created the atmosphere of evil it will be our job to disperse."

Lord John smiled ruefully. "You have me there, Father; that's precisely what I was thinking. And who should know better than you?"

"One hardly has to be a sensitive to see what's on your mind, John. Let me see if I can't provide a somewhat different viewpoint on it. Do you remember your First Proposition?"

"I think so." Lord John smiled. The Nine Propositions were the first things the fledgling sorcerer had to learn. *"Magic is the art of causing change in accordance with the will."*

"Indeed; and the important word for us now is *will*." Not, you notice, nature. Magic has little interest in what you are, only in what you *do*. We do not choose—as far as we know—our situation of birth; we do have free will to make of that situation what we will." Father Adamsus paused, struck by a memory. "One time, oh, it must have been a dozen years ago, it happened that I was in conversation with His Majesty—it was to do with the problem of the St. Arthur gargoyles, do you recall? No matter—anyway, I said something to him about how proud he must be to bear the Plantagenet name. He looked at me for a moment in a disappointed way and said, 'I try not to be. I had no say in my being born with this name. If I do have pride—and I do, probably to a sinful degree—it is that, insofar as I can tell, I have been lucky in my advisors. But then, if I get to feeling smug, the row of Plantagenets stare down at me from the Palace wall, and I am reminded of what others with that name have done, and I am again humble. And then I pray that I may continue to do my best, and that I am judged by no greater standard than that I did my best. I would hope to do no less had I been born into a family of coopers or draymen.' "

Lord John Quetzal stared into the glowing embers in the fireplace for several seconds. Presently he said, "The King is as wise as I am foolish."

"Don't be so hard on yourself, Your Lordship. You're certainly not the only man who has ever brooded on the eve of a difficult task. Not even the only man in this room."

This drew a smile without shadow from Lord John.

"Now," continued Father Adamsus as he poured himself a small glass of xerez, "what's the rest of the trouble? Just what did I gallop through mud and rain to listen to?"

"You're right, of course," he said several minutes later, after Lord John had told him of their Imperial observer. "The King, probably through His Grace the Duke, must have some reason for requesting de Maisvin's presence; a reason that His Majesty doesn't feel it necessary to burden us with. It's just one of those things one has to contend with, but I share your misgivings. Like you, I don't really foresee any great difficulties; we'll be using fairly standard rituals all the way through. But—also like you—I am not entirely comfortable about our task, and the presence of Count de Maisvin is just one more thing to think about. We would be responsible if anything were to happen to him."

"That had occurred to me," Lord John said. "Have you met the Count?"

"No," said Father Adamsus. "I haven't. And, uncharitable as it may sound, at the moment I don't particularly want to. Tomorrow will be soon enough."

3

THE ICY WIND whipped across the bow of the small cutter; above Lord John's head the new heavy canvas sails creaked in a random pattern of small whipcrack sounds.

Against all odds, the dawn was bright and clear. More than that; the sun shone down with a brilliance almost unnatural, turning the choppy water of the bay into countless blinding mirrors. Lord John hugged the slick mahogany rail and found himself thinking about the weather.

Any other time I'd be pleased if the rain stopped, especially when I had outdoor work to do.

Then:

Huitsilopochtli is a Sun god.

It was silly; it was absurd. If it *had* been raining, Lord John thought, I'd have found some sort of omen in that. *I'm going to have to pull myself together.*

He retreated toward the warmth of the small cabin. With his hand on the brass turnlatch, he stopped and looked at the commanding figure standing alone at the very front of the foredeck.

Count Maximilian de Maisvin was of no more than average height, but he somehow gave the impression of being a tall man. It was perhaps partly in the ramrod-straight posture, but to a far greater degree it was sheer force of personality, a force which could be sensed even when, as now, de Maisvin was paying attention to naught but the approaching island.

The Count's face was striking in appearance: deep-set dark eyes, a hawklike nose above a cruel mouth, a small, carefully tended black goatee. Most striking of all, however, was the blue-black mane of hair, far richer than Lord John's own, which fell to his shoulders and which sat above the broad forehead in a pronounced widow's peak.

His clothes were of a severe, almost formal, cut—and they were all black—from the silk neckcloth to the polished boots. Three touches of silver offset the black: the Imperial insignia on the coat lapel, the massive finger-ring set with a huge black pearl, and the .40 caliber MacGregor revolver in the tooled pigskin holster at his hip.

Lord John knew that the revolver was a special one; the engraved crest—the lions of England quartering the lilies of France—showed it to be a personal gift of His Majesty John IV. MacGregor & Sons only made the .40 caliber weapons for His Majesty to bestow as favors, and each bullet was hand-loaded in the company's Selkirk factory.

Lord Darcy, who also had such a weapon, had told Lord John that the King did not intend these gifts merely as presentation pieces, but as tools to be used. All the MacGregor skill went into crafting the weapons, which were dead-accurate man-stoppers. Those few who possessed them wore them proudly—and used them well.

Lord John stepped inside the cabin. At a table sat Father Adamsus, warming his hands with a mug of steaming caffe. He looked up.

"How's our friend doing?"

Lord John glanced out the forward porthole. "He seems as unhappy to be here as we are. He barely made it to the dock before we sailed, and since boarding he hasn't said more than ten words."

Father Adamsus frowned. "He shows good sense. No one with a choice would be out here now. Did he tell you why he has come along?"

"The Duke commanded it. And de Maisvin is subject to the Duke's commands. But for no stronger motive than ducal anxiety, apparently. D'Arc is very concerned that all goes well with the various ceremonies, so I suppose he wants personal reports about everything, preferably from a disinterested party."

Father Adamsus grinned, surprising even himself. "At the moment, he looks very disinterested indeed." After a pause, he continued, "How can he stay out there without a cloak? Doesn't he feel the cold?"

"He doesn't seem to. But—" Lord John glanced again out the port, "—you can ask him yourself. Here he comes."

Count de Maisvin stepped inside and carefully latched the door behind him. He did not shake, nor shiver; for all the effect it seemed to have on him, the weather outside might have been that of high summer. Pouring himself a mug of caffe, he turned to face the priest and the sorcerer.

"Sorry we didn't have an opportunity for more than brief greetings at dockside," he said. His voice was deep and resonant. "Of course I imagine we've all had a great deal on our minds." He paused for a long moment and gazed at each man in turn with a curious, intent expression. "I do know what you're thinking—not, I hasten to add, in a literal way; I'm not a sensitive, Father—and believe me, I will stay out of your way completely. When a magician knows what he's doing, I am quite content to just stand there quietly and watch."

Lord John couldn't resist the opening. "And when a magician doesn't know what he's doing?"

"Then," responded de Maisvin as he took a sip from the steaming mug, "I don't want to be anywhere in the vicinity."

The three men paused at the top of the long wooden staircase that led from the pier, and gazed at the pyramid before them.

They were alone on the island. Father Adamsus had been prepared to insist that the captain and his crew of four stay aboard the cutter, but this had turned out to be unnecessary; the sailors had no intention whatever of setting foot on the island, and the captain had made it clear that the sooner the landing party's task could be completed and departure could be made, the happier he would be.

The gray-and-white stones of the pyramid shone brightly in the intense sunlight. For a structure five centuries old, subjected to the extremes of weather on New England's Atlantic coast, it appeared remarkably undamaged. In fact, with the exception of a few cracked stones here and there, it might almost have been built yesterday. Lord John realized that he had been carrying in his mind the image of a crumbling ruin, as the many pyramids he'd seen as a child had led him to expect. The weather conditions were certainly as severe here; perhaps the difference was in the northern granite. But it was unnerving; the pyramid looked new. It looked—ready to be used.

Father Adamsus found that he too was upset, in a paradoxical way. Because he wasn't.

He had prepared his shielding ritual as soon as they had stepped from the ship, before he had even ventured up the wooden steps. Even with such a shield, the sensitive can detect the presence of Entities, of psychic vibrations; it is the ravaging emotional content of such impressions that is screened out. So Father Adamsus had been prepared, and now, as they reached the foot of the pyramid, he sensed—

—nothing. Nothing at all.

Oh, there was the avoidance spell, put on by Angevin sorcerers to keep the unwary off the pyramid for the past century, but that was a familiar sensation and had no overtones of evil, for no evil was intended.

He tried to persuade himself to feel relieved about this development, about not having to deal with a psychic onslaught such as he had experienced at Tenochtitlan; but he could not. It was as strange as seeing someone stand in the sunlight and cast no shadow.

Even de Maisvin seemed to be affected by the place, saying nothing, but watching the other two men with an expression of doubtful concern on his face.

As they approached the stone steps the avoidance spell became stronger, which Father Adamsus found especially annoying as he didn't want to be there in the first place.

Lord John placed a small brass brazier from his sorcerer's bag on the first step and carefully set fire to the charcoal inside. It blazed up unnaturally fast, and then began glowing brightly. "This will take but a moment," he said. "The spell is a simple one." He poured some powders into his thurible and placed one of the glowing coals on top. As Lord John swung the thurible around his head, muttering some indistinct words to himself, it emitted green smoke from one side, and red from the other.

Suddenly, after two sharp words that sounded like Latin— although they were unfamiliar to Father Adamsus—the smoke ceased, the air cleared, and Father Adamsus no longer felt any more than his natural aversion to climbing the pyramid.

"I'll bring the brazier with me," Lord John said, picking it up gingerly by one of its tripod legs. "I'm going to need it in a minute. Let's go on up."

They mounted the central staircase, with Father Adamsus and Lord John in the lead and Count de Maisvin a few steps behind. About a third of the way up, Father Adamsus paused and looked at Lord John Quetzal with a questioning glance. Lord John shook his head.

"Nothing," he said. "Nothing at all."

By this he meant that there was no trace of the presence of black magic. That was Lord John Quetzal's very special gift, in addition to his Talent as a sorcerer. While not a sensitive, he was psychically attuned to sense the presence of magic that was used in evil or negative ways. Commonly known as "witch-smelling," it was a rare gift; of the psychic gifts, rarest of all but for precognition. It was the one of the reasons Lord John had been chosen for today's tasks.

Father Adamsus shook his head, puzzled. There should be *something* that one or the other of them could sense. With Lord John now preceding Father Adamsus, the three men resumed the climb toward the pair of temples that shared the top of the pyramid.

As they drew level with the temples, the psychic pressure Father Adamsus had been expecting finally made itself known. Yes; there was the sense of evil here, of blood and death. But again there was something wrong. What he sensed now was not the collective death agony of many, but of just one or two—a sudden, jolting shock, not that of a long-drawn-out torturous death. But none the less horrible for that.

And whatever he was sensing had not happened five centuries ago, or even five weeks ago. This was a horror that had happened within days—perhaps hours. "Do you sense it?" he asked Lord John Quetzal, realizing he was whispering.

Lord John looked puzzled. "Sense it? No. As I told you, there is no trace of sorcery used with evil intent here."

For the very briefest of moments Father Adamsus thought he might be losing his mind, but that thought vanished as an iron-hard determination took over. *I am not mistaken; there is death here. And if it is not magic, then it is something else.*

The right-hand temple, consecrated to Tsaltsaluetol, where the Eternal Flame would be rekindled, stood open and empty, its great wooden doors fore and aft swung wide, as they had been for the past week or so, awaiting the ritual cleansing and reconsecration by the Azteque priests. But the left-hand temple, formerly the home of Huitsilopochtli, bloody god of all bloody gods, was the object of their present interest. Its massive double doors were sealed with a heavy bronze lock, put into place a century before, along with the avoidance spell, to protect the interior of the temple from those strange sorts of people who would be attracted to a house of the Devil, even when the Devil was no longer in residence.

A wax seal impressed with the ducal arms was affixed over the keyhole. Father Adamsus had been given the huge key for the lock by Duke Charles himself, an hour before the boat had left the Palace dockyard. The seal and lock, however, were only the visible parts of the closure; a hermetic spell had also been placed on the door and lock, and this—if not removed—would prevent anyone from shifting the bronze wards inside the lock, with or without the key. According to the Palace records, this spell, like the one already removed, had been renewed eight times in the past century.

Father Adamsus examined the ducal seal. It was intact. Carefully peeling if off, he inserted the key in the lock and, experimentally, tried to turn it. It would not budge. He turned to Lord John Quetzal.

"It's all yours now."

Lord John nodded. He put down the brazier and took some small items from his sorcerer's bag. Dropping a small handful of some dark substance into the brazier atop the charcoal, he set it alight. As the plume of smoke began to rise, Lord John sprayed powder from a small insufflator onto the lock and key. Then, from a small phial, he sprinkled more of the same powder onto the burning brazier.

Immediately, the smoke turned a bright crimson, and now—instead of rising straight up until it was whipped away by the wind—it curved in toward the door and began to surround the lock and key with a rolling red cloud.

Lord John now took from the bag a small wand with a blue stone set into its tip. He held it in the stream of smoke for several seconds as his lips soundlessly formed strange words. Then he withdrew the wand from the smoke and held it horizontally by its center.

He twirled the wand between thumb and fingers. As he did so, the key rotated in the lock. There was a click from somewhere within the mechanism, and the door moved open slightly.

"Excellent," said Father Adamsus. He had become so involved in watching the young sorcerer at work that, for a few moments at least, he had been able to forget his greater problems. "Master Lord John, I've never seen it done better."

Lord John Quetzal almost blushed at the compliment. "You've never seen Master Sean O Lochlainn," he said. "He taught me that technique himself."

"Well. Shall we go in?"

Lord John nodded, and pulled the door fully open. The three men stepped in, and sunlight flooded in behind them to illuminate the temple interior. It might better have been left in darkness.

Father Adamsus stared bleakly at the scene before him, and found that he could not even be surprised. He knew that in some strange way he had expected this, or something like it, since the sensation he had experienced while mounting the steps. All he could feel was a tiredness, and exhaustion of the soul.

In the center of the temple was the *techcatl*, the great sacrificial altar stone, a nine-foot-long block of some white mineral. It was indelibly stained with the blood of centuries past.

On it lay a young man, no older than Lord John, and with skin of the same reddish-brown color. He had been stripped to the waist. On the stone, near the young man's head, lay an ornately-decorated knife of bone and obsidian, glinting in a random shaft of light. The obsidian blade was caked with dried blood.

There was a gaping hole in the man's upper torso, where the heart had been severed and ripped from the chest. The blood had stopped flowing from the horrible wound some time before, but to an experienced eye it was freshly dry. The man had been dead less than a day.

The heart was nowhere to be seen.

4

"LAND HO! TWO points off the starboard bow!"

At this call from the lookout in the crow's nest high above his head, Lord Norman Scrivener, one of the fourteen first-class passengers on H.I.M. Steam Packet *Aristotle*, poked his carefully shorn blond head into the first-class passengers' lounge and relayed the good word. "The fabled New World awaits us, my lords, gentlemen," he stated with evident relish. "And you too, my lady."

The slender man in the red cloak looked up from the book he was reading. "A quick passage," he said to his tubby companion. "We've been at sea barely a week. With any luck we'll be in port by nightfall."

His companion, who wore a black traveling-cloak over his brown workaday Master Sorcerer's robes, was concentrating on suspending a silver hoop and spindle in the air in front of him, with the spindle centered in the hoop. He relaxed his concentration and allowed the objects to drop to the table before him. "Aye, my lord," he said, gathering them up to put them in a small flannel bag. "And I hope we have that good fortune, for my stomach's sake."

"It has been a rough passage, Master Sean," Lord Darcy said sympathetically. "March is not the month I would pick for transiting the Atlantic."

"Nor I, my lord," Master Sean O Lochlainn, Chief Forensic Sorcerer to the Court of Chivalry, pointedly told his old friend, and superior, Lord Darcy, who was the Chief Investigator of that same Imperial court.

Lord Darcy raised an eyebrow. "Now, Master Sean," he said, "surely you cannot blame me for this hasty voyage. It was His Majesty's express wish that we conduct this investigation for him."

"Aye, my lord," Master Sean agreed. "And is it merely a coincidence that but two weeks ago Your Lordship was complaining to me about the dearth of interesting crimes anywhere in Europe? I recollect Your Lordship's very words. 'The European criminal today is sadly lacking in imagination,' Your Lordship said. 'There are no crimes of scope for the fine inquiring intellect to hone itself on. Merely an endless series of piddling problems.' "

"Did I say that?" Lord Darcy asked, amused.

"Yes, my lord. Word for word." Master Sean nodded. "And when Your Lordship tempts the fates like that, what can Your Lordship expect but to be flung across the ocean in mid-March to investigate a crime that's more to Your Lordship's liking?"

"Well, it was true," Lord Darcy said.

"The matter of the Comfiture Diamonds?" Master Sean asked.

"A simple task," Lord Darcy said, "once you understood the meaning of the footprints on the ceiling."

"The business with Lord Champhire and the trained pelicans?"

"An elementary exercise in deduction," Lord Darcy explained, taking a sip of his caffe.

"I found it compelling enough," Master Sean commented. "And, as I'm sure you remember, you had the excitement of a bullet from a .23 caliber Douglass-Bizet in your calf."

"Ah, yes," Lord Darcy said, rubbing his right leg reflexively with the memory. "But with all that, nothing to stimulate the intellect, Master Sean; and the intellect is all!"

"It was sufficiently stimulating for me," Master Sean insisted stubbornly.

"Ah, but there, my old friend, you see the difference between us," Lord Darcy said. "You are a master magician, and a creative forensic sorcerer. And thus the problem, for you, is in the objective evidence, the residue of facts left for magic to uncover and explain. It is, so to speak, Nature herself who is your antagonist, from whom you wrest her secrets. You are always expanding the bounds of magical knowledge with your experiments. Forensic magic is much more advanced today than it was twenty years ago, largely as a result of your work."

"Thank you, my lord," Master Sean said, his round face beaming with the unexpected compliment.

"But I have no body of knowledge to expand," Lord Darcy said, "except those skills of systematic thinking that enable me to develop an accurate image of an obscure crime from the few accidental and unintentional clues overlooked by the criminal. Rather as an osteomantic wizard is able to recreate a long extinct animal from its ossified lower jawbone, I must piece together the substance of a crime from a few overlooked bits of its skeleton. And to keep my problem-solving ability properly honed, I have a constant need for new, baffling problems to pit it against. I thirst after the obscure, Master Sean. The ordinary dulls my abilities; the bizarre, the grotesque, the utterly baffling—these provide the stimulation I need!"

"You may consider your skill merely systematic thinking, my lord," Master Sean said. "But, as I've often told you, there's more to it than that. You gather what facts you can, and then make a wild leap into the unknown, somehow landing squarely on the truth. It isn't magic, my lord, as far as I can tell; but I'm damned if I know what it is."

"And as *I've* said," Lord Darcy told him, "it may look like that to an outsider—if you will excuse me calling you an outsider even in this context—but all you're seeing is the exercise of a well-trained and practiced deductive facility. There's nothing miraculous in it."

"Aye, my lord," Master Sean agreed, "so you've said."

Lord Darcy smiled at the doubt in his friend's voice. "Look at it this way, Master Sean," he said, "What you do, with your smoking thuribles and your twirling wands, seems just as miraculous to an observer."

"Nothing miraculous about it, my lord," Master Sean said, sounding slightly offended. "It's just good, clean, applied magic."

"It is as a miracle to me," Lord Darcy told him.

"Ah, Your Lordship, that's as may be. But you see, I could

teach my techniques to anyone else with the Talent. And often have."

"And you think that what I do is unteachable? Well, perhaps it is, but I trust that you are mistaken. Perhaps my Talent, whatever it is, is just more rare."

"I would say it's unique, my lord," Master Sean said.

"I wouldn't like to think so," Lord Darcy said. "But we may soon find out. I have been thinking recently of putting together another monograph, a little book on the art of deduction, which would force me to codify exactly how I do what I do."

"I shall be one of the most earnest readers of that book, my lord," Master Sean told him. "Right now I think I'd better go back to the cabin and get packed. I don't think there'll be any delay in our debarking once the ship is docked."

"You're probably right, Master Sean," Lord Darcy said. "But, as I am already packed, I believe I shall remain here and have a last ouiskie and splash before we take up our new problem."

Master Sean got up and made his way with cautious deliberation across the gently swaying lounge floor to the corridor door, while Lord Darcy signaled the steward to bring him a ouiskie and splash and turned to stare out through the large, double-paned porthole by his table. He pulled the curved, blocky meerschaum pipe from his left pocket and the waterproof pouch holding tobacco and matches from his right. Thoughtfully tamping the Robertia plug tobacco down into the wide bowl, he reviewed the events of eight days ago, the day before they boarded the *Aristotle*.

It was late in the evening, and Lord Darcy had been in his apartments in London, working on the galley proofs of his latest monograph, an essay entitled "Reflexions on the Criminal Mind," when the summons came, and a queer summons it was. For Lord Darcy to attend His Majesty was no longer an unusual occurrence; as Chief Investigator of the Court of Chivalry for the past six years, he both took orders from and reported directly to His Majesty on many of the cases that were sufficiently important for him to take personal charge.

But to be summoned personally by Lord Peter Whiss, chief of the Most Secret Service, at ten at night, and taken immediately in a bread delivery van to a side entrance of Winchester Palace, was unique in Lord Darcy's long experience. To then be wrapped in a dark cloak and surrounded by six of the Palace Guard with drawn pistols before being whisked upstairs into the Royal Presence added a bizarre quality that made the entire interview, in retrospect, seem unreal.

But real it had been.

"As always, it is a pleasure to see you, my lord Darcy," King John said, turning from the window he had been staring out as Lord Darcy unraveled himself from the cloak, crossed the small room adjacent to the Royal Chambers and knelt to greet his sovereign.

John IV, *Dei Gratia* King of England, Ireland, Scotland, and France; Emperor of the Romans and the Germans; Premier Chief of the Moqtessumid Clan; Son of the Sun; a handsome, powerful-looking man in his sixth decade of life, had been well-used by the years that had passed over him as he, in turn, had used well the passing years. Not that he looked older than his years; his hair was still largely blond, although the beard was graying faster than that above, and the thin straight hair, combed straight back, was, perhaps, thinner than it once had been. But he looked every day of every one of his years.

It showed largely in the Plantagenet face, where the fine lines about the eyes and mouth reflected thirty years of truths that could not be spoken, burdens that could not be shared, and decisions that could not be undone.

"You will, we are sure, forgive the unceremonious way in which you were delivered," John said, gesturing with his hand for Lord Darcy to rise. "We will more than make up for it in the grateful way in which you are received. For you have all of Our gratitude, my lord, for a life of devotion to the Crown and the Empire."

"And, as my life is not over, sire, neither is my devotion to my sovereign's projects," Lord Darcy said, standing and stretching a bit to relieve his tensed-up muscles.

The King smiled. "A subtle way, my lord, of saying 'What the hell am I doing here at this hour, in this way?'—is it not?"

"I would not for the world disagree with Your Highness," Lord Darcy said, bowing slightly, the ghost of a smile on his lips.

"Come, sit down, my lord," King John said, preceding him to the heavy wooden table in one corner of the room, "Once again We require your services. All will be explained to you presently. We merely await the arrival of Lord Peter Whiss, who had to stop at the Ochre Room on the way up here. Join us in a glass of our great-grandfather's brandy while we wait."

King John took the bell-shaped bottle of Imperial cognac from the sideboard and poured about three-quarters of an inch of the reddish-amber fluid into each of two green crystal glasses. He handed one to Lord Darcy, and then sat in one of the six massive oak chairs surrounding the table, allowing Lord Darcy to be seated in another. One did not sit while the king stood.

"I am doubly honored, Your Majesty," Lord Darcy said. "To be served the Imperial cognac of eighteen—as I see by the label—ninety-two; and to be served by Your Majesty's hands. It makes me very nervous."

"The King serves all his subjects," King John said, leaning back in his chair and taking a sip of his great-grandfather's cognac, "although usually not in quite so direct a manner. What do you mean, 'nervous'?"

"It makes me think that the secrets that I am about to hear are secret indeed, and that whatever has occurred to cause Your Majesty to send for me is serious indeed. Therefore I am concerned both about the threat to the Realm and about living up to Your Majesty's expectations." Lord Darcy cupped the glass and raised it to his lips, inhaling deeply of the mature bouquet of the Angevin Empire's finest cognac before taking a small sip. The brandy, as with all fine things, was something to be savored in unhurried enjoyment.

"Secrets? Threat to the Realm?" His Majesty leaned forward and stared intently at Lord Darcy. "What secrets, my lord? What do you know of a threat to the Realm?"

"Oh, come now, Your Majesty," Lord Darcy said. "I am your Chief Investigator, after all. Of what use would I be to you if I were unable to deduce the existence of a State secret in the events of the last half hour? As to what that State secret may be, I confess I have no idea. As to the threat to the Realm, which is somehow involved in or with the secret, what else would command the attention of both Your Majesty and Lord Peter in such an urgent manner at ten o'clock at night? Besides including a visit to the Ochre Room, which it is commonly believed is the entrance to a suite of rooms in the Palace occupied by Your Majesty's Most Secret Service."

"Ah, my lord, We are relieved," His Majesty said. "Your ability to deduce the existence of an ocean from a few drops of water is well known to us, but sometimes We fail to allow for it. For Our own curiosity—how did you hypothesize the existence, and the importance, of this State secret?"

"In this case the deductive process was hardly called into play at all, Your Majesty," Lord Darcy explained. "When a man is brought secretly into the Palace, and then bundled up the back stairs, it is not a great exercise in deductive reasoning for the man to conclude that it is not desirable for his presence to be known. Likewise, when, in a small room off the Royal Chambers, the King pours his own cognac, not to speak of serving a guest, it is a reasonable deduction that servants are forbidden to enter that room. And why else but for security? And, as the Palace servants are highly reliable, the secret must indeed be of a high order to routinely exclude them. As to there being a possible threat to the Realm involved, as I explained, the very identities of those concerned would certainly indicate that."

"That is so," the King admitted. "And it surely seems obvious when you explain it. We will have to rethink our security precautions to exclude the unusual. Although in this case, with time at a premium, We hardly see how We could have done otherwise."

There was a perfunctory knock at the door, and Lord Peter Whiss entered the room. A small, intense man with a wonderful mind for detail, Lord Peter, as always, managed to look studied and unhurried in the midst of the most intense activity. "Your Majesty," he said, "Lord Darcy. I apologize for the delay. There is nothing new to report from the link, Your Majesty. I have arranged passage for two on the Steam Packet *Aristotle*, which sails at seven tomorrow morning. I trust Lord Darcy can be ready by that time."

"We think you'd better explain to Lord Darcy where he's going," His Majesty said dryly, "and why."

"Certainly," Lord Peter said, sitting down.

"One moment," Lord Darcy said, taking his fountain pen and a small notebook from an inner pocket of his jacket. "If, as I suppose, the second passage is for Master Sean O Lochlainn, kindly have someone take him this note. The longer he is given to prepare, the better. It is wise not to hurry wizards."

"I will have the note sent immediately, my lord," Lord Peter said. "Please reveal no more than is necessary."

"That will be easy," Lord Darcy told him. "At the moment, I

know nothing beyond the bare fact that there is something to know."

"Do not convey even that, my lord," Lord Peter said.

"Just the essential information that Master Sean had better pack for an extended trip," Lord Darcy said, scribbling a couple of lines on the page and then ripping it out of the book. "And that we'll be leaving first thing in the morning. It will come as no surprise to him, although the destination may. We often leave for an investigation on scant notice." He passed the note to Lord Peter, who took it to the door and called for a guard.

"Now," Lord Peter said, after handing out the note with appropriate instructions, "let me tell you of an interesting problem, which seems to be in your line of business."

Lord Darcy took another sip of the Imperial cognac and listened.

"The Angevin Empire is about to sign a treaty of amity and assistance with the Azteque Empire; one which we have been negotiating for some time," Lord Peter said, pacing back and forth before the table as he spoke. He kept his gaze focused on his own hands, which were clasped in front of him. "It will define boundaries between our New England territory of Robertia and the Azteque lands, codify the complex bipartite situation of our Duchy of Mechicoe, establish trading rights and trapping rights, and the like, and allow for the exchange of emissaries and missionaries and commercial travelers of various sorts."

"I have heard something of this," Lord Darcy said.

"Yes, well, you will be hearing a lot more in the near future," Lord Peter said. "I imagine you're going to have to become something of an expert on it."

"How does the Duchy of Mechicoe come into this?" Lord Darcy asked. "Nothing, I trust, that reflects adversely on the present Duke."

"Ah, yes, a friend of yours, isn't he, Darcy?" His Majesty asked.

"His son, actually, Your Majesty. Master Lord John Quetzal. A fine young man, and a promising forensic magician."

"Of course," His Majesty said. "We've met the lad. Good blood."

"You understand, my lord," Lord Peter said, "that there are two Dukes of Mechicoe. One of ours, your friend's father; and one of theirs. And there are two Duchies. But it happens that the territory each claims to control is the same as the other's."

Lord Darcy thought this over. "Interesting," he said. "How does—how *can*—it work?"

"Up until now it has been working based only on the fear the Azteques still harbor after the 1789 Three Prisoner incident. They regard the ridiculous ease with which their army was crushed as a sign of our military and magical superiority. Which, they feel, has increased over the years. We have carefully nurtured this feeling."

"I see," Lord Darcy said.

"The Azteque ruling class has a very restricted view of themselves and the world around them," Lord Peter said. "All those who they can best are their slaves—or should be. And all those who can best them—which, so far, has only been the Imperial Legion—are fools for not enslaving them. It is a rather abrupt, simplistic, and unsympathetic philosophy.

"The native dukes who came over to the Angevin Empire, and embraced Christianity, like de Mechicoe and d'Eucatanne, are accepted for what they are. But new dukes were appointed to take their place. It makes a strange sort of sense. After all, the Azteque nobility also has a religious function, which their Christian cousins cannot take part in."

"This treaty is of great importance to Our government, my lord Darcy," King John said, hunching back in his seat. The gaslight reflecting off his hair created a halo effect, reminding Lord Darcy of a medieval painting of Saint Thomas he had once seen. "There are those on both sides who are interested in seeing that it is never signed."

"*Both* sides, Your Majesty?"

"On our side," Lord Peter explained, "some of our less enlightened citizens believe that the sins of the fathers carry through to the sons and the grandsons, and down through the generations. On the basis of his ungenerous belief, they feel that it is sinful for the Angevin Empire to have anything to do with the Azteque Empire, whose rulers worshiped Huitsilopochtli, a war god who demanded human sacrifice, until we discouraged the practice. His victims had their hearts torn out on bloody stone altars atop massive pyramids."

"I've read of the ceremony," Lord Darcy commented.

"Well then, as you know, the ceremony was abandoned hundreds of years ago, and since then has not been practiced anywhere in the civilized parts of the Azteque Empire. Religions, like people or cultures, grow up. And we all tend to be pretty barbaric in our youth. But there are those in the Empire—clerics and others—who selectively forget the barbarisms of our own youth and insist that these evil practices of the early Azteques make their great-grandchildren unacceptable as treaty partners. The 'blood-can-never-be-cleansed-from-these-stones' sort of thinking."

"There is a sense," His Majesty said mildly, "in which the blood never *can* be cleansed from those stones."

Lord Peter paused and glanced at his sovereign, and then back down at his clasped hands. "That is so, Your Highness," he said. "But the guilt of those responsible has long since been determined by a higher court than we can convene." He looked up at Lord Darcy. "And then there are those who believe we should go to war with the Azteque Empire, to support the claim of the Dukes of Mechicoe and Misogohelli and the other native nobility who have embraced the Christian faith and who owe fealty to His Majesty."

"What claims?" Lord Darcy asked.

"Aye, there's the rub," Lord Peter said, resuming his pacing. "The native Christian nobles have made no territorial claims beyond what they already possess. And this treaty would endorse those very possessions. They are at peace with their Azteque brethren. And His Majesty has taken on the title of Premier Chief of the Moqtessumid Clan and has appointed a Bishop of Mechicoe to show continuing royal interest. The Christian nobles, it would seem to me, have the best of both worlds at the moment. They'd be very foolish to do anything to rock the boat. And they do not strike me as being particularly foolish.

"On the Azteque side, there is what they call a 'war party,' within the nobility that believes they should not give away their ancestral right to the territory we call New England,' and by that, they mean the whole Eastern Coast of the continent. The fact that they retreated from it over four hundred years before we arrived, and that the Fifteen Nations—the loose confederation of native tribes of the Northeast—have much more claim on it than they, should we disappear, is somehow not relevant to them." Lord Peter sounded personally aggrieved.

"We are having a dossier prepared for you, Lord Darcy," said the King, "to study at your leisure. You will have about a week of enforced leisure, while crossing the Atlantic."

"So far, Your Majesty, I have heard no secrets," Lord Darcy said. "What has happened that puts this treaty in jeopardy?"

The King looked at Lord Peter.

"There has been a murder," Lord Peter said. "In an ancient Azteque temple to Huitsilopochtli which sits atop a pyramid on a small island in the harbor of Nova Eboracum, or New Borkum, as it is commonly known. A priest-exorcist and a magician went there to cleanse the temple in anticipation of the arrival of the Azteque treaty party. As a symbol of something—I'm not sure just what—an Eternal Flame is being brought from the Azteque capital city to be kindled in the temple next to it atop the pyramid.

"When they climbed the pyramid and opened the temple—it had been sealed for the past century—they found a body within. Freshly dead, with its heart ripped out. They couldn't find the heart."

"Interesting," Lord Darcy said, pulling thoughtfully at his ear. "Who was the, ah, victim?"

"His name was Prince Ixequatle. He was an unofficial representative of the Emperor of the Azteques. I believe he was the Emperor's nephew. Apparently he came along a few weeks early to make sure we did everything right in welcoming the High Priest and the Eternal Flame. His Grace of Arc says Prince Ixequatle had been very helpful."

"I see," Lord Darcy said. "I will refrain from asking the obvious questions that can be better answered at the site of the crime, or at least on the same continent. When did the murder happen?"

The King looked at Lord Peter, who stopped pacing and looked back at the King. For a long moment neither of them said anything.

Lord Darcy looked from one to the other. "Is this, then, the secret?" he asked. "What is the problem, Your Majesty?"

King John nodded. "We grant it is a problem," he said. "My lord Darcy, you are indeed one of Our most trusted advisors, and the one We have time and again called upon to solve knotty problems. As, indeed, We are doing now. There are perhaps five secrets held by the Empire that you are not privy to, or would not be if you asked about them— and those only because you have no need to know of them. This is—was—one of the five. And now you are about to become one of the three dozen men and women who have access to this information."

"Thirty-four," Lord Peter said.

"Guard it well," King John said.

"This is known as the Gemini Secret," Lord Peter said. "You are to take it as a sacred trust not to divulge it, or even mention its name, to any living soul; not to speak of it even with someone who shares the knowledge, unless there is immediate and pressing need and you are quite alone and have actively verified that you are."

"Well!" Lord Darcy said.

"Do you so swear?" Lord Peter asked.

"On my oath as a peer of the Realm, and by my honor, which I hold most sacred," Lord Darcy replied, repeating an ancient and hallowed formulation.

Lord Peter nodded. "I shall add your name to the list," he said. "Now there are thirty-five."

"If We have a rule, my lord," King John said, looking slightly embarrassed, "it must be enforced for everyone, or else it isn't really a rule."

"I quite understand, Your Majesty, and agree," Lord Darcy said.

Lord Peter sat down and, with clasped hands, stared across the table at Lord Darcy. "In answer to your question," he said, "this morning."

"My lord?" Lord Darcy asked.

"The murder, or at least the discovery of it, occurred this morning."

Lord Darcy thought that over for a second. "But—" he said.

"Exactly," Lord Peter said.

"How?" Lord Darcy asked. "Have you found a way to make the teleson work over water?"

"No, my lord," Lord Peter said. "Our best theoretical thaumaturgists seem to think that is an unattainable goal. Magic-at-a-distance does not work over running water."

"Then how—?"

"There would seem to be other forces in the universe besides magic, my lord," King John said. "The method by which we are enabled to receive information from various distant parts of Our realm has been of great service to Us, and its secret must be preserved."

"I understand, Your Highness," Lord Darcy said.

"Let us take it that we do have some means of communicating with the Ducal Palace at New Borkum, and perhaps with one or two other places, that is, effectively, instantaneous," Lord Peter said. "If there is ever any reason for you to know this method, then you shall be informed of it. The very fact that the method exists is the essence of the Gemini Secret, which you are requested and required to maintain."

King John smiled. "They didn't want to tell *Us*, my lord Darcy," he said, "but We insisted."

"I shall ask no more questions concerning method, my lord," Lord Darcy told Lord Peter. "Tell me more about the murder."

"Regrettably, you now know as much as we do," Lord Peter said. "We assume the case is being handled by Lord John Quetzal, at least as far as the forensic sorcery goes. After all, he is on the scene. The Duke of Arc's chief investigator is a man named De Pemmery—but last we heard he was some distance away, visiting the territory around FitzLeeber Land and Garretton, investigating disturbances concerning Angevin subjects among the Fifteen Nations."

"Will they know I am coming?" Lord Darcy asked.

"Two will," Lord Peter said. "His Grace the Duke of Arc, and one other. But they will not appear to. Your trip must seem to have been accidental and fortuitous."

"I see," Lord Darcy said. "The, ah, Gemini Secret must be maintained."

"Indeed," Lord Peter said. "The resident agent of the Most Secret Service in Nova Eboracum is named Muffin—code name, of course. My assumption is that Muffin will check to see whether there is anything of interest to the Service in this killing. Let us hope that there is not, as that would probably mean a Polish connection. If Muffin needs to contact you, the code name and the word 'opera' will be used in the same sentence."

"Opera, my lord?"

"Yes. You know, one of those Italian musical things—"

"I am familiar with the word, my lord."

"It was chosen as an unlikely but vaguely plausible combination of words, my lord," Lord Peter said.

"It is that," Lord Darcy agreed. "And if I wish to speak to Muffin?"

"Tell the Duke," Lord Peter said. "And wait for someone to whisper 'Muffin' and 'opera' in the same sentence."

"Ah!" Lord Darcy said.

"Now remember about this Gemini business," Lord Peter said. "It is not to be discussed."

"Master Sean O Lochlainn will have to know," Lord Darcy said. "I can see no way to keep the secret from him. He is an intelligent, perceptive man, and a master magician. The anomaly in dates will occur to him, if he is not informed."

Lord Peter considered. "That is so," he admitted. "We will leave it to Your Lordship to swear him into the Gemini conspiracy, and I shall enter his name on the list. Number thirty-six."

"Is there any more you can tell me concerning the murder?" Lord Darcy asked. "I take it our mission, Master Sean's and mine, is to identify the murderer. If there is any more you would have of us, you should tell me now. If not, I'd better get home and pack."

"You must catch the killer, my lord Darcy," King John said, "if possible before the Azteque Imperial Retinue d'Ambassade reaches Nova Eboracum. We say 'if possible,' because We have no idea when they will arrive. It could be before you do. We do not know what the response of the Azteques will be to the murder of one of their royal princes, but it could hardly be favorable. We sincerely hope that the killer was not an Angevin subject, but the murder happened on Angevin territory and the victim was a guest of the Imperial Governor, and thus of Us. Whoever the killer was, he must be apprehended and punished."

"What makes this treaty so important, Your Majesty?" Lord Darcy asked. "Could the killing be an effort to sabotage the treaty?"

"That is certainly one possibility," His Majesty replied. "And, indeed, it might have that effect. You, my lord, must see that it does not."

"As to the treaty's importance," Lord Peter said, "of itself, there is little; the Empire of the Azteques and the territories of New England and New France are in no way in contention at this time. But we fear that the hand—and right arm—of His Polish Majesty, King Casimir, is beginning to take an interest in the Western Continents."

"Ah!" Lord Darcy said. It was really not surprising. The Polish Empire, under Casimir IX, was always looking for ways to tweak the Angevin Empire. And, if the tweak was successful, it would be followed shortly thereafter by a sharp blow. The *Serka*, the Polish Secret Police—the name came from a phrase meaning roughly "The King's Right Arm"—could not be expected to allow the Angevin Empire's hold on two entire continents to remain undisputed.

"We think we had better let you go now, Lord Darcy," His Majesty said. "We are sure Your Lordship must have much to do before the ship leaves."

"To whom shall I report, during the course of my investigation?" Lord Darcy asked.

"We have full confidence in our cousin the Duke of Arc, who is the Royal Governor of New England," His Majesty said. "You may feel free to report fully to His Grace. You and Master Sean will probably be staying in the Residence in New Borkum."

His Majesty rose, causing Lord Darcy and Lord Peter to scramble to their feet. "We also have full confidence in you, my lord, and we are certain it is well placed." He extended his hand, and Lord Darcy took it and bowed.

"Thank you, Your Majesty," he said.

His Majesty shook his head. "We are indeed fortunate," he said. "We present our subjects with onerous and impossible tasks, at a moment's notice, and they thank Us. Go with God, Lord Darcy."

"I trust you won't mind going back to your apartment in a covered meat-wagon?" Lord Peter asked. "It's the best we could do on such short notice."

5

IT WAS SIX in the evening when H.I.M. Steam Packet *Aristotle* drew alongside the Imperial Navy pier in the Arthur River. Lord Darcy and Master Sean waited on the main deck with the other passengers for the Nova Eboracum Port Admitting Officer to examine them before they were permitted to debark. On the pier below, all their luggage was being piled in neat rows at the foot of the gangway.

A wide wooden table had been erected beside the gangway for the Admitting Officer's use, and several ship's officers were waiting with the passengers.

Lady Ephram, a stout matron in her forties and the only woman passenger on the voyage, complained loudly to her husband while they waited. "I just don't see why we have to go through this," she said. "We are Angevin citizens, subjects of His Majesty, going from one part of his Realm to another. There are no such inspections when you go from France to England or to Belgium."

"That's so, my dear," agreed her husband, a short man, even stouter than his wife. Lord Ephram was dressed in a bright scarlet tunic and green trowsers, and bore an unfortunate resemblance to a huge, overripe strawberry. "And, even if they need inspections for others, surely, as members of the nobility crossing on an Imperial Navy ship we should be exempt. Pure officiousness, I'm sure, my dear," he said. "These colonials, you know. I shall write to the *Courier* about it."

"These Imperial Navy steam packets take passengers as a courtesy, my lord, and not as a sign of status," a tall, bearded man dressed in the powder-blue-and-gold uniform of a naval officer said mildly, taking his pipe out of his mouth and knocking it against a bulkhead-mounted ashtray. "The Admitting Officer is a New England Coast Guard officer, under the direct command of His Grace the Duke, and I'm sure they have excellent reasons for what they do."

"You should not speak disrespectfully to the nobility, young man," Lady Ephram told the officer, looking haughtily up at him. "I should report you to the Captain."

"I am the Captain, my lady," the officer told her, mildly puffing on his pipe.

The Admitting Officer, a husky little red-faced man with black hair, who wore the red-trimmed dark blue uniform of the New England Coast Guard, climbed up the gangway and strode to the group on the main deck. "Hi!" he said, waving a pouch full of forms at the passengers. "Welcome to New England. I'm Lieutenant Assawatan, at your service. There are a few formalities that we must go through before you debark. Please be patient, I'll keep you as brief a time as possible.

"First, a general speech of introduction and caution, which I must give to all who first come to these shores. While I'm giving it, why don't you all fill out these forms. They're self-explanatory."

Lieutenant Assawatan distributed the forms, and pencils for those without their own fountain pens, and then pushed himself up onto the table and sat there. "On the maps you see back home," he told them, "the whole northern half of this huge continent, from the Isthmus of Von Helsing north, is labeled 'New England,' and the southern half, 'New France.' This is what we might call a polite fiction. In reality, the situation is not nearly that simple.

"'New England' is a group of Angevin colonies plastered haphazardly along the eastern shores of this vast continent, completely surrounded by aboriginal tribes. Most of the land around the more northern of these colonies is under the control of one or another of the Fifteen Nations, a loose confederation of native tribes. The ones in this immediate area—as a matter of fact, right on the other side of the Arthur River—are the Pequot and the Wappinger. Further inland, around the royal trading companies at FitzLeeber Land, Garretton, and Martensville, where I venture several of you are headed, you'll meet up with the Mahican, the Mohawk, the Seneca, the Cayuga, and several lesser tribes."

"Excuse me, Lieutenant, but why this lesson in ethnography?" Lord Norman Scrivener asked, patting back his hair, which had become somewhat disarranged in the light wind.

"Because we have discovered that most of you have no idea of what it means to leave the boundaries of the Angevin Empire," Lieutenant Assawatan said bluntly. "Many heretofore useful, law-abiding citizens go into the wilderness and begin behaving like irresponsible fools. They get themselves in trouble; sometimes they get themselves killed. Well, that's their business, if they so choose. But they also get the colony and the town they came from in trouble with the local tribes. If they have behaved like big enough fools, they give the whole Empire a black eye."

Lieutenant Assawatan looked around at his audience. Some were regarding him with an amused, tolerant stare; others appeared mildly frightened; the rest, including Lord Darcy and Master Sean, listened impassively but closely to his words. "Our job is to prevent that," he continued. "So I should warn you; you are accountable for your actions even when out of the boundaries of the Imperial colonies. We are at peace with the Fifteen Nations, sort of, and will not look kindly on anyone who breaks that peace. And the other tribes, not part of the Fifteen Nations; well, the best that can be said of them is they're unpredictable. If you get in trouble with one of them, there is little we can do to help you, no matter the right or wrong of the case."

"You're a native yourself, aren't you?" Lady Ephram asked loudly.

"I am by ancestry," Lieutenant Assawatan affirmed. "Tuskegee. They live down by Nova Burgundia. My grandfather converted to Catholicism, and sent my father to school at St. Thomas' Academy in London, and then on to Oxford. He, in turn, sent me when I was of age. But I'm the first to join the Coast Guard. At any rate, it is a good idea not to get into trouble with any of the native tribes; they are not all Catholic, and some of the native religions encourage practices that you don't even want to know about."

"You said the Government couldn't protect us. Well, what about the Imperial Legion?" one of the passengers asked. "Are they not stationed over here?"

"Twelve companies of Legionnaires for the entire coast, from Nova Centium to Nova Hebridia," the Lieutenant said, "and they are kept busy, believe me. Now—" he took out a card and read from it, "—the following items are forbidden by Imperial regulations, as you should have been informed before you left England: Firearms, aside from one sidearm and one hunting piece for personal use—which you will be asked to show when you leave, so you'd better not lose them; living plants; uncooked fruit or grain; animals, except dogs or licensed familiars; stonewort; magical paraphernalia, apparatus, goods or supplies, unless under the seal of a bishop and consigned to a licensed user or dealer, or in the personal possession or under the personal control of a properly licensed master or journeyman magician, wizard, or thaumaturge.

"If you have any of the proscribed items, please indicate them on the form, and state any special circumstance which would allow you to keep them in your possession. Otherwise, they will be confiscated and kept in bond here at the Coast Guard warehouse, and you can retrieve them as you leave. If the item in question is a living animal, you will be charged a reasonable board fee."

"Stonewort?" Lord Darcy muttered.

"I'll explain it to you later, my lord," Master Sean whispered to him.

"Ah!" Lord Darcy said. "If it's magical, don't bother, Master Sean. I wouldn't understand."

The group filled out the forms, which merely asked for names, titles, professions, addresses, destination, expected length of stay, and next of kin. Lieutenant Assawatan collected them all, and nodded. "That's it," he said. "Your luggage will be checked as you pick it up on the pier."

"Excuse me, Lieutenant, but what college?" Lord Norman Scrivener asked.

The Lieutenant turned to face him. "College?"

"At Oxford," Lord Norman explained. "What college were you? I'm St. David, myself."

"Magog," the Lieutenant said. "Seventy-seven."

"Ah!" Lord Norman said.

"You may all leave now, and I wish you a pleasant and successful stay. Enjoy New Borkum. Master Sean O Lochlainn, would you step over here for a second? There are a couple of additional forms you have to fill out in regard to your magical bag."

As the rest of the passengers filed down the gangplank, Master Sean and Lord Darcy went over to the young officer. "Sorry to inconvenience you, Master Sean," Lieutenant Assawatan said. "And you must be Lord Darcy. I understand you were a Magog man yourself, my lord."

"Fifty-four," Lord Darcy said.

"And we still heard stories about you when I was there," the Lieutenant said.

"The forms, Lieutenant?" Master Sean asked.

"Ah, yes." Lieutenant Assawatan watched the last passenger descend the gangplank. "Actually, I was just sort of segregating you and Lord Darcy out of the herd, if you see what I mean. I have orders to take you two to the Residence, but not to make a fuss about it. So, if you'll please come with me . . ."

"As soon as we pick up our luggage," Lord Darcy said.

"My men will have already loaded your luggage onto my launch," Lieutenant Assawatan told them.

"There's a dozen people down there who will see us leaving with you," Lord Darcy objected.

"I'm taking you to see the Bishop," Lieutenant Assawatan told him, "to get your—Master Sean's— magical apparatus permit signed."

"I see you've thought of everything," Lord Darcy said.

"We try," the Lieutenant said. "Actually, Master Sean will have to get his permit signed; something about verifying that he understands the different type of magic practiced here—I'm sure you know better than I what that's all about, Master Sean—but ordinarily we would have trusted him to go by himself. Besides, your visit to the Residence will soon be known all over the island anyway. My instructions were only not to make a fuss about it, and so we won't."

"I see," Lord Darcy said. "Tell me, Lieutenant, do you have any idea of what this is about?"

"None at all, my lord," Lieutenant Assawatan said cheerfully. "When they want me to know, they'll tell me."

He escorted them down the gangway and over to the Coast Guard steam launch, which was across the pier. "Have either of you ever been here before?" he asked. "No? Well, the Residence is about two miles upriver. It's one of the three largest structures on the island: the Residence, the Cathedral, and Fort St. Michael."

"'The Residence,'" Master Sean said, musingly. "That'd be your name for the Ducal Palace, wouldn't it?"

"That's so," Lieutenant Assawatan agreed. He gave the order to cast off, and shouted some hurried instructions to his small crew, then turned back to his guests. "I hope I have a chance to speak with you while you're here, Lord Darcy," he said. "Fellow alumni, and all that. Perhaps I could invite Your Lordship to dine with me in the officer's mess sometime during your stay. And you too, of course, Master Sean."

"It would be our pleasure," Lord Darcy told the young officer.

"Are you going to be with us long?" the Lieutenant asked. "Are you here on His Majesty's business, or your own?" He saw the slight frown pass over Master Sean's face, which wiped the smile off his own. "Oh!" he said. "I'm terribly sorry. What a personal question to ask. I do apologize. How presumptuous of me. We're so informal around here, and, with only each other to talk to, I sometimes forget my manners."

"No, no, that's quite all right," Lord Darcy said, smiling. "As a matter of fact, we're here for both business and pleasure, and for His Majesty's business and our own. I have some small land holdings here—family inheritance, you know. They're being run quite well by the factor, as far as I can tell; but there's nothing like the personal touch once in a while. And, while we're here, Master Sean is going to look into the state of forensic sorcery. He is a—"

"I know, believe me, I know all about Master Sean, in as much detail as a layman can understand," Lieutenant Assawatan said, laughing. "You'll excuse me, Master Sean, I mean no disrespect, but Master Lord John Quetzal is a good friend of mine, and we dine together regularly. All I heard about is Master Sean O Lochlainn. Especially if I try to compliment him on something he has done well. 'That was a nice bit of magic you used today,' I'll say. 'If you think so, then you've never seen Master Sean O Lochlainn working,' he'll reply. Then he'll describe something he saw you do in the classroom, or on a case, and it will sound like a miracle indeed. If you're as good as Lord John thinks you are, Master Sean, then you're no magician, you're a saint!"

Master Sean came as close to blushing as Lord Darcy had ever seen. "Well," he said, "His Lordship is one of my favorite pupils, and one of the best I've ever taught. Aside from his own native ability at witch-smelling, he's just one of the best natural all-around magicians I know. Forensic magic will not be the poorer for his decision to practice it."

"I'd tell him you said so, Master, only he wouldn't be fit to live with for a week after," Lieutenant Assawatan said.

Lord Darcy watched with fascination as the noisy vessel chugged upstream toward the Residence. To the right, Fort St. Michael at the tip of Saytchem Island, and then a mile of farmland before the town of New Borkum started. To the left, a granite palisade separating the river from a thick virgin forest that came right to the cliff's edge. Ahead of them a flat-bottom barge was gliding across the river toward the distant palisade, with no visible motive power.

"What is that?" Lord Darcy asked, pointing to the rectangular barge crossing their path.

"The Langert Street Ferry," the Lieutenant told him. "It's operated by ropes from below. Best and fastest way to cross the river, even if it is a little out of the way, being a bit south of town to be entirely convenient."

In another ten minutes they had reached the Residence, a squat stone building that stretched out over several city blocks and couldn't quite decide whether it was a palace or a fort. It had its own private dock, and a quarter-hour after they left the deck of the *Aristotle*, they were being ushered into the Throne Room, and the presence of His Grace, Duke Charles of Arc, Imperial Governor of New England.

The Throne Room was gay with color; crowded with courtiers in the multicolored splendor of the elaborate court garb, and stuffed with military officers in the rich dress-uniforms of a variety of services from a multitude of lands. There were also a sprinkling of plainly dressed, hard-bitten men who projected an air of competence that was as tangible as the scent of the courtiers.

Lord Darcy and Master Sean approached the throne and knelt on bended knee before it, in the thousand-year-old ceremony of acknowledging their obedience to their sovereign, and his representative the Duke of Arc.

His Grace was a slight, handsome man in his early sixties, with the look of someone who led a full and active life and spent a great deal of time outdoors. At the moment he looked worried. "Welcome to Nova Eboracum, Lord Darcy, Master Sean O Lochlainn," he said. "You have come at a propitious moment—for us, at least. But I fear that I may intrude upon your plans. When I heard of your impending arrival from your cousin, Lady Irene Eagleson, I arranged for you to be brought here from the ship. I trust you will forgive the needs of Government, my lord."

"There has been a murder, I understand, Your Grace," Lord Darcy said, rising to his feet.

"Indeed," His Grace said. "A vile and pointless crime has been perpetrated; one that could affect the relations between us and the Empire of the Azteques. And our own chief investigator, Major DePemmery, is in the neighborhood of Garretton, some three hundred miles west of here. I have sent a message to him, but it is unlikely that he has received it yet. I fear we must impose on you, Lord Darcy, and ask you to investigate this crime."

"As Your Lordship requires," Lord Darcy said, "we will, of course, comply. We can put off our personal business for the time being and devote ourselves to the Crown's needs."

"As you have for so many years, my lord, and, if the stories I have heard about you and Master Sean are true, so well. I have arranged for you to have a suite of rooms in the Residence. Lady Irene will show you to your chambers; I'm sure you and your cousin have a lot to talk over. When you are settled, I would speak with you. Shall we say at nine this evening, my lord?"

Lord Darcy bowed. "I think Master Sean and I can be settled in by then, Your Grace. Thank you."

Very good, my lord," his grace said. He turned and called, "Lady Irene?"

A slim young woman stepped from the group to Lord Darcy's left and approached the throne. Lord Darcy's first impression was of light-blue skirts and a cloud of blond hair. She curtsied to His Grace and turned to Lord Darcy. "Cousin. How good to see you again."

Indeed, my pleasure," Lord Darcy said. "You've, ah, changed a lot since we last met. I don't think I would have recognized you."

Lady Irene laughed. "I surely have," she agreed. "A woman does change from the time she's seven until she's twenty-six."

"Has it been that long?" Lord Darcy asked. "Come, show Master Sean and myself to our chambers, and we'll talk over old times."

Lady Irene led the way along the complex of corridors in the Residence to the suite of rooms that had been put aside for Lord Darcy and Master Sean. When they were safely inside the entrance door, she closed it behind her and leaned up against it. "We really are related, you know, my lord, although we've never met, and the degree of consanguinity is considerably wider than would normally be embraced by the term 'cousin.'"

"Lady Irene Eagleson?" Lord Darcy said. "I am delighted to discover such a beautiful and charming relative, but I confess that the details of the relationship elude me."

"My mother, the Baroness Saltire, is the first cousin of the Duchess Pemberton, my lord. And, as the Duke is your mother's brother, that makes us—um, second cousins once removed."

Lord Darcy laughed. "I'll take your word for it," he said. "Genealogy has never been my strong point, although once or twice I've had to bone up on it for a case I was working on. Master Sean, meet my cousin Lady Irene. I've known her since she was in pigtails. Or, at any rate, I'm sorry that I haven't."

" 'Tis a pleasure, my lady," Master Sean said.

"I'm not sure why I'm supposed to have known you for ever so long," Lady Irene said, "but it's going to make me quite popular with the ladies in town. You two are quite the most eligible bachelors to have arrived at New Borkum for some time. You are unmarried, aren't you, Master Sean?"

"Aye, my lady," Master Sean said, looking rather alarmed. "But I believe that magicians make very poor husbands."

6

COLONEL HESPARSYN GRUNTED and stirred in his bedroll. Somebody was shaking him by the shoulder. He opened one eye. It didn't help; the world around him was pitch-black. For a second he was disoriented. Then memory—and responsibility—returned. "All right, I'm awake," he said in a low voice. "What is it?"

"Corporal Buchanan, sir," came the whisper in the dark. "Corporal of the guard tonight, sir. Lieutenant MacPhearling ordered me to wake you. He thinks something is about to happen, sir."

"What?" the Colonel asked, pushing himself out of his bedroll and sitting up.

"He's not sure, sir."

Colonel Hesparsyn resisted the impulse to say, "Well, come back when he is sure." That was merely his subconscious, in a desperate desire for more sleep, searching for some excuse. Years of Legion discipline had trained him to override such bodily needs. Instead he said, "Thank you, Corporal. Tell the Lieutenant that I'll be right along," and reached for his boots.

The first vague hints of the approach of dawn were showing in the eastern corner of the star-washed sky as Colonel Hesparsyn left his tent, and a damp, predawn March chill seeped through his woolen uniform and enveloped his slowly waking body. He trotted to the command tent, slapping his hands against his arms in an effort to warm them up.

The red glass was in place over the alcohol lamp in the command tent; red light was least damaging to night vision. Lieutenant MacPhearling and Lieutenant Duggen, the Duty Officer, were sitting at the small table. The Magic Officer held a small, gold dowsing fork over a crude map tacked to the table-top.

"No, no, stay seated, gentlemen," Colonel Hesparsyn said, as his two officers started to rise when he entered the tent. "Keep at whatever you're doing, and tell me what's happening." He went over to the large caffe pitcher that was kept in the tent, and poured himself a steaming cupful. The caffe was kept hot by casting a variant of the preservation spell over it.

"I'm not sure, Colonel," Lieutenant MacPhearling said, peering down at the roughly drawn chart. "There's all sorts of activity going on around the perimeter of the camp, but I can't pinpoint just what it is." Holding the dowsing fork gingerly between the ring-finger and thumb of each hand, he moved it over the surface of the map, watching it carefully as it dipped and jumped. "There are people out there—many people—moving around in small groups."

"Horses?" the Colonel asked.

"Yes, I think so. The dowser is tuned to people, but I'm getting a response that appears to be some kind of large animal. So, unless the elk are migrating early this year, there are probably horses out there."

"Hmm," the Colonel said, looking at his two officers. Unspoken but in everybody's thoughts was the fact that the local tribes were superstitious about fighting at night. They would not attack until dawn. But dawn was rapidly approaching.

"Colonel, are we really going to fight to protect those— Azteques?" Lieutenant Duggen asked. "That's not exactly a popular idea with the troops now."

"I know," Colonel Hesparsyn said. "Frankly, it's not a popular idea with me, either. But His Grace, Duke Charles of Arc, would probably be rather annoyed if we allowed his treaty party to get slaughtered on the way to New Borkum to sign the treaty."

"So we have to prevent the chaps we like from attacking the chaps we don't like," Lieutenant Duggen said. "Isn't that the way it always is?"

"It is not for us to decide Imperial policy," Colonel Hesparsyn said. "His Imperial Majesty's government is slowly and subtly applying external pressure, trying to turn the Azteque nation into one we can like better. But it won't help to get their treaty party, which includes Lord Chiklquetl, who is one of the highest of their assorted high priests, murdered and scalped."

"That's so, sir," Lieutenant Duggen admitted.

"On the other hand, sir," Lieutenant MacPhearling added, "it isn't going to be a good thing for our relations with the local natives if a bunch of them get slaughtered in the attempt. Which I believe is a distinct possibility; I think Lord Chiklquetl and his boys have something up their long, flowing sleeves."

"That's interesting, Lieutenant," Colonel Hesparsyn said. "Have you any idea what it could be?"

"Not in the slightest, sir. But I don't trust those fellows while they're in my sight, much less when they're out of it."

"What are they doing now—can you tell with that silver stick?" Hesparsyn asked.

Lieutenant MacPhearling played his dowsing fork over the map for a little while as the others watched. "Well, they're awake," he said. "Or at least many of them are. I can't tell what they're doing, but they don't seem to be moving around much."

"They know of the gathering warriors?"

"Of course they do," Lieutenant MacPhearling said. "Probably better than I."

"They'll certainly be outnumbered some three or four to one by whoever is out there," the Colonel said. "Maybe better. But their warriors are quite good, I understand. How does their battle magic stack up against the locals?"

"I'd be guessing," Lieutenant MacPhearling said. "But I think they'll pretty much cancel each other out. As you know, it's hard to use magic effectively in the heat of a battle. Their priest-magicians should be able to do a good job of defending themselves, but I don't think they'll be able to do much damage to their opponents in the process. Not nearly as much as the warriors are going to do with the variety of edged and pointed implements they carry. The magical efforts of the two sides should balance."

Colonel Hesparsyn shook his head. "What a wonderful position to be in," he said. "Caught between two groups that hate each other." He went to the tent flap and spoke through it to the guard outside. "Trooper, will you get the herald? And wake up the cook; tell him to put on an urn of caffe for the men and something to break their fast."

"Yes, sir," the guard said. "Cook's up, sir. Been up for hours. You can smell the biscuits."

Of course, the Colonel realized. Silly of him. The cook's day normally started well before dawn, so that the men could have something of a hot breakfast. Too little recognition was given to the cooks in this man's legion.

Within three minutes Captain Humphrey Flagg, the Company Herald and second-in-command, came into the tent. A tall, solidly built man with a rugged, ugly face, the Captain was one of the most reliable and capable officers Colonel Hesparsyn had ever served with. He somehow lacked that quality of leadership that would make him a top-rate commanding officer, but he seemed to know it and never let it worry him. "Yes, sir?" he said. "Fine time to wake a man up."

"These things get passed down the line, Flagg," Colonel Hesparsyn said, holding out a cup of caffe for him. "If I get up, you get up."

"So I've noticed, Colonel," the big man said, smiling and taking the tin cup in his hands. "Well, what's it to be today, fellows?" he asked, turning to the two officers hovering over the table. "Furious battle to defend the indefensible? Are the clouds of war marshaling against us?"

"So it would seem, Captain," Lieutenant MacPhearling told him.

"The hordes are gathering around us, with hatred in their hearts toward their Azteque cousins," Colonel Hesparsyn said. "The Lieutenant believes our Azteque friends have something up their collective sleeves. Personally, I think that they merely suffer from an overweening conceit. But, in either case, we're going to be in the middle."

Lieutenant Duggen looked up at the Colonel. "The Legion's Pride," he said without thinking.

"How's that, son?" the Colonel asked.

"I was just remembering the poem, sir," Duggen told him, looking embarrassed. "*The Legion's Pride*, by Lord Dif."

"That's right, Lieutenant," Colonel Hesparsyn said, remembering. "It does, ah, reverberate in the present situation, doesn't it?" Lord Dif, called the unofficial poet laureate of the Legion, had written the ditty called *The Legion's Pride* on the occasion of the border wars of the German principalities, around 1892.

"I would say so, sir," Lieutenant Duggen said. In a clear, low voice, he recited:

It was a border skirmish,
  A thousand on either side,
But the Legion was sent to maintain the peace,
To stand between them and keep the peace
And pay the price they demand for peace,
  And that was the Legion's pride.

The Legion stood between them,
  Taking neither side,
And the Legion stayed till the fighting ceased,
Stayed in place till the fighting ceased,
And some were killed, but the fighting ceased
  And that was the Legion's pride.

I stood that day with the Legion,
  The precious few who defied
The border barons and made them cease
And stayed to uphold the Legion's peace
And I paid the price for the Legion's peace
  For I was one that died.

All you sons of the Legion
  Scattered far and wide,
Mark well the coin of the Legion's peace
The awful price of the Legion's peace
And if you must pay for the Legion's peace
  Lay you it down with pride.

"Yes," Lieutenant MacPhearling said. "A rather trite poem, I've always thought. But, when it's staring you in the face—"

"Just so," the Captain said. "What was, shall be. The wheel turns, but it is a wheel. And shortly comes the dawn. I'd better go and wake the men."

"Without blowing reveille," the Colonel told him. "No bugle calls."

"Of course not, sir," Captain Flagg said.

"See that the men get some breakfast, if we can manage it, Humphrey," Colonel Hesparsyn said. "At least a biscuit and a mug of caffe. Biscuits should be ready; cook's been up for hours."

"Right, Colonel," Captain Flagg said, saluting and pushing his way out of the tent.

The Colonel held his wristwatch up to the red lens on the alcohol lamp and peered at it. "Five thirty-five," he said. "About twenty minutes to dawn. The tribes won't attack for at least half an hour after that, and probably more like an hour." He rubbed his hands over his face and brushed his thinning hair back. "We have one hour to decide what to do. Then, I fear, the clouds of war will indeed be upon us."

"The clouds—" Lieutenant MacPhearling looked up. "Colonel, I may have an idea."

"I would welcome that," Colonel Hesparsyn told him. "How do we get out of this mess with honor—and most of our troops—intact? I can't come up with an answer that isn't magic, Lieutenant, so magic it will have to be. Is there a spell that would do the job?"

"There may be," Lieutenant MacPhearling told his commander. "I've been looking at this wrong, sir. We're not interested in *fighting* these people—on either side."

"Not by choice," the Colonel agreed.

"We're interested in keeping them from fighting," the Lieutenant continued, talking faster and with more expression as the ideas worked themselves out in his mind. "We want to create conditions that will prevent a battle. This is a special case, and certain magical techniques are available to us that are not usable by the, ah, combatants."

"What are you suggesting, Lieutenant, a rain dance?" the Colonel asked, smiling.

"No, sir," Lieutenant MacPhearling said. "As you know, a rain dance requires a lot of preparation, for which we have insufficient time. And, besides, the success rate is only about thirty per cent. And I have a feeling these two groups might not stop fighting when they get wet. But perhaps, sir, the *rain* isn't necessary! After all, neither will be expecting anything from us, beyond the usual spells of self-defense. Anything we do will come as a complete surprise."

"And you've thought of something we can do?" Colonel Hesparsyn asked.

"I believe so, sir. Something we couldn't do if we ourselves were fighting. But we're not. Something that wouldn't stop them if they were ready for it. But they won't be."

"Tell me about it, Lieutenant," the Colonel said.

Colonel Hesparsyn swung easily onto his mount. The surrounding area, he noted without conscious thought, was a rolling grassy plain with a slight downhill slope from left to right. About a mile ahead of him, to the north, was a line of old, massive evergreen trees, which looked like the edge of an extensive forest. To his right, about two miles off, was the river, which was unfordable at this point.

The sun had risen in the east, as expected, and was blazing earnestly in a clear blue sky, with only the faintest traces of clouds way overhead.

The Azteques had finished their morning exercises, and were lining up to continue the march as though nothing were out of the ordinary. The only hint that all was not as it had been yesterday was that each of the priests—high and low—was painted with gaudy, contrasting red and blue stripes all over his body. The red, Colonel Hesparsyn strongly suspected, was some mixture of the priests' own blood. The warriors—exactly six hundred and twenty-seven of them for some reason steeped in Aztequean mythology—had only restrained, simple designs on their faces; but the Colonel noted that they were wearing the hardened leather greaves and armlets that they normally carried in their packs.

Across the horizon to the left, spaced about ten yards apart, a line of copper-skinned, silver-armored warriors from the local tribes stood stolidly, watching the Azteques as they prepared to move. Each of them carried a spear, and either a bow or what looked suspiciously to Colonel Hesparsyn like one of the new Dumberly-FitzHugh repeating rifles. He'd have to look into that when—if—he got back to Fort St. Michael. If somebody was supplying the natives with Dumberly-FitzHughs, somebody would have to be spoken harshly to.

The local warriors made no motion to approach, and the

Azteques ignored them completely as they finished their preparations to move on.

The main force of locals must be in those woods ahead of them, Colonel Hesparsyn decided. But the Azteques must surely realize that also, and would not enter the woods. Never let your opponent pick the time and place of battle. The Azteques would stop in the field before the woods and change to their battle formation. The locals would shoot arrows at them from the woods, but with little effect because of the distance. The Dumberly-FitzHugh repeating rifles, if that's what they were, might have more effect, but they were not designed for distant aimed fire. So the tribesmen would have to come out and fight. But they could pick when and where along the Azteque line to strike hardest. It was like a giant chess game—one where the pieces at risk didn't get taken off the board but merely lay where they had fallen and bled to death.

And what, Colonel Hesparsyn wondered, *will we be doing?*

The interesting thing was that neither side seemed to care. Probably both sides hoped that the Legion would simply not interfere in something that was none of its business.

Unfortunately, Colonel Hesparsyn couldn't agree.

The Colonel, along with his Company Sergeant, rode along the double column of mounted men, giving each man and horse a rapid but keen-eyed inspection. Three hundred smartly dressed, battle-ready men on three hundred well-trained, powerful mounts. Each man holding a steel-pointed eight-foot lance rigidly upright in its holder by his right stirrup. The steel tip of each lance was carefully wrapped in rags that had been soaked in cooking oil and tallow mixed with certain other oils and essential powders supplied by Lieutenant MacPhearling.

At the end of the column, Hesparsyn reined in his horse and turned to Sergeant Tavis. "Very good, Sergeant," he said. "I always knew that someday those lances would come in handy."

"Sir!" the Sergeant said, sounding offended. The lances were an ancient tradition, used these days only for dress parade. Which, as far as Sergeant Tavis was concerned, was sufficient reason for anything.

"Ready the men to move out, Sergeant," the Colonel said. "Watch for my signal."

"Yes, sir!" Tavis saluted, and his horse reared and pawed the air briefly.

I'd swear he was teaching that horse to salute, Colonel

Hesparsyn thought as the Sergeant trotted off down the line, *if that hadn't been the animal's left hoof*.

The sun was bright but the air was chill. The Azteque party was moving out; their drummers beat out the rhythm of the march on puma skin drums. The platform carrying the Eternal Fire was flanked by the palanquins carrying the higher-ranking priests, the whole surrounded by lesser priests and then warriors. It was a fierce and splendid display.

Lieutenant MacPhearling trotted up to the Colonel. The mounted magician's special wide saddlebags gave his horse the appearance of wearing stubby little wings. "I'm all ready, Colonel," he said.

Colonel Hesparsyn nodded. "You want the middle of the line?" he asked.

"That would probably be best," the Lieutenant agreed.

"Then let's get to it." The Colonel took his place at the front of the line, his thin face expressionless. He raised his right arm and moved his hand in a small circle, the signal to move out. The bugler sounded the brassy strains of "England and St. George," and move out the company did. Lances up, the double column trotted forward toward the trees.

The double column of Legionnaires passed the Azteque marchers and trotted up to a position about fifty yards from the forest. There they swung around and spread out until they were stretched in a single line between the trees and the approaching Azteque columns. Colonel Hesparsyn positioned himself in the middle of the line, and Lieutenant MacPhearling joined him there.

"It may be a little late to ask, MacPhearling, but, is this going to work?" The Colonel was looking at the wide brass bowl affixed to the front of the Lieutenant's saddle.

"I think so, Colonel," MacPhearling said. "The magic part of it will."

The Colonel glanced over at the end of the line, where Captain Flagg and his five picked men were waiting. If nothing went wrong, the plan would work like a charm. But there were two groups of warriors out there determined to see that things did go wrong. And, Colonel Hesparsyn reflected wryly, there were all sorts of charms.

The Azteque party reached a point about fifty yards from where the Legion was spread out and, as predicted, began to arrange themselves in battle formation. The palanquins were grounded, and Lord Chiklquetl and the other senior priest-magicians took their places at the front of the line, Lord Chiklquetl in the center. The platform bearing the Eternal Flame was placed behind the line on the right-hand side, closest to the river. They seemed unconcerned that a thin line of mounted Legionnaires stood between them and their forest foe.

With their placement and preparations complete, the Azteques froze in place, waiting. Theirs was not a mere lack of motion, it seemed to Colonel Hesparsyn, but a positive acceptance of immobility. They seemed able to wait all day—all year if necessary.

There was a slight flicker of movement in the woods, and then a runner carrying a white flag appeared. He loped steadily to where Colonel Hesparsyn waited, looking neither left nor right, and handed the Colonel a scroll, rolled into a tube and tied with a bit of thong. With hardly a perceptible break in his stride, he turned and raced back to the forest.

"Well, at least they didn't try another message arrow," Colonel Hesparsyn said wryly to Lieutenant MacPhearling. "God knows where it would have hit!" He unrolled the scroll and read it.

"Terse," he said, handing it to the Lieutenant.

> Colonel,
> You are in the way.
> Not a good place to be.
> Sincerely,
> Laughs-Last

"How long before they attack, do you think?" Lieutenant MacPhearling asked. "I'd like to wait until the last possible moment."

"Any time now," Hesparsyn told him. "There would be no reason to delay. They will be attacking the center of the line with foot troops, and then their cavalry will sweep around the left end."

"Prophecy, Colonel?"

"Tactics, Lieutenant. That's what I would do, to cut off the Azteque line of retreat."

The Lieutenant stared musingly at the battle-assembly of Azteque troops. "I don't think they have any intention of retreating," he said.

"I agree," Colonel Hesparsyn said. "If your scheme doesn't work, we're going to be very busy."

"Well, sir, we'll soon find out," Lieutenant MacPhearling told him. "I think it's time to commence."

"Good luck, Lieutenant," Hesparsyn said. "Although I am fully aware that luck has nothing to do with magic, still, it couldn't hurt." He nodded and rode off toward the front of the line.

MacPhearling opened the flaps on his overlarge, symbol-decorated saddlebags and removed a thin metal tripod with legs of different lengths. One leg of the tripod fit into a leather projection by his right stirrup, and the other two fastened to clamps at the front and rear of the saddle, forming a fairly stable projection canted off to the right of man and horse.

The Lieutenant slid the brass bowl into the gimbaled ring at the tip of the tripod and tightened three brass set screws to hold it securely in place. Now, as long as his horse didn't decide to roll over, he could make magic.

Three small lumps of charcoal from his saddlebag went into the brazier, followed by an already-prepared packet of finely divided charcoal mixed with various pulverized metals and earths, plus a few carefully picked and powdered organic materials.

A bright blue light flashed from the brazier as MacPhearling fit a slotted lid into place over it. The light continued to shine brightly through the narrow openings for about a minute, before muting itself. A dull purplish glow now surrounded the brazier, seemingly independent of the fire inside, which still shone a quiet blue through the intricate pattern of slits in the lid.

The magician held his hands out over the glow and stared into it, reciting secret, unintelligible words in a low-pitched, firm voice. His eyes, and the eyes of his horse, seemed to glow green in the strange light.

The double drumbeat of the Azteque warriors sounded over the meadow, and the triple bugle-call of the natives responded. Both sides were ready to attack. And the thin line of troops of Company B of the Duke's Own was all that stood between them.

Fine streams of blue smoke poured out of the slits in the brazier top and writhed about each other in a pattern no air current could have caused. And then, when they were about twelve feet off the ground, the streams separated and moved down the line of troopers. As the tip of each stream met with the rag-wrapped tip of a trooper's lance, the rags burst into silent flame, and billows of yellow-tinged white smoke poured from each ignited lance.

A smell reminiscent of roasting turnips filled the air. The line between the opposing forces was filling with the dense yellow-white smoke, punctuated with mounted, lance-armed Legionnaires.

The triple *ta-tra* of the horn sounded again, and the native troops began moving forward all along their line. The Azteques, drums beating, also moved forward. The smoke thickened and spread.

Colonel Hesparsyn stared into the billowing smoke and tried to make out the movement of the native warriors in front of him. Not a rifle had been fired yet; not an arrow had cut through the air. Both sides were waiting until the last possible second to start hostilities. They wanted to be so close that the first volley would count. And the first volley would have to go through his men to reach the enemy. Not, Colonel Hesparsyn reflected wryly, a good place to be if his war magician's scheme failed to work.

And so far it had produced nothing but smoke.

Colonel Hesparsyn resisted the urge to ride over to the Lieutenant and peer over his shoulder. It was not wise to disturb a wizard at work, even if you were his superior officer.

The smoke had spread out now, until it formed a wall between the opposing forces, running the full length of the front; about three hundred yards. It was some twenty feet thick and twelve feet high. Inside the smoke, visibility was limited to your hand in front of your face.

But this in itself would not stop the battle; it would merely curtail the effectiveness of guns and bows. Hand-to-hand combat—when you had to be closer than three feet from your opponent to even *see* him—would be particularly deadly.

The First Sergeant's whistle sounded—two sharp blasts—and the mounted troops of Company B diverged by the numbers. Even-numbered men moved forward at a walk. Odd-numbered men swiveled their horses to face in the other direction—back toward the Azteque column—and headed out at a walk. The smoke screen widened.

The Azteque column moved forward at a trot, determined to get into the protective shielding of the smoke before the natives raced through it from the other side and attacked.

On the other side, the main body of the natives marched out of the wood and double-timed in to the ever-expanding wall of smoke.

Now the smoke covered all, and everything smelled of roast turnips.

Now the first shots were heard, but who fired them and at whom they were aimed, was impossible to tell. An arrow whizzed by Colonel Hesparsyn's ear with a high-pitched droning sound.

The Colonel slowly rode over to where he had left Lieutenant MacPhearling, and found him in the process of adding to his brazier a small bundle of dried twigs from some black, oily plant. "Nothing's happening," the Colonel told the magician, "beyond the smoke screen itself."

"You will continue to think so," the Lieutenant told him without looking up, "for a while after the spell has commenced work on the opposing forces. It is designed to affect most strongly those in a fighting frenzy and those with hate in their hearts. If we were involved in the battle, we couldn't use this spell. Even so, there will be some effect on our troops. But at least they have been warned, and know what to expect."

Somewhere off to the Colonel's right someone screamed; a high, unexpectedly shrill scream. It was not the scream of combat, but the scream of fear.

"I think it's starting to work," said the Lieutenant, nodding in satisfaction. "If it were not that these two groups hate each other, a journeyman, such as I, couldn't have made the spell work. If we *were* involved on either side, the greatest master sorcerer in the Empire couldn't have done it."

Guns were being discharged freely now. Amid strange, unwarlike screams and cries of terror, the firing came rapidly and from all directions. *Sound like Dumberly-FitzHughs to me*, the Colonel thought. *His Grace of Arc is not going to be pleased*. Something appeared in the corner of his vision, but darted away as he turned to look at it. Although he hadn't clearly seen it, he knew it had been something horrible. *It's begun*, he thought.

Copliquetle the Invincible, Warrior Chief of the Puma Sept of the Azteque Horde, crouched on the ground, his feet buckled under him, his shield raised protectively over his head. With his right hand he stabbed his spear repeatedly at the mist above him, muttering the words of the charm his mother had taught him to ward off evil. All around him, grinning and chattering, and

weaving from side to side in the dense fog, he saw the skulls of
dead warriors. They stared at him, they laughed at him, they
whispered to him; they challenged him to play *tlachtli*. They told
him they would make him the ball.

"I am not afraid!" he yelled at them. "A Puma warrior knows
no fear! Come, put your bodies on and fight me! I can't fight
naked skulls."

One of the skulls weaved in toward him until it was facing him,
eye-socket to eye. "Life is fear," it whispered. "When you are
dead, you will not say you are not afraid. It will be evident. Hit
me with that spear, oh warrior, thrust it in this empty eye-socket,
for I am you. Am you. Am you . . ."

Copliquetle screamed.

Something moved in the white fog. Wise Fox, War Chief of the
Catahaw Tribe, caught the motion out of the corner of his eye. He
lowered his bow, useless anyway in the fog, and unslung his
battle-ax. There it was again. He turned to meet the threat.

At first he saw nothing, although he could sense that it was
there. And then—

It was tall—taller than a tree. A formless mass of black that
blotted out the mist. No, not merely black; it was *empty*. A large,
grotesque writhing mass of something that wasn't there.

Wise Fox, his battle-ax raised to forehead level, tried to yell the
Catahaw battle cry, but the inside of his mouth was dry as dust,
and the words stuck in his throat. The formless black thing
approached. Inside it he could now see various lights, colors,
shapes, beings—that flitted back and forth restlessly and glared at
him as they passed.

The blackness enveloped him, and he found himself standing
on a featureless plain that receded at unnatural and ever-changing
angles, in all directions. A naked woman with large breasts and
the head of a snake hissed at him, and then fell away; falling to the
right as though that direction had become down. A large elk
bounded at him, and then another, and a third, kicking down at
him with their hind feet as they passed over his head. They were
slit open, breast to belly, and their intestines were trailing on the
ground, and still they leaped.

The ground opened beneath him, and a hand reached out and
groped about, feeling for his feet. With a scream of terror, he
jumped aside.

• • •

The white smoke was rapidly clearing away. Colonel Hesparsyn signaled to Captain Flagg, who wheeled his small body of hand-picked men around, and raced back through the lines to the Azteque encampment.

The Azteque warriors were still in place, but they were unaware of the approaching Angevin detachment. They were, each of them, fighting a private battle. Some stood firm, mouthing inarticulate war cries, and thrusting at invisible opponents with their spears. Others were writhing on the ground, in the grip of some private hell. The priest-magicians seemed to have the worst of it: Some of them were frozen in place, staring at an unimaginable horror; some, pursued by invisible demons, ran unceasingly in small circles, screaming simple words, until they dropped from exhaustion.

Captain Flagg's men reached the back of the Azteque line, where the platform holding the Eternal Flame was grounded. The twelve slaves of the flame were sitting on the ground by the edge of the platform, looking bewildered, as their Azteque masters fought unseen enemies.

The Legionnaires prodded the slaves to their feet and indicated that they were to hoist the platform. Captain Flagg contributed his few words of pidgin Nahuatl to the prodding process. "Come, we move," he said. "Quick—quick!"

Stolidly the slaves picked up the platform and trotted through the chaotic battleground, oblivious to the strange and frightening scene surrounding them. Theirs was not to remark or wonder or consider the world around them. Theirs was but to lift and carry and eat gruel and sleep when they could. And thank whatever god it was that watched over slaves—if there were such—that their masters practiced *almost* no human sacrifice anymore.

Colonel Hesparsyn signaled for his company to form up while Lieutenant MacPhearling put away his magical apparatus. Around him was surely the strangest battlefield scene he had ever seen in twenty-seven years with the Legion. Hundreds of men, scattered about a narrow plain, fighting furiously or collapsed from exhaustion—or crouched in pitiable postures of defeat; and nowhere any enemy to be seen. Each of the men locked in his own private hell, fighting his own private fears, unaware of ally or foe.

"You've done well," the Colonel told his Magic Officer. "At the very least, you have saved many lives. How long will the effects of this spell last?"

Lieutenant MacPhearling closed and secured his saddlebag. "Hard to say, sir," he said. "The spell interacts with the—let's call it the psyche—of the individual experiencing it. Most of our men, because they were not involved, got but a small taste of it, and that has washed out by now. For these others"—he indicated with a wave of his hand the battlefield scene before him—"several hours, or possibly longer."

"Then Lord Chiklquetl should be caught up to us, and his precious Eternal Flame, by the end of the day," the Colonel said. "With his flame platform up here with us, he won't stand around to fight the locals."

"If he figures out what happened, which he will," Lieutenant MacPhearling said, "he just may decide to fight us instead."

"Now wouldn't that be a pretty mess of beans," Colonel Hesparsyn said, waving his arm for Company B to move out. "But he won't, Lieutenant. Not after that display of magic you've just shown him."

"But we can't use it against him if he attacks us," Lieutenant MacPhearling protested. "It won't work if we're involved in the battle."

"That may be so, Lieutenant," the Colonel said, "but *he* doesn't know that."

7

A ROW OF green-coated guardsmen stood at attention as the cutter came alongside the pier. One of them grabbed the line tossed out to him and tied the boat off. The Chief Master-at-Arms in charge of the guard unit came out onto the dock. A man with a craggy, good-humored face bearing a carefully trimmed beard, he stepped alongside the craft to get a good look at its occupants. "Is one of you gentlemen Lord Darcy?" he called.

"I am." Lord Darcy jumped nimbly from the bobbing cutter to the pier and paused to look up at the giant pyramid that dominated the island. Then he turned back to the guardsman. "What can I do for you, Chief?"

"Not a thing, Your Lordship," the guardsman said, touching his hand to the rim of his uniform cap. "Chief Master at Arms Karlus of the Duke's Guard at your service. We were told to expect you, and not to allow anybody except Your Lordship's self and companions on the island."

"Very good, Chief Karlus," Lord Darcy said. "Allow me to present my companions: Master Sean O Lochlainn, Father Adamsus, and Master Lord John Quetzal. I am acting as Duke Charles's

Special Investigator, and these are my assistants. We are here at the Duke's direction to investigate the crime of murder which was committed here."

"Very good, Your Lordship," the Chief said, stepping back and giving Lord Darcy a formal salute. "However we can help, please let me know."

The importance of tradition was not underestimated in the Angevin Empire. The Duke's Guard was supposed to render all assistance to a ducal investigator as a matter of course—but not until the Guard was officially informed that the man was an investigator, and was currently investigating a crime. Lord Darcy's official title of Chief Investigator of the Court of Chivalry would warrant more than the usual courtesy—but not one whit of assistance from a guardsman on duty, unless he was investigating a crime. When an investigator was not actively engaged in his employment, he was entitled to the full courtesy of his rank—but not his title. Only when investigating a crime did a ducal or royal investigator speak with the full voice and authority of the Duke, or the King.

Such rules could be found, or extrapolated from other rules, in the Guardsman's Handbook, but they were merely a compilation of age-old accepted behavior. The force behind them came not from any act of parliament or royal fiat, but from centuries of tradition, which had a meaning and a force greater than law.

"How many men have you on the island, Chief?" Lord Darcy asked.

"Twenty-six, my lord. Twenty-eight, counting myself and my sergeant. I have twelve stationed around the shoreline, six roaming about, and eight in reserve."

"Have you had any trouble?"

"Nary a sign of anything, my lord."

"Very good. Keep at it. I suppose your relief is provided for?"

"Yes, my lord."

"If anything should happen, no matter how slight, see that I am notified at once, Chief Karlus. I depend on you."

"No fear, my lord," the craggy-faced chief assured him. "Nothing is going to happen while I and my lads are here."

"Well then, if anything should attempt to happen, let me know."

"I shall, my lord."

"Very good." Lord Darcy turned to his companions. "Well,

lords and masters, shall we ascend the pyramid and see what awaits us?"

The four of them made their way up the wooden steps from the pier and began the climb to the twin temples atop the ancient pyramid. "I see, or should say I feel, that you didn't reactivate the aversion spell on the pyramid," Lord Darcy commented to Lord John Quetzal when they were about a third of the way to the top of the massive stone structure.

"That's true, my lord," Lord John replied. "The guardsmen were sent here immediately, and it would have made things extremely uncomfortable for them. The original spell wouldn't have, I confess, but I wasn't sure how to prepare that one."

"And why is that, Lord John?" Master Sean asked.

"The original spell, which I removed when Father Adamsus and Count de Maisvin and I arrived here, was carefully attuned to the purpose of the visit. Anyone visiting for a legitimate purpose would not have felt its effect."

"That's a very complex and difficult job—to have, so-to-speak, 'windows' built into a spell like that," Master Sean commented. "Why would anyone go to the trouble?"

"And why, then, would you and Father Adamsus have felt its effects?" Lord Darcy asked.

"Master Sean's question I cannot answer," Lord John said. "We would have to investigate the ducal records to find the one authorizing the spell."

"And even that might not mention it," Master Sean added. "It might have been a whim of the sorcerer's, don't you see."

"That's so," Lord John agreed.

Lord Darcy paused for a second, and looked down at how far they had come, and then back up at how far they still had to go. "This is quite a climb," he added. "I didn't realize that these things were so steep."

Father Adamsus sat down on the steps, wiping his forehead with a large white handkerchief that he pulled from his cape. "I believe I can answer your question, Lord Darcy," he said, puffing slightly from the effort of the climb. "We felt the effects of the aversion spell because we were not there to engage in anything that the original creator of the spell would have considered legitimate business. Indeed, quite the reverse. We were there to reactivate one of the temples. Not the unholy temple of Huitsilopochtli, to be sure, but I doubt whether any spell could be set fine enough to tell the difference."

"I see," Lord Darcy said, thinking that over as they continued to make their way up the high and narrow steps. "This case has some interesting aspects. I look forward to—ah! Here we are at the top." Lord Darcy pulled himself up and paused to look around. "A noble view," he said. "I believe this must be the highest point in the entire area."

"That is so, my lord," Father Adamsus agreed.

Lord Darcy turned around to examine the façades of the two temples which crouched together atop the massive pile of stones. They were not built to be in harmony with each other, he observed. The two were of different sizes and shapes, their proportions were different, and the structural details did not agree in form or style. Either would have looked impressive centered atop the pyramid, but the two side by side looked to be a hasty and ill-advised compromise.

The two temples were crowded together at the top, with a walk space from the walls to the edge of the pyramid, which varied from about eight feet in front to less than four feet at the rear. The temple of Huitsilopochtli, on Lord Darcy's left, was by far the more massive structure. Although tiny compared to the pyramid it rested upon, it bulked large on the small platform at the apex. About thirty feet wide and fifteen feet high, it had a peaked roof that added about ten feet to its height, and was surrounded by intricately carved waist-high stones, which were set into its walls every few feet. Ten feet high on the outer wall, going all around the building, a wide frieze had been cut into the stone. Lord Darcy stared at it for a minute before realizing that the carving was made up of a triple row of grinning skulls.

Snug up next to it, with less than a foot clearance between the two walls, was the smaller temple of Tsaltsaluetol, the God of Fire, where the Eternal Flame was to be rekindled. The stone walls of this temple were covered with Azteque pictoglyphs, which seemed to be arranged in descending rows, right-to-left, to tell a continuous story. There were, Lord Darcy noted, far fewer skulls among the designs carved into its surface. The roof of the temple was slightly domed.

The foot of space between the two temples was filled waist-high with the debris and clutter of building, as though the stone masons had not wanted to bother taking their fragments back down the pyramid. There were signs that the space had once been closed off by a thin cement barrier, but it had worn away over the centuries.

The great wooden front doors of both temples were standing wide open, and Lord Darcy walked over to the right-hand one, the temple of Tsaltsaluetol, and peered inside. The interior consisted of one room, essentially square, lit by a series of horizontal slits cut into the walls right under the roof. Aside from a very small back door, which also stood open, the room was devoid of furnishings or other appointments.

"This is the temple to Tsaltsaluetol, the God of Fire, is it not?" Lord Darcy asked.

"Tsalt*sal*uetol," Master Lord John said, correcting Lord Darcy's pronunciation. "Yes, it is."

"Where is the Eternal Flame going to be placed when it arrives?" Lord Darcy asked. "There is no altar or fireplace."

"The High Priest, Lord Chiklquetl, is bringing the altar," Lord John told him. "When the temple was abandoned, three hundred years ago, the priest of the temple took the Eternal Flame with him. Now it is being returned."

"Ah," Lord Darcy said. He entered the temple and looked curiously around at the bare walls.

"The murdered man is in the other temple, my lord," Father Adamsus said, finding, not to his surprise, that he couldn't bring himself to say the name of the god who had once occupied the house next door. Certainly not while this close to that absent god's home.

"I know, Father," Lord Darcy said. "That's why I'm in this temple."

"Oh," the good Father said.

"These doors have not been open long," Lord Darcy commented.

"That's so, my lord," Lord John told him. "The doors to this temple were opened a few days before we arrived to cleanse the, ah, temple next door. Three days, I believe."

"By someone who had a legitimate purpose, no doubt," Lord Darcy said, smiling. "Else he would have had to suffer the effects of that overly elaborate century-old aversion spell."

"Prince Ixequatle," Lord John said quietly.

Lord Darcy turned to look at him. "The young man whose body lies next door?"

"That is so."

"And what was he doing here?" Lord Darcy asked. "Was he alone?"

"He came here to see what preparations would be necessary before the temple of Tsaltsaluetol could be reconsecrated and receive the holy fire," Lord John told him. "I believe he was alone."

"Fascinating!" Lord Darcy said. "No doubt he came by cutter, and the boatmen waited below. We shall have to locate those boatmen and speak with them. I take it he could not have entered the temple of Huitsilopochtli at that time?"

Father Adamsus felt himself wince as the ancient name was pronounced. *I'll have to watch that,* he thought. *Either I'm getting overly sensitive, or there's something that, as a sensitive, I'm feeling in this location. I had better determine which.*

"There's no way he could have opened those doors, my lord," Lord John said. "The locking spell had not been disturbed, and at any rate, he didn't have the key."

"You checked for dematerialization, of course, my lord?" Master Sean asked.

"Well, actually, I didn't," Lord John said, looking faintly embarrassed. "But, as Prince Ixequatle was not himself a wizard, I thought it highly unlikely."

"It is, it is," Master Sean assured the young master magician. "But we'll check for it, nonetheless. It isn't until we've eliminated the dross of the unlikely, as my lord Darcy is fond of reminding us, that we can find the remaining golden grain of truth."

"I expect that's why this room is so clean," Lord Darcy remarked. "I had expected to find a century's worth of dust in here, but the Prince must have swept it out." He looked keenly at each of his companions for a second, as if expecting a reaction. When he got none, he resumed his careful investigation.

Lord Darcy spent another ten minutes looking systematically about the small room, peering into the shadowy corners with the aid of a pocket lantern and a magnifying glass, which he produced from an inner pocket of his cape. Then he stood up and surveyed the entire room, slowly turning on his heel to bring it all into view. "Fascinating," he said.

The others looked blankly around the empty room.

"What is there in here that you find fascinating, my lord?" Master Sean asked.

"It's what isn't in here, Master Sean," Lord Darcy told him.

"It's that missing dust that fascinates me. There's so much of it, you see."

Father Adamsus rubbed his hands together. "Surely we have here a conundrum," he said. "You point out to us the presence of the absence of dust, my lord. And yet you yourself offered an explanation of that a few short minutes ago, when you suggested that the poor unfortunate lad whose body awaits us next door must have swept out the room himself when he opened it."

Lord Darcy turned to the exorcist. "Oh, come now, Father," he said. "Can you picture a young Azteque prince carrying a broom up here in the first place, or using it in the second? I find the idea highly unlikely, and incompatible with my views of either youth or royalty."

"Well now," Father Adamsus said, putting his forefinger to his lower lip, "when you put it that way— "

Lord Darcy turned to Master Sean. "Is there any spell, or enchantment, or other diversion that would recall the dust that covered this floor, let us say a week ago?"

Master Sean thought it over for a minute before shaking his head. "I'm afraid not, my lord," he replied. "There's a lack of relevance, don't you see. It doesn't matter to the dust where it lies—here or elsewhere. It has never been attached or associated with this room."

"That's what I was afraid of," Lord Darcy said. "But, I suppose, one can't expect miracles. Come, let us go next door and investigate the scene of the crime."

The temple of Huitsilopochtli was as it had been last week. As it had been, for that matter, five centuries before. Three parallel vertical slits high in the south wall admitted the rays of the afternoon sun, spilling them across the ancient altar that dominated the room. Nine feet long, three feet wide, four feet high; carved from a solid block of once-white granite, the humpbacked altar, stained with the blood of centuries of human sacrifices, crouched before them, chuckling of ancient horrors. They all felt it; Father Adamsus perhaps more than the others. On the stone was the body of Prince Ixequatle, reposing there as it had the week before.

"What's to be done with this temple?" Lord Darcy asked. "I take it it is not to be used for anything?"

"Certainly for nothing religious or ritualistic, my lord," Father Adamsus said. "I am going to insist to His Grace that it be sealed up with cement, and the most powerful spells a Church sorcerer can manage, and eventually razed to the floor, and every stone broken to powder and scattered to the winds."

"A bit strong," Lord Darcy said.

"The—being—who was home here, cannot be treated lightly," Father Adamsus said.

"I understand that you did not perform the exorcism rite on the day you discovered the body," Lord Darcy said to Father Adamsus. "You had come up here to do so, but it was never done."

"I, ah, dissuaded him, my lord," Lord John Quetzal said. "Likewise, I suggested that Father Adamsus not give the deceased the last rites. Didn't want to destroy evidence."

"Oh, of course, of course—you did right," Lord Darcy said. "I was just wondering if that would explain the odd feeling I have that that bit of stone there is watching me."

"I have the same feeling, my lord," Father Adamsus said. "But, oddly enough, whatever physical or psychic evil was in this temple—and I feel sure that there must have been a myriad of, ah, undesirable presences—they are none of them present any longer. The stone altar, although washed in blood, is totally innocent of malevolence."

"Really?" Master Sean said. "That's very odd—very odd indeed. How do you account for that, Father?"

Father Adamsus shook his head. "I cannot," he said. "It is a puzzle."

"Couldn't an exorcism have been performed at an earlier time?" Lord Darcy suggested. "Perhaps a century ago, when the temples were sealed and the avoidance spell was first put on the pyramid?"

"It could have, my lord, no question about that," Father Adamsus replied. "The only thing is—it wasn't! As you know, any exorcism procedure has to be authorized by the local bishop. And there is no record of any such authorization."

"Very curious," Lord Darcy said, looking about him at the stones of the temple floor, dark-stained as the altar, with the blood of centuries. "One would expect the presence of the Dark Force—if I may use that imprecise expression in the presence of my professional confreres—to be overwhelming in this, ah, place. Wouldn't you say, Master Sean?"

"Aye," Master Sean replied. "Very much so, my lord. Father

Adamsus, what say you? Were you surprised at the absence of hostile entities to submit to your exorcism?"

"Master Sean, I was astounded," the slender priest said, lacing his hands together in front of his chest. "My only other experience with one of these—pyramids—had led me to expect otherwise."

"We must assume, then, that the rite of exorcism *was* performed in this temple, at some time in the past—regardless of the Cathedral records," Lord Darcy said. "Since these beings do not of themselves go away, I believe."

"Indeed not," Father Adamsus agreed. "They are bound to the brick and mortar that called or created them—or, in this case, the stone and blood. Only the Holy Rite of Exorcism of the Mother Church can relieve them of the geas that compels them to remain where they are. Even then, as I had occasion to remark to the Bishop a few weeks ago, they may, under some circumstances, decided to return home. Which is why I feel so strongly that the, ah, home be removed—destroyed— obliterated—before the being who once dwelled here decides to return."

"I understand," Lord Darcy said. "Master Sean, is there anything in that carpetbag of yours that would give us an indication of just how long ago this putative exorcism was performed?"

"I'm afraid not, my lord," Master Sean said. "The beings of the *demi-monde* are not, strictly speaking, the concern of the licensed magician. Some forms of sorcery may strive to control or direct them, but all of these forms fall within the realm of black magic."

"Are there not some priest-magicians who deal with these creatures?" Lord Darcy asked.

"Aye," Master Sean agreed. "But only to enquire of them, neither to control nor direct, if you see what I mean."

"It is a curious thing," Father Adamsus said, "that none of the priests who have the gift of exorcism are among these priest-magicians. They can communicate with the spirit world, but they cannot banish it, for some reason."

"I think I can explain that, Father," Lord John said, a slight twinkle evident in his black eyes. "It is a question of belief."

"Belief?" Father Adamsus looked puzzled.

"Yes. You see, in an exorcism you must say, with all your heart, 'begone spirits—return here no more.' This is one of the key exhortations, is that not so?"

"In Latin," Father Adamsus said, nodding his head. "For some reason most creatures of the *demi-monde* seem to respond better to Latin."

"And you must mean it," Lord John said.

"Absolutely," Father Adamsus agreed.

"But, when the priest-magician says it, the priest in him means it, but the magician in him is whispering 'now wait a minute—there are a few more questions I'd like to ask.'"

Master Sean chuckled. "Aye, that'd be so," he agreed. "Cats and sorcerers are more prone to die of curiosity than anything else."

Lord Darcy was prowling around the room, bent over, with his glass in his hand. He examined the bare stone floor and walls of that ancient temple, with the rigorous care and attention to detail that he always paid to the immediate area in which a crime has been committed. "Lord John," he said, "would you mind telling me just what steps *you* took upon discovering the body?"

"First, I sent Lord de Maisvin back with the cutter, to notify the authorities and to bring back a chirurgeon," Lord John replied. "Then I examined the body and the area around it for any physical clues. I discovered little beyond the obsidian-bladed knife found by the body. Father Adamsus was good enough to stay with me and verify my notes, of which there are but a scant half-page of any value, I'm afraid." Lord John shook his head ruefully.

"Ah, well, you can't very well find what isn't there," Master Sean said. "Sometimes it's like that."

"It's true," Lord John agreed, "but you can't help asking yourself whether this is one of those times, or whether you're overlooking something that someone cleverer or more experienced would find. At least I can't."

Lord Darcy turned to look at the young Mechicain forensic sorcerer. "I trust you will keep asking yourself that throughout your whole career," he said. "It will give you that extra edge that will keep you at the top of your craft. It is those who are complacent who get sloppy and undependable. You are an exemplar of your craft, my lord. If Master Sean were unavailable, I cannot think of anyone I would rather have at my side in an investigation."

"Thank you, my lord," Lord John said.

"What did the chirurgeon say?" Lord Darcy asked, turning back to his investigation of the bare floor in the left-hand back corner of the temple.

Lord John shrugged his broad shoulders., "What could he say beyond making it official? Prince Ixequatle had been killed some hours earlier, presumably with the bone-and-obsidian knife found by the body, and his chest had been ritually torn open, and the heart removed."

"Yes, and then?" Lord Darcy asked. "What did you do?"

"I placed a preservation spell on the body, leaving it as you see it there, and I came away." Lord John said, speaking very carefully. "I did nothing else. What else could I do? I was not authorized by the Duke to conduct a forensic investigation, and so I did not do so. If I did any tampering with the body, it will show up when Master Sean conducts his tests, but I assure you I did not."

Lord Darcy stood up and turned to face Lord John Quetzal, looking slightly puzzled. "What—" he said. "Oh! Of course. My apologies, Lord John, for not making this clear earlier. You are not under suspicion in this case. Not any more than anyone else who doesn't have the near-perfect alibi of being on the other side of the Atlantic when it happened. You have my word."

"Lord John under suspicion?" Master Sean asked, sniffing. "Incredible!"

"That's what he has been thinking," Lord Darcy said. "Am I right?"

Lord John nodded. "So," he said. "What was I to think? The only master forensic sorcerer in town, and not asked to investigate? Duke Charles had no way of knowing that you and Master Sean were on your way. Why else would he have kept me away? He thought that because the Prince and I were of the same race, I might have committed the crime. That, at least, was my reasoning when the Duke made it clear that the body was to be left alone for the time being."

"I can assure you, my young friend, that the Duke did not indicate any such suspicion to me when we discussed the case this morning," Lord Darcy said. "It was suggested to Duke Charles that your presence, as a Catholic Mechicain, might offend the approaching Azteque treaty party. I understand that there is a thinly veiled hostility between the two groups."

"That is so," Lord John admitted. "When my great-grandfather, the then Duke of Mechicoe, embraced Christianity, Quachititiquotl, the then Emperor of the Azteques, declared my great-grandfather and all his relatives dead, and the Duchy of

Mechicoe vacant. He appointed a 'new' duke, whose family retains the title to this day. Our two families very carefully ignore each other."

"Now, just how large is the Duchy of Mechicoe?" Master Sean asked. "And just how do the two dukes decide who controls what facility or collects what revenue?"

"It is a medium-sized chunk out of the north-central area of the Mechicain arm—or perhaps I should call it a leg—of New England. It includes Tenochtitlan, the capital city."

"Ah, yes," Father Adamsus said. "I was there once, four years ago. I stayed at your father's palace, as a matter of fact. You were away in England, studying sorcery. Your father is very proud of you."

"Magic is very important in our family," Lord John said. "We keep our title, our palace, and probably our lives, only because of the superiority of Christian magic to Azteque magic. It is the sort of thing that can shape one's life."

"I can well believe it," Lord Darcy agreed. "Now you must relieve your mind of any thought that you are suspected of this crime. *I*, certainly, do not suspect you. And neither does the Duke. His only concern was that by asking you—a Mechicain, who is not on His Grace's regular staff of investigators—to investigate the killing, he might offend your prospective Azteque guests. He was hoping that Major Sir John DePemmery, his regular investigator, and Master Bryce Comrich, his regular forensic sorcerer, might return from wherever they are in time to conduct the investigation. And, instead, he got me and Master Sean."

"Ah, my lord," Master Sean said, looking slightly troubled, "I trust there won't be any difficulty with allowing Lord John here to work as my assistant?"

"If you need him, and he is willing," Lord Darcy said, " I don't see any difficulty. As long as the investigation is under our control, we can use whatever assistance we require. And, as always, I leave such choices in your capable hands, Master Sean."

"Good, good," Master Sean said. "I anticipate the need for a few rather lengthy and difficult procedures, and Sir John's assistance will be invaluable. That is, if you'll agree to help me, Sir John?"

"I should be delighted, Master Sean," Sir John said earnestly. "Working with you has always been a learning experience in the past, and I trust that I am never too old nor too conceited to learn."

Lord Darcy went over to the ancient altar and stared down at the corpse. "A young man," he said. "Somewhere between twenty-five and thirty, I should judge. Skin and facial features consistent with Azteque heritage. Has he been positively identified?"

"As positively as possible," Lord John said. "That is, I cannot identify him as Prince Ixequatle, since I never met the Prince back in Tenochtitlan. But he is the man who arrived in New Borkum, claiming to be Prince Ixequatle. All his servants believe him to be the Prince."

"A nice distinction," Lord Darcy said.

"What tests do you want me to perform, my lord?" Master Sean asked.

"Let's see," Lord Darcy mused. "What can we hope to find out?" He walked slowly around the altar, his hands clasped behind his back, examining the body from each side. Only the nervous twitching of his thumbs showed the suppressed energy under his passive exterior. "Cause of death would be a good place to start," he said.

"You mean aside from that great gaping hole in his chest?" Father Adamsus asked, staring at the corpse. It was as though time had just looped around and brought him back to a week ago. The preservation spell on the corpse kept it as it had been; even to the not-completely-congealed blood which had run out of the body. It remained semifluid, and kept the red color of life, belying the awful stillness of the body from which it had spilled.

Lord Darcy turned to Lord John. "You are familiar with the Azteque ceremony in which they performed human sacrifice?" he asked.

"I have had it described to me," Lord John said quietly.

"Describe it to me, if you don't mind," Lord Darcy requested.

Father Adamsus gasped. "My lord!" he said sharply, "not here!" He waved his arm to indicate the interior walls of the temple. "That would be most unwise."

"Of course," Lord Darcy said. "Pardon me, Father. Master Sean, I would like to know how Prince Ixequatle met his death and where. I should like you to examine that rather complex loincloth he is wearing—"

"*Maxtlatl*," Lord John said. "The garment is called a *maxtlatl*."

"Thank you, my lord," Lord Darcy said. "I would also like you to check the blood surrounding the body. See if it's all his. That's all that comes to mind at the moment. If you yourself, or Lord John, think of anything else that might be of use, please go right ahead."

"Um," Master Sean said, setting his symbol-decorated carpet-bag down and staring speculatively at the murder scene. "The Law of Synecdoche is useful for such questions," he said. "But how to best apply it? Lord John, perhaps you'd busy yourself by removing the preservation spell you've placed on the body while I see what I have handy in my bag here."

Lord Darcy and Father Adamsus walked outside the temple while the two thaumaturgists busied themselves at their tasks. "How are you going to go about this?" Father Adamsus asked. "Finding the poor lad's killer, I mean."

"That depends on exactly what information about himself he has left behind," Lord Darcy said. "In some cases—in many cases—the forensic sorcerers do my job for me. When Master Sean tells me to look for a tall brown-haired man in his mid-forties of Burgundian extraction, with a scar on his right arm, whose first name is Guiliam, I can just turn the case over to the guardsmen. There are times when Master Sean is able to report the exact identity of the killer; and, as you know, a licensed forensic sorcerer's report is accepted as evidence in criminal cases."

"In this case?" Father Adamsus asked vaguely.

Lord Darcy shook his head. "I don't think that's going to happen in this case," he said. "I will, of course, be damned grateful—excuse the language, Father—for anything that Master Sean and Lord John can determine; but I doubt it will be that simple."

A slight smell of incense wafted out through the open temple doors. The murmur of Latin phrases, intoned with a strong Celtic accent, could be heard.

"Well," Lord Darcy added, "we'll soon find out."

8

CHARLES, DUKE OF ARC, was not pleased. It usually came to pass that when Charles was not pleased, those around him had little reason to congratulate themselves. "Three days, my lord Darcy," he enunciated in his high, precise voice, leaning forward in the massive oak chair behind his oversized desk and jabbing the desk with this forefinger, "three days you've been here, you and your magical Master O Lochlainn. You've puttered about, and visited here and there, and you have nothing to show for it. Nothing! I might just as well have let that young Mechicain fellow do it."

His Grace of Arc was troubled, and his trouble was beyond his own skills to patch. His Grace had gone to great lengths, and risked a state secret, to send for Lord Darcy. The least Lord Darcy could have done was to solve the crime in as brief a time as possible. After all, was not Lord Darcy a wonder worker in his chosen profession?

Lord Darcy recognized the attitude and bowed silently to the Duke, not allowing any emotion to cross his face. The reputation for being an almost clairvoyant crook-catcher was sometimes a drawback, he reflected. He was somewhat in the position of the court jester who is perpetually being asked to "say something funny."

"Well?" His Grace asked testily. "Sit down, man, and tell me something. We're three days closer to the Azteque retinue arriving, and they're overdue already. I do not wish to have the murder of an Azteque prince unsolved when they get here."

"I understand, Your Grace," Lord Darcy said, sitting in the chair opposite the Duke. "But you must understand that investigating a crime is not cut and dried. It is like trout fishing; you can cast your line many times without success, and there's no way to rush it."

"You can always drain the pond, my lord," the Duke said, leaning back in his chair without changing his intense gaze at Lord Darcy.

Lord Darcy raised an eyebrow. "Hoist by my own simile, Your Grace," he said. "Would that I could 'drain the pond.' I do realize the need for haste, and I'm doing what I can. I have commandeered twenty plainsclothes guardsmen to help with the investigation of Prince Ixequatle's servants and friends, and his movements since he arrived here, and I would take more if I could think of anything to use them for."

"You believe the answer lies there?" the Duke asked. His ire spent, he was now prepared to listen. Lord Darcy knew that His Grace, despite the occasional outbursts of petulant anger, was a fine administrator in a difficult post; Governor of the Empire's largest, newest, and wildest domain.

"Truthfully, I don't know, Your Grace. It seems logical. Usually you have to have had some interaction with someone to have a reason to kill them. We are seeking that interaction."

"What do you think of it being a ritual murder?" the Duke asked. "That's what de Maisvin thinks. Either some fanatical Azteque who lives about Nova Eboracum, or one of the Prince's own staff that he brought with him. They used to sacrifice their own royalty, de Maisvin says. He's been researching it."

"What sort of man is the Count de Maisvin?" Lord Darcy asked, "and just what was he doing out there with Father Adamsus and Lord John Quetzal?"

"Sort of an unnecessary appendage, eh?" the Duke asked. "Well, it's my fault, Darcy. I sent him. I use the Count, in effect, as my general busybody and surrogate. If I can't get to see something myself, I send de Maisvin. I don't mean State occasions, of course.

"As to what sort of man the Count is, he is highly intelligent and intensely loyal." Duke Charles stared at Lord Darcy for a moment. "You're thinking of him as a suspect, eh? Well, very natural. But, in that case, I should tell you that all my officers swear a bound loyalty oath: 'I shall, as I hope for salvation, truly obey the commands of my sovereign, in person or through his liege lords and adjutants, and shall hold his interests paramount in all of my actions. So do I swear with all my heart, and so do I affirm.'

"I don't think that would stop one of them from committing murder, if it *didn't* involve the Empire, or if he believed it to be for the good of the Empire, but an act of murder that was also harmful to His Majesty's interests would probably burn something out in their head, or so my own sorcerer, Master Poul Hosmer, tells me."

Lord Darcy noted that the thought had occurred to Duke Charles, else he would not have questioned Master Poul. "Well, Your Grace," he said mildly. "What if the killer is one of your bound officers, and he thought he *was* doing it for the good of the Empire."

Charles, Duke of Arc, thought that over for a moment. "You do come up with the strangest ideas," he said. "As for Count de Maisvin, he didn't want to go out to the Pyramid Island with Father Adamsus and Lord John; it was my idea. I wanted to make sure everything was done right. In this case, I admit, a ridiculous excess of zeal, since neither de Maisvin nor myself could tell if either a sorcerer or an exorcist did something wrong. My wife tells me I'm fussy, and perhaps it's so."

"Better to be too careful than too lax, Your Grace," Lord Darcy suggested.

"Yes, yes," the Duke agreed. "Just what I say. De Maisvin is really an impressive man, you know. Good at whatever he puts his hand to. I'm lucky to have him. Carries a MacGregor .40 caliber handgun given him by His Majesty, you know. I believe you have one yourself, don't you, my lord?"

"I do," Lord Darcy admitted. "A special caliber and a special gun, made by MacGregor only to the King's order. I am very proud to carry mine."

"Well, I'm lucky to have both of you here, then," Duke Charles said. "But I trust one of you will solve this little mystery very soon."

"Is de Maisvin also investigating the murder?" Lord Darcy asked.

"At my order," the Duke said. "He'll follow your instructions, of course. He should look you up sometime this morning. But I do want him to follow through on his theory. It *could* be a ritual killing, you know."

"Master Sean O Lochlainn and Lord John Quetzal await me in the anteroom," Lord Darcy said. "May I have your permission to bring them in? You might be interested in Lord John's description of what the Azteque sacrifice ritual was like."

"I confess I'd be fascinated," His Grace said. "Secondhand, I trust." He raised his hand, palm outward. "I jest, my lord; you know I jest. Bring them in, by all means."

Lord Darcy rose and went through the heavy door into the anteroom. There were a variety of court persons waiting there to catch the Duke's eye, with a guard at the door to keep them out, and a seneschal at a small desk by the door to weed them out.

"Would you ask Master Sean O Lochlainn and Lord John Quetzal to join His Grace and me," Lord Darcy whispered to the seneschal. His two compatriots were sitting only four feet away, but protocol must be observed.

"Lord John explained this to me two days ago," Lord Darcy told the Duke when the Mechicain sorcerer and Master Sean had seated themselves across the desk. "I asked him to describe the sacrifice ritual. Among other things, I learned that there was not merely one, but a host of sacrificial rituals."

"That's so," Lord John said, nodding. "And a score of gods to sacrifice to; some of them even crueler than Huitsilopochtli. The priests of Xipe commonly wore a freshly flayed human skin during their religious ceremonies."

"Tell His Grace the story of Huitsilopochtli," Lord Darcy said.

"Huitsilopochtli was—is—one of the most important gods, the God of the Sun," Lord John said. "According to the ancient ritual, he fed on human blood, and he needed to eat daily.

"Once a year—or more often in troubled times—he fed on the blood of a prince."

"A prince!" Duke Charles turned to Lord Darcy. "Then de Maisvin may be right!"

"It is possible, Your Grace," Lord Darcy said, "but there's more to the tale—"

"A captive, or on occasion a volunteer, was made a prince for the ceremony," Lord John went on. "For up to six months he *was* a prince: He lived in the palace, he wore rich clothing and ate the finest food, he was married to a princess, his advice was sought with the other princes in matters of policy. In word, deed, and behavior, he was as the other royalty in the land.

"Then the holy day would arrive when a prince's blood must feed Huitsilopochtli. Lots are cast, and our six-month prince is chosen. It's very symbolic—the ballot is rigged to show that life is rigged. The prince is stripped of his fine clothes to show the transitory nature of wealth and possessions. He is taken to the water's edge and put in a rowboat, where he is deserted by his wife and servants. Thus showing the ephemeral quality of human relationships. He rows himself out to the pyramid. As he climbs it, the rest of his clothes are ripped from his body.

"When he reaches the temple of Huitsilopochtli, four priests grab him and throw him face-up onto the altar. The top of the altar stone is humped so that when his arms and legs are held down, his chest protrudes. This also widens the space between the ribs to make the knife-thrust easier.

"The Chief Priest thrusts his obsidian-bladed knife between the third and fourth ribs, and rips the wall of the chest open. The still-beating heart is cut loose and held aloft for Huitsilopochtli's approval."

There was a silence as Lord John stopped talking. Then Duke Charles said, "Well!" and stared off into the middle distance.

"Not nice," Master Sean said. "No wonder that Father Adamsus expected to have a difficult exorcism; the creature that fed—psychically—on that blood must have grown in power until he was possessed of a horrific malevolence."

"I have been long fascinated by the study of pantheistic theologies," Lord John said, "as you can probably understand. When a minor demon is treated as a god for a few centuries, his power in the Underworld, and among humans, can grow to unbelievable proportions. If the early Angevin missionaries and explorers who came here had not had a full knowledge of both magic and demonology, then those bloodthirsty savages who were my ancestors would probably have overwhelmed them with ease."

"Don't denigrate your ancestors, my lord," Duke Charles said. "Bloodthirsty, perhaps. Savages, no. For a people who refuse to use the wheel, they have an exemplary road system. And their irrigation methods, I understand, are brilliant."

"They got them from the Mayans, Your Grace," Lord John said, smiling. "Anything clever the Azteques have, they got from the Mayans. Just as Master Sean tells me that everything clever the Angevins have they stole from the Irish."

"Ah, hem, my lords," Master Sean said, looking embarrassed. "That's not *precisely* what I said. Near enough, I'll grant you, but not *precisely.*"

Lord Darcy chuckled. The Duke laughed. "After all, Master Sean," the Duke said, "you may be right."

Lord Darcy rose. "We'd best be on our way," he said. "We have a day's work ahead of us. If anything is discovered, Your Grace, rest assured that I shall have it relayed to you immediately."

"What about de Maisvin's theory?" Duke Charles asked. "Do you think it has merit?"

"It may, Your Grace; but if anyone thought they were duplicating the ancient sacrifice to Huitsilopochtli, they didn't do their research. This man was dead before his heart was ripped out, which I am given to understand is definitely not how it is supposed to be done."

"Is that so?" His Grace asked. "Killed first, and then the heart ripped out?"

"Aye, Your Grace," Master Sean agreed. "No question about it. The blood from a living heart would have behaved quite differently. And the body was moved onto that altar stone after it was dead. There was no psychic shock resident in the stone, you see. Of course, the faint traces of ancient death were evident, but they were quite easily blocked out."

"How strange," the Duke of Arc said. "What would anyone rip the heart out of a corpse for?"

"A good question, Your Grace," Lord Darcy said. "Also, where was the body moved from? I have a feeling that the answer to those two questions will give us the killer. But the answers are not going to be easily come by. We'd best go hunting for them. If you will excuse us, Your Grace?"

The Duke stood up. "Keep me closely informed, Lord Darcy. If you need anything—anything—take it."

"Thank you, Your Grace." Lord Darcy bowed, and he and his two forensic sorcerers left the room.

9

LORD DARCY PUSHED aside the papers on his desk and glanced up at the ornate Horry clock on the wall. This gilded masterwork from one of the Duchy of Uberstein's finest clockmakers had four dials, and a profusion of hands for each. It told the date, the phases of the moon, the tides in any of four locations, the times of sunrise and sunset; it showed the astrology sun and moon signs, the positions of the major planets, the locations of eclipses of the sun across the surface of the earth for the next century, sidereal time, the exact longitude at which it was now midnight, and the correct local time.

It was ten minutes before two in the afternoon.

At two o'clock Count Maximilian de Maisvin and Lord John Quetzal would arrive to accompany Lord Darcy on personal interviews of the entourage and acquaintances of the dead prince. Lord Darcy had read the reports of the interviews conducted by Plainclothes Chief Master at Arms Vincetti and his men; indeed he was just rereading them now. But words on paper, especially words cast into the stilted language used in official reports, were lifeless things; no substitute for talking to the people involved.

He gathered the reports together and put them back into their file. Then he yawned, stretched, reached for his notebook, and rang for his valet.

Mullion, the rather plump, balding man in carefully tailored Duchy of Arc livery who answered his ring, was but a poor substitute for Ciardi, who had been Lord Darcy's personal servant for the better part of three decades, since he was at Oxford. It was not merely that the slender, ascetic Ciardi occupied himself with Lord Darcy's well-being, it was that he had the judgment to recognize what a being looked like when it was well. Ciardi's interests were limited to taking care of Lord Darcy, reading French romances, and keeping up with Court gossip. Lord Darcy found him an ideal servant, and valued and trusted him.

But when the King's command had come, Ciardi had been on his semiannual visit to his aged mother in Burgundy—she must be coming on to ninety by now—and Lord Darcy had to leave him behind.

The stout Mullion was a minion of the Duke, assigned to Lord Darcy to tend to his needs for the length of his stay in the Residence. He performed his job well enough, was cleanly, punctilious, and did exactly what was required of him. Exactly. Without fear, favor, imagination, observation, forethought, or resources. If Lord Darcy asked for a cup of caffe, he would get a cup of caffe. If he hadn't mentioned that he needed cream, Mullion would have to go back for the cream. If there was no cream in the kitchen, Mullion would be baffled. After three days of going back for the cream, he was well on his way to breaking Lord Darcy of the habit of not mentioning the cream when he ordered the caffe. It wasn't stubbornness or rebellion at his position as a servant, Lord Darcy thought, nor invincible stupidity. The man seemed bright enough. It seemed to be a sublime lack of interest in his work, combined with a positively glowing naiveté.

"Tell me, Mullion," Lord Darcy said when the servant was standing before him, arms at his side, incurious face pointed toward His Lordship, "do you have any hopes or dreams of advancement?"

"Excuse me, Your Lordship?" the plump valet asked, a puzzled expression washing across his untroubled features.

"Would you like someday to become, say, major-domo of the

Residence?" Lord Darcy asked, "Or leave His Grace's services and open an inn of your own?"

"No, Your Lordship."

"Do you aspire to one of the professions then? Are you studying for the Arthur Threes?" Lord Darcy referred to the annual scholarship examinations given to applicants of all ages for admittance to the Royal University system, and thence a career in the professions or in the Imperial bureaucracy, named after King Arthur III, who had first set them up.

"No, Your Lordship."

"Well then, are you interested in an opening in the Legion? Start as a trooper and advance up the military ladder? Or are you hoping to colonize one of the Western territories when they open up?"

"No, Your Lordship," Mullion replied, showing no interest in any aspect of his inquisition. It was clear that he was going to volunteer nothing beyond the monosyllabic negative, so Lord Darcy, recognizing the limp hand of placid intransigence when it slapped him in the face, stopped his questioning for the time being.

"Excuse the unnecessarily personal questions, Mullion. I trust I haven't offended you," he said. "Would you bring me a cup of caffe please—with cream. And fetch my heavy brown cape from wherever it's gotten to and hang it on a peg by the door. I think it's going to snow."

"Very well, Your Lordship," Mullion said, giving a careful half-bow and retreating silently the way he had come.

There was a puzzle there, Lord Darcy felt. But it would have to wait on the larger puzzle. He centered his notebook on the desk and turned to the next empty page. For a minute he gazed at the page, waving the pen in his hand in an idle pattern over the blank, lined paper. Then, neatly and precisely, he listed what he knew of the Prince's followers, and what he would like to know. In the fullness of time Mullion returned and placed the caffe tray on the table before him. Lord Darcy poured himself a cup and sipped it thoughtfully, staring at the blue lettering on the page in his notebook.

Prince Ixequatle had been in Nova Eboracum for a little over three weeks when he was killed, having arrived on Friday, the thirteenth of February. He and his party had traveled by ship from Mechicoe to England, and thence to Nova Eboracum. The coming of winter had precluded an overland trip. Lord Darcy wondered whether the Azteques had superstitions about the number thirteen.

The Prince's traveling companions were Lord Lloriquhali, an elderly man who advised the Prince on things Azteque, and Don Miguel Potchatipotle, a Spaniard who had married into a noble Azteque family and taken his wife's surname. Don Miguel was to advise the Prince on matters Angevin, being the closest thing to an expert around Tenochtitlan when the Prince left. Nothing was known of his past, at least not by his Angevin questioners. He claimed to be the younger son of a younger son of a noble Spanish family, and that was being checked. Unfortunately the report of the Aragonese authorities would not arrive in time to be of any use, as the request would take two or three months to make the round trip to Zaragoza and back.

The Prince's personal manservant, a young, undersized creature named Chichitoquoppi, and his personal warrior bodyguard of a dozen men, and a flock of additional slaves who had also traveled with him, were all now living together in—apparently—a rented house somewhere in New Borkum.

Don Miguel was the primary informant; Lord Lloriquhali spoke no Anglic, nor did any of the warriors, and the slaves didn't communicate very well even in Nahuatl. Chief Master at Arms Vincetti had pretty much had to take Don Miguel's word for what the others were saying. Which, Lord Darcy reflected, was not good investigative procedure. Which was why he was taking Lord John Quetzal with him.

The preliminary reports were clear on one thing: Except for Lord Lloriquhali, who evidently saw a plot under every bush, nobody knew any reason why the young Prince should be killed, nor anybody who would wish to kill him. There were, to be sure, many Azteque haters among the native tribes in New England, but mostly in the South. Here in the North the Azteque occupation had taken place too long ago for anything but legends, and the natives who wanted to hate something either picked another tribe or the Angevin presence.

But there were other reasons to kill someone besides hate. Some people, Lord Darcy thought wryly, kill people they don't even know.

There was a loud knock at the apartment door. Two minutes later there was a soft knock on the study door, and Mullion entered to announce Lord John Quetzal and a dark, somber-looking man dressed in black and silver, who was announced as Count Maximilian de Maisvin.

"Lord John," Lord Darcy said, rising. "An expected pleasure. Count de Maisvin. I have been looking forward to meeting you."

"And I, you, my lord," de Maisvin said, striding forward to take Lord Darcy's hand. "I have heard so much of you from His Grace, and in such strong terms, that I confess I expected to find you breathing fire and overturning stone walls with your voice. It is something of a disappointment to find you mortal. At least, in appearance."

"His Grace gives me too much credit," Lord Darcy said. "The pleasure of receiving an accolade is somewhat diluted by the problem of living up to it." He smiled. "His Grace speaks very highly of you, too, my lord."

"I shall do my best to live up to it," de Maisvin said. "Shall we be off?"

"Before we leave," Lord John said, drawing his cloak around him, "I would like to suggest that we make a point of using my services merely as a translator. I don't think I should initiate any of the questions put to Prince Ixequatle's retinue."

"How is that, my lord?" Lord Darcy asked.

"I think, considering my position—that is, who I am— that the Prince's people might well resent any suggestion that I am personally interrogating them. If it's clear that you are merely using me as a translator, then there should be less of a problem."

"That makes sense, my lord," Lord Darcy said. "If any questions occur to you, we will carefully place them in my mouth." He pulled his heavy brown cape on and took a thick brown felt hat from the rack by the door. "Was it, indeed, snowing when Your Lordships came inside?"

"Large, thick white flakes," Lord John told him, his expressive dark eyes lighting up. "You know, I never saw snow until I arrived in London at the age of twenty-three. I still find it quite remarkable."

They left the Residence by the great front doors and turned left, to walk north along the Great Way. Lord Darcy waved aside the carriage that was waiting for them. "If you two gentlemen don't mind," he said, "I'd rather walk. I understand it isn't very far. I am unfamiliar with the town, and would like a chance to get something of the feel of it."

"I enjoy walking through snow," Lord John said. "Although it seems to be melting as fast as it hits the ground."

The Count de Maisvin swung into step silently alongside them. Whether he got pleasure from walking through snow or found it a nuisance was impossible to tell from his emotionless expression. "It's a bit over a mile from here," he said. "I'll show you."

"You don't happen to know," Lord Darcy asked the Count, "why the Prince and his party weren't put up at the Residence? It would seem the natural thing to do, given his status."

"Indeed," de Maisvin agreed. "He was offered a suite of rooms, but he turned it down. I think the Prince would have liked it, but the old man who travels with him vetoed it."

"Lord Lloriquhali," Lord John muttered.

"That one," de Maisvin agreed.

"His dislike of my family is matched only by his intransigence," Lord John said. "He takes every change that has taken place over the past two hundred years as a personal affront."

"And he was sent to give advice to Prince Ixequatle?"

"I doubt whether the Prince was taking his advice," Lord John said. "My guess would be that the conservative faction in court foisted him on the Prince. You should enjoy talking to him, my lord; you will get a glimpse of a fascinating world view."

The Great Way was a broad, well-paved avenue at this point; with a cobblestone street and stone-slab sidewalks. Traffic was light, and made up mostly of goods-wagons bringing produce to the downtown markets. The houses that lined the street were two- and three-storey wood-frame buildings with shops downstairs and living quarters on the upper floors. Lord Darcy's first impression was that, except for the width of the street, uncommon in the centuries-old towns of Europe, it could have been a town anywhere in the Angevin Empire. Then gradually he began to notice other differences.

The houses were cleaner, for one thing, and spaced further apart, with carriageways between them. The predominant color was white; every bit of exposed surface was gone over with a white-wash, as though the sight of raw wood were an offense against nature. White picket fences surrounded the neat yards. Most of the buildings had red trim, although there was a smattering of blue and just a touch of brown. The people they passed were the goodmen and goodwives of any town; neatly dressed earnest shopkeepers for the most part, and some men of a rougher sort, who drove the wagons and worked as day laborers in the streets.

But, Lord Darcy noted, there was another sort of man they passed, a sort that he had seen represented in Duke Charles's audience chamber. These were men who looked ill at ease and confined in the narrow streets of New Borkum; who dressed and walked as though they needed open space around them, and a distant horizon to gaze at. They wore fringed leather garments, most of them, and wide-brimmed leather hats, and they took no more notice of the snow falling around them than a hawk takes of the mist.

"Those men," Lord Darcy said, indicating a group of four who were talking together outside a livery stable. "Who are they? What do they do?"

De Maisvin shrugged. "Trappers, mappers, hunters, surveyors, explorers, guides, scouts; call them what you want to, and hire them for that purpose. We call them frontiersmen as a group. It's hard to realize that this trim little town is on the edge of a vast untamed frontier. These are the men who are pushing back the boundaries of the New England territory as fast as there's anyone to move in, as fast as the native tribes will let them. Sometimes faster."

"I thought something like that," Lord Darcy said. "Who are they?"

De Maisvin looked at him sharply. "You mean where are they from? What social class? What is their background?"

"Yes," Lord Darcy told him. "I suppose that's what I meant."

"They come from every class, every location, and every occupation in the Empire," de Maisvin told him. "There are gaolbirds and clerks, the sons of barmaids and the sons of dukes, dissatisfied dentists, inquisitive magicians, bored attorneys, and adventurous seneschals. There are strong men who come to pit their strength against the unknown, and weak men who come to gain strength or die trying. There are some who come to live life to its fullest, and some who come to die. Each, to some extent, gets what he has come after."

"You seem to have made something of a study of these people," Lord Darcy said.

"I have," de Maisvin said. "I find them of great interest. I would like to understand the impulses that moved them to become what they are, and also, the impulses that continue to drive them."

"Are there any women amongst them?" Lord Darcy asked.

"Oh, yes. Of as many types, and for as many motives as the men. I do not count the hangers-on, the local demoiselles who find these strong silent men fascinating; I speak only of the women who go as they go, do as they do. They range from the highborn to scullery maid, from plain to breathtakingly beautiful; and the only trait they share, aside from the wanderlust, is that any man who approaches one of them without being invited to do so is liable to wind up with a split skull."

"Hardy ladies," Lord John commented.

"Hardly ladies, as that term is usually applied," de Maisvin said, "but a very impressive group of women. Just as these are a very impressive group of men. And well they should be, my lords; they are winning a continent for the Empire, and paying for it with their own blood."

With that, de Maisvin turned right and led them across the street and onto Garvey Lane, a narrow curving street that headed east toward the Igerne, as was called the narrow east branch of the Arthur River which turned Saytchem Island into an island. The houses fronting the lane grew smaller and farther apart as they progressed, each standing on its own plot of land.

"What part of town is this?" Lord John asked. "I am not familiar with it."

"The 'town,' as such, has grown up along both shores of the island," Count de Maisvin told him. "We are now cutting across the middle, which is occupied by small farms that grow the fresh produce we enjoy in such abundance."

The snow was letting up, and in a few minutes it had stopped entirely, except for a few random windborne flakes which still fluttered to the ground. It had melted off the road as fast as it landed, but there was still a fine white layer on the fields on both sides.

A few minutes later they were through to East Road, which paralleled the Igerne and led to docks and wharves on the river side, and warehouses on the other. Six or seven large merchantmen were berthed along the row of docks immediately before them, their prows pulled almost up to the road, and their bowsprits thrusting out over the road until they almost met with the upper storeys of the buildings across the street. From the pier alongside the nearest of these great ships a gang of stevedores was busy with the unloading, while a row of drayage wagons waited patiently for their cargo, their draymen gathered about a small fire with pewter mugs cupped in their hands.

"What do you suppose is in the mugs," Lord Darcy asked idly as they passed the huddled group of draymen, "caffe, tea, or ouiskie?"

"Probably hot rhum from the southern islands, my lord," Count de Maisvin said. There's no duty collectible on rhum."

They walked north along the East Road. "A strange district for our Azteque friends to have settled in," Lord Darcy remarked. "Don't you agree, Lord John?"

"I do," Lord John said. "Perhaps they felt a need to be as far from the Residence, and the Cathedral, as possible."

"That may be," Count de Maisvin said. "But, you'll note, they are still within easy walking distance. Nothing is very far from anything else in New Borkum. The town only takes up a part of the southern third of Saytchem Island, which is, in any case, not that big an island."

"Why does such a small place have such a large amount of commerce?" Lord Darcy asked, indicating the great ships ahead of and behind them.

"Goods to and from all of New England, my lord," Count de Maisvin told him. "My lord Duke's domain is much larger than the size of this town would indicate, even though it is the ducal seat. The spaces here are just—vast. It's hard to imagine. This is the major port of entry in the North, and quite the best harbor on this side of the Atlantic. It services settlements for hundreds of miles in every direction. Except, of course, East."

"Of course," Lord Darcy said.

"Ahead of us on the corner and across the street you will note three inns," the count said. "the Lord of the Sea on the corner, the Bon Richard, and the Earl Orkney, across the street. The last was named after the last royal governor of New England but one. The Bon Richard has been taken over, lock, stock, and beer kegs, by the Azteque advance party. Their deal with the landlord even included having him and his staff move out for the duration. *They* are putting up at the Earl of Orkney."

"They value their privacy," Lord Darcy commented.

"I think it's a matter of trust," Lord John said. "They don't trust Angevins, and they *certainly* don't trust the local tribes."

"That's understandable, given their world view," Count de Maisvin said. "They know what they would do to us, given the chance, and they are constantly amazed that we don't do it to them."

Lord John nodded. "That expresses it well," he agreed.

They walked over to the Bon Richard, a rectangular three-storey building in the middle of the next block. On a swinging sign over the entrance a knight in full armor with plumed helm stared belligerently out at the world. The door was locked and, from peering through the casement window, they could see that the downstairs barroom was empty. "They are not expecting guests," Lord Darcy said.

Count de Maisvin pounded on the door. "They never go out," he said, "so they must be in there somewhere."

"Excellent logic," Lord Darcy said.

A pair of muscular copper-colored legs appeared on the stairway, followed shortly by the rest of the body, as one of the Azteque warriors came down to see who was banging on the door. He approached the window and peered out at them, "No come in," he shouted through the glass. "No come in! Not want nobody in! Very busy!"

"We are guardsmen," de Maisvin yelled back, "investigators. Must talk to Don Miguel. Get Don Miguel!"

"No come in!" the warrior insisted. He turned and headed back toward the stairs.

"I don't think he's going to get anybody," Lord Darcy said.

Lord John called out in the harsh, guttural Nahuatl language, and the warrior spun on his heels, looking amazed.

"I trust you'll excuse me for demoting you to guardsmen, my lords," de Maisvin said. "I felt that the subtleties of rank were beyond the gentleman in the loincloth."

The warrior returned to the door, and he and Lord John had a loud colloquy before he turned away and dashed upstairs.

"They are completing some sort of religious ceremony for the dead prince." Lord John said. "But he will send someone down as soon as he can."

Less than a minute later another pair of legs appeared on the stairs, and an elderly man garbed in much wicker-and-feather finery, and carrying an ornate six-foot stave, stormed down and across the barroom and flung the door open. A torrent of Nahuatl burst forth from him, as though it had been under pressure inside him for some time, and he gesticulated emphatically with each phrase.

"What are we being told?" Count de Maisvin asked Lord John.

"This is Lord Lloriquhali," Lord John told him. "He wants to know why the body of his prince has not been returned to him. He wants to know just what we are doing with Prince Ixequatle's body."

"Tell His Lordship that the body will be returned to him as soon as possible," Lord Darcy said. "I don't see any reason for holding on to it; we've completed all the tests. We have, haven't we, Lord John?"

"Oh, yes," Lord John told him. "Master Sean was quite thorough."

"Then let us return the body to His Lordship. Ask him where he would like it brought."

While Lord John spoke, Lord Lloriquhali stared straight at Lord Darcy, as though the young master magician were not there. When Lord John paused, Lord Lloriquhali replied in a spate of words aimed directly at Lord Darcy.

"He is pretending I do not exist," Lord John said. "Which, believe me, does not offend me. He would like to go fetch the body himself, so no further profane hands will touch the empty shell of the Prince."

"Make a note, will you, de Maisvin?" Lord Darcy said. "Lord John, tell His Lordship that it shall be as he wishes. In the meantime, tell him that we would like to know more about the Prince, and his entourage, to help catch his murderer. Tell him that I have been put in charge of the investigation and I need his help. Tell him we would like to speak to everyone, ah, in the house."

Lord John spoke. Lord Lloriquhali did his best to make it clear that he was *actually* listening to Lord Darcy. Finally he nodded, and then turned and went back into the house. He stamped three times with his staff on the staircase before going through to the room beyond.

"Do we follow?" de Maisvin asked. "I assume we do."

"Come," Lord Darcy said, and led the way after Lord Lloriquhali.

The room Lord Lloriquhali had entered was the public room of the tavern: a large rectangular room with a serving bar across one side, a stone fireplace centered in the far wall, and space for a lot of tables. Most of the room was bare, however, the whole lot of tables and their accompanying chairs having been piled up along one of the side walls. In the center of the floor a group of breadloaf-sized stones had been made into a circle about two feet across, and a charcoal fire was smoldering in the middle of it. Lord Darcy looked up, following the thin line of rising smoke, and saw that a smoke hole had been chopped in the ceiling right above the stone ring.

"A very phlegmatic landlord they must have," Lord Darcy said, "if he knows about this."

"I would say he'll be none too pleased," de Maisvin said. "And neither will Duke Charles, if it comes to that; His Grace had to promise to indemnify the innkeeper before that worthy would allow the Azteques to move in."

"Against such damage?" Lord Darcy asked.

"Against anything; fire, flood, and acts of God included," de Maisvin told him. "The innkeeper, Goodman Malterby, didn't hold with having heathens carrying on in his house, as he told the Duke."

"It looks like he had a point," Lord Darcy said.

The rest of the Azteque party came trooping down from upstairs and, without so much as a glance at their visitors, gathered in a double circle around the embers and squatted on the floor. Lord Lloriquhali sat on a small three-legged stool, almost over the fire, and began a long, monotonous chant that the others listened to attentively.

After it had continued for a few minutes, Lord Darcy drew Lord John aside. "What is going on?" he asked.

"A brief prayer to an unspecified god, to commit various indignities of an intimate and highly painful nature upon the person of whoever murdered their prince," Lord John told him. "It's quite imaginative."

"I believe it," Lord Darcy said. "Will it continue long?"

"I don't think so. There—it's winding down already. Another minute or so."

The chanting died down and stopped, and Lord Lloriquhali hopped up on top of his stool and talked rapidly and shrilly for about two minutes to the men squatting around him. "He is telling them to cooperate with you," Lord John said, sounding surprised. "He says you are the great Lord Darcy, who makes the gods jealous with his ability to catch murderers. He says that you will soon catch the assassin of Prince Ixequatle and turn him over to them for punishment. He says the gods have told him that this is so."

"Well!" Lord Darcy said. "He says that, does he? I'll try not to disappoint him, although I'm not sure about the turning the killer over to them part of it."

"He says that this example of good faith on the part of the mighty Emperor of the Angevins will make it possible for his people to sign the treaty when they arrive," Lord John added.

"The implication there is clear," Count de Maisvin whispered. "No assassin, no treaty. His Grace will surely be pleased."

"Well," Lord Darcy said, "since I'm to get cooperation, although at a rather higher price than I am accustomed to, I had better begin. Is the Spanish gentleman here?"

"Don Miguel?" de Maisvin asked. "He is squatting over there. The one with the double row of feathers in his helmet."

"I should have known by the mustache," Lord Darcy said. "How is your Spanish, my lord?"

"Adequate," de Maisvin said.

"Well presumably Don Miguel speaks some Anglic. Wait for a minute or two, and then have him come to see me in the front room," Lord Darcy said. "The others can wait in here until I call for them. You can use him to translate; I'll send him back to you. Lord John, you come with me."

Lord Darcy and Lord John returned to the front room, where Lord Darcy pulled a small table away from the wall and slid a straight-back wooden chair around behind it. "It's dark in here," he said. "I assume our Azteque hosts would object if we opened the door and windows to let more light in, so we'll have to resort to artificial aids. This house doesn't seem to have gas laid on; perhaps it hasn't reached this far uptown yet. Lord John, will you see if you can locate a few lanterns and put them about? I like to see who I'm talking to."

Lord John found a cluster of kerosene lamps in a closet, where presumably the absent landlord had hidden them, and hung them on wall brackets before lighting them. Lord Darcy in the meantime located another chair and placed it on the other side of the desk. "Put one of the lamps over here," he said. "Off to one side, so it won't shine directly in anyone's face. I don't want to make my witness nervous, but I do want to get a good look at them."

"Where do you want me, my lord?" Lord John asked.

"Pull a chair into that corner," Lord Darcy said. "You'll be sitting in the shadow behind my right shoulder. Now, to lessen the possibility of any of these Azteque gentlemen getting upset because you are doing the actual questioning, I will not look at you, but keep staring at the witness. In a polite and inoffensive manner, of course. That should keep his eyes on me, and make him less overtly aware of your presence. You will become, psychologically, an offstage voice, if you see what I mean."

"I could, with very little effort, become entirely invisible, my lord," Lord John said.

"You could— Oh, you're referring to the Tarnhelm Effect; the magical ability to cause others to look everywhere but where you are." Lord Darcy chuckled. "I think the effect on my witnesses of an entirely disembodied voice would outweigh any possible advantage that your apparent absence would generate. But thank you for the suggestion."

Lord John shrugged and took his place. "It was just an idea," he said.

Lord Darcy swiveled in his chair. "A question for you, my lord," he said. "Would your witch-smelling ability sense evil in a crowded room—like the one we just left?"

Lord John considered. "In a specialized sense, my lord," he replied. "And it depends on how you define evil. Someone practicing black magic to any extent, certainly. Someone stealing twelfth-bits, probably not."

"Let us consider this scenario, my lord, Lord Darcy said. "Let us assume that one of the people in that room sacrificed their prince in a pagan ceremony to their Sun God. Would that be evil enough for you to have sensed it?"

"Yes," Lord John said. "Black magic is a matter of symbolism and intent, as you well know. "The symbolism of that ceremony and its intent would surely have left its mark on the mind of the perpetrator. And a powerful one. I would have sensed it."

"Thank you, my lord," Lord Darcy said. "As I know your abilities well, that settles one possibility rather thoroughly."

Don Miguel Potchatipotle stalked down the short hallway to the front room. "You want to speak of me?" he asked, smiling ingratiatingly with his stubby gold-filled teeth. His Anglo-French was distorted by what might once have been a Spanish accent, and was now further burdened with a random tonality and erratic mangling of consonants. Lord Darcy sighed as he rose to greet the Azteque-cum-Spanish grandee.

"Please sit down, Don Miguel," Lord Darcy said, speaking slowly and distinctly. "I am pleased that your Anglic is so good, so that we may converse in a mutually understandable language."

Don Miguel's smile broadened, displaying more gold. "You do me too much of a goodness," he said.

"That may be," Lord Darcy said in an undertone, smiling and gesturing to the chair. They sat simultaneously.

Don Miguel Potchatipotle was a short, dark-haired man with a slight pot belly, and a wide, substantial mustache, which was carefully waxed and turned up at each end. A superlative example of the noble Spanish mustache, it was definitely misplaced on the upper lip of a man in the region of an Azteque chief.

"How long have you lived among the Azteque, Don Miguel?" Lord Darcy asked, pulling out his notebook and flipping to a blank page.

Don Miguel looked up at the ceiling and muttered to himself, counting on the fingers of his left hand with his right. He went around the fingers several times. "It would be much of twelve years now," he said. "I am married the better piece of nine years, which is why I am of the Azteque name at the present. My wife is a lovely girl. All her own teeth. Her family is noble—very noble. I am being of much use to them in things European."

"I see," Lord Darcy said. "Tell me, did you have to give up your religion to marry into this Azteque family?"

"Oh, no," Don Miguel said, crossing himself. "*Santa Maria*, no." He reached into the neck of his brass-studded leather cuirass and pulled up a small gold cross at the end of a fine gold chain. "I am still good Christian," he said, "good Catholic. I maybe convert my whole family. It takes time. I go to church maybe two-three times a year. When I can."

"Your Azteque family knows this?" Lord Darcy asked.

"Oh, yes. It is mutual accommodation. I good for them—they good for me."

Lord Darcy nodded. It was indeed a complex and wonderful world they lived in. "How long have you known Prince Ixequatle?" he asked.

"Not long—not well. The Prince, he royalty. Prince—you know? I know *of* him much well. He very serious young man. Going to reform the religious of his people. He pushing Quetzalcoatl, as God Who Help Man. Much like Christian God. Get rid of other gods. Get rid of blood sacrifice. No good."

"I thought your adopted people gave up blood sacrifice a century ago," Lord Darcy commented.

"Oh yes, they did—they did," Don Miguel said earnestly. "But, like hedge magicians back in old country, highly illegal but still being done.

"A real problem?" Lord Darcy asked.

"No, no—not a problem. An annoyance. A bother. You see?"

"Yes, I do," Lord Darcy said. "Tell me, what sort of European help are you giving your Azteque in-laws?"

"Very ambitious program," Don Miguel told him, smiling earnestly. "They want teachers in things European—things Angevin. They want to give up old ways and take on new, better ways."

"Are you having much success?" Lord Darcy asked.

Don Miguel's smile disappeared, and he cast his gaze sadly down at the table. "Is much difficult," he admitted. "On two sides: Many Azteques have little desire to change; like most people most places, they are comfortable with what they know. Contrariwise, many Europeans not want to teach Azteques. Is easy to get missionaries, but not teachers. The Azteques, even so as want change, do not want to change religions. Teachers *si* missionaries *no*."

"I thought missionaries make good teachers," Lord Darcy said.

"In places where they do not have to give up being missionaries," Don Miguel explained. "Teachers, healers, others of fine profession. But missionaries not willing to give up their god to teach, or heal. And Azteques have their own god. Is a difficult problem."

"I can see that," Lord Darcy said. "How did you happen to come along with the Prince?"

"Needed someone who spoke Anglo-French, and understood mores and manner of thinking of Angevins," he said seriously. "I am the closest thing to an expert presently in Tenochtitlan. I am, in truth, hardly qualified, as I spent my youth in Spain without ever crossing the border to any neighboring kingdoms. But Spain is a lot closer than Tenochtitlan, so I am become an expert. It is better, as the Azteques say, then even a small earthquake."

"What was the Prince like?" Lord Darcy asked. "Did you like him?"

"He was earnest young man," Don Miguel said. "The sort who is not easy to like, even when you agree with him. With the same point, it would be hard to dislike him enough to do anything about it. He was so serious—so intense. And yet there was nothing of harm in him, if you see what I say."

"I do," Lord Darcy said. "And yet somebody killed him. And ripped out his heart."

"Is a puzzle," Don Miguel said. "All I can think is maybe somebody did it to discredit Azteque peoples. But seems a far way to go for such a little effect."

"I agree. Do you think it could have been a ritual killing by someone within the Azteque community? Not necessarily someone you came with, but someone else?"

Don Miguel shrugged. "Who?" he asked. "There are not many people of Azteque background here in Nova Eboracum, and most of them are like your friend Lord John Quetzal there—they are not any longer of the old religion. These people that I came with certainly would not have done such a thing. Besides, on the morning it was done, the only one absent from this house was the Prince himself."

"Why did he go alone, without a guard?" Lord Darcy asked.

"He did not know he had reason to need one," Don Miguel said. "He was going to meet someone."

Lord Darcy raised his head from the notebook. "He was what?"

"He went to meet someone."

"Whom?"

Don Miguel shook his head. "None of us knows. Prince Ixequatle mentioned to Lord Lloriquhali that he was meeting someone who had information about the pyramid, but he did not say who it was."

"What sort of information?"

"That, also, he did not say, alas."

Lord Darcy stood up. "Thank you, Don Miguel." he said, "you have been a great help."

"It was my pleasure," Don Miguel said, rising. "I, also, feel the necessity of capturing the assassin. Please, if there is more I can do, you will call upon me."

"I shall," Lord Darcy assured him.

Lord Lloriquhali marched in as Don Miguel left. He stood across the desk from Lord Darcy, ignoring the chair, raised his right hand, and made his speech. He enunciated his Nahuatl clearly so that even a child could understand, and ignored the voice of Lord John as he translated.

He made it clear that he had warned Prince Ixequatle not to go out that day. That whoever the Prince had gone to meet must have been one of the assassins. That everyone was plotting against them. That he, Lord Lloriquhali, trusted Lord Darcy because it was clear that he, Lord Darcy, was an agent of the gods who would avenge the Prince.

"What do you suggest that I do?" Lord Darcy asked.

"Arrest everyone who could have been connected with the plot," Lord Lloriquhali said firmly. "Torture them until the guilty ones confess. Then give them to us."

"Why do you think that there was more than one assassin?" Lord Darcy asked.

"Because this was the work of cowards, and no coward would ever face an Azteque alone," Lord Lloriquhali explained.

"Ah!" Lord Darcy said.

Lord Lloriquhali wheeled and stepped firmly back into the other room. In a few moments his place was taken by Chichitoquoppi, the dead Prince's personal manservant.

Chichitoquoppi was a small, thin man in his twenties, with stooped shoulders and a large head, dressed only in a bleached white *maxtlatl*, the Azteque version of the loincloth, and a plain wool mantle, knotted over his left shoulder. His hair was close-cropped, and his few garments were meticulously clean. He sidled into the room, as though unconvinced that he wouldn't be yelled at, and stood behind the chair, holding its back for support.

"Tell him to sit down," Lord Darcy said over his shoulder. Lord John did so, and the thin, nervous man pulled the chair out and lowered himself gingerly into it.

"How long were you Prince Ixequatle's manservant?" Lord Darcy asked.

Chichitoquoppi glanced at Lord John Quetzal as he translated, and then focused on Lord Darcy. "For the past six months," he said. "Before that I worked in the place. I was a barber. Prince Ixequatle liked the way I trimmed his beard, and he took me into his personal service when his previous man had to stop work because of stomach problem." Chichitoquoppi held his stomach to illustrate. "He was in great pain."

"How is he now?" Lord Darcy interrupted.

"Stuppitiquti? He is much improved. He has retired and opened a *pulque* shop."

"It's a sort of wine made from agave sap," Lord John added at Lord Darcy's questioning look.

"What sort of man was the Prince?" Lord Darcy asked.

Chichitoquoppi considered, scratching the side of his head. "Firm," he said. "Smart," he added. "When he decided to learn your language, it took him six months to become fluent."

"He spoke Anglic?" Lord Darcy asked.

Chichitoquoppi nodded. "He spoke it well, they tell me. I do not understand it myself."

"Well," Lord Darcy said to Lord John, "that explains something that has been puzzling me. It's easier to imagine the Prince going off with somebody, now that I know he could talk to him." He turned back to Chichitoquoppi. "What did you do for your master?" he asked.

"I brought his food. I saw that his clothes were clean, and that he dressed properly. His mother made him promise to dress warmly, so I made sure he had his wool mantle when he went out. I brought him things and delivered messages. I did whatever the Prince wished me to."

"Did you give him his wool mantle when he went out the morning he was killed?" Lord Darcy asked.

Chichitoquoppi nodded his head emphatically. "It was cold," he said. "The Prince wore his embroidered wool mantle. Also cotton foot-wrappings under his sandals."

"Thank you, Chichitoquoppi, you can go now," Lord Darcy said. The little man scurried out of the room.

"What do you suppose happened to that wool mantle?" Lord Darcy asked, getting up and stretching.

"He certainly didn't have it when we found him," Lord John said.

Lord Darcy strode to the connecting door and opened it. "I want to see the Prince's room," he told Don Miguel Potchatipotle, who was sitting cross-legged on the floor by the fire.

"Right away, Your Lordship," Don Miguel said, pushing himself to his feet. "I, myself, will take you."

"Indeed," Lord Darcy said.

10

MASTER SEAN O LOCHLAINN set his symbol-covered carpetbag on the large, plain wooden table and spread it open by its crocodile-jaw hinges. "This will be tricky, my lord," he said, "but, with any luck, it will do the job."

Lord Darcy, Master Sean, and Lord John Quetzal were in the inner room of a small suite of offices in the Residence, which Duke Charles had turned over to them for the investigation. The rooms were just past the regular guardroom, to the right of the main door as one entered. Plainclothes Chief Master At Arms Vincetti controlled his minions from the outer office, and his clerk sorted the steady influx of reports into file folders. Every hour he added new folders to a growing pile. "You are to gather as much chaff as you can," Lord Darcy had instructed the lanky Chief Master At Arms, "so that when we learn to recognize the wheat, it will be somewhere in there waiting for us to separate it."

Master Sean lit a beeswax candle and placed it to one side of the table. Then he took a roll of fine, bleached-white vellum from his carpetbag and unrolled one sheet, placing it on the table. Using a long, thin gold wand with a cat's-eye opal clutched by five golden fingers at its tip, he touched each of the four edges of the sheet, and then the center, while intoning some Latinate phrases. The parchment became visibly stiffer on the table, as though it had just been magically starched and ironed. He nodded his satisfaction. "Would you take all that material you gathered from the Prince's room, Lord John, and place it at one end of this sheet, if you please?" he said. "State clearly what you are doing as you do it, if you'd be so kind. Intent is all."

Lord John pulled the drawstring on the leather pouch he was holding. "The material in this pouch, being detritus which I collected personally from the room formerly occupied by the Azteque Prince Ixequatle, particularly the area around his wardrobe, I now place at the near end of this magically charged sheet of vellum for separation," he said clearly, shaking the contents of the pouch gently onto the white sheet and spreading them out with the blunt end of a silver pen which he took from his shirt pocket.

"Very good, my lord," Master Sean said. He took the beeswax candle, which now had a little cup of melted wax at the top under the wick, and pinched the wick with two moistened fingers, putting it out. With a small brush made with hairs from a fox's tail he drew a line of melted beeswax across the parchment. "As is well known," he said, "like attracts like, and, by proper application of the Law of Similarity, the attraction can work at a distance. Not a great distance, in this case, but sufficient for the purpose."

With a smile, Lord Darcy listened to his Master Magician lecture as he worked. Master Sean worked better if he talked out his actions; the necessity for clear description made him focus his mind intently on what he was doing. It also made him a superb teacher in the art and craft of magic. After long years of association, Lord Darcy now understood fully most of the more common magical procedures associated with forensic sorcery. Of course he still couldn't *do* any of them; no amount of magical knowledge could substitute for the Talent, and if it was absent, the magic just wouldn't work. It was one of the mysteries of the universe that was not even close to solution: why the laws of magic would work for one person and not another. But it was certainly so.

Like hair and eye color, color blindness, high intelligence, and the ability to govern, the trait seemed to run in families. You had a much better chance of having at least a trace of the Talent if your parents were Celtic rather than, say, Frisian. If they were Norman, you could peer into a crystal all your life and never see anything beyond your own reflection. The Poles, also, were a people devoid of Talent. But King Casimir's Magyar subjects were possessed of it to a high degree, so the balance was maintained.

"Now I'll take this charged bit of wool," Master Sean was saying, "and put it on the far side of the beeswax barrier. It's a sort of magical version of the lodestone, do you see, but type-specific. Like attracting like, as I said. Now it is on the same plane as the particles to be tested, and we'll shortly find out—There, now!"

Some of the particles in the little spread-out pile of princely detritus had begun a jerky motion in the direction of the strand of wool; a sort of drunkard's walk when the drunkard really wants to get home. Slowly and erratically they separated themselves from the surrounding bits of debris and staggered across the stark white parchment surface until they had reached and crossed the wax line. Once on the far side, they seemed to lose interest, and after a few more jerks to one side or the other, they lay where they were.

"That isn't how a lodestone attracts bits of iron," Lord John commented.

"There are no exact analogies," Master Sean said, removing his woolen lodestone from the vellum.

"So now what do we know?" Lord Darcy asked. "Merely that those dancing bits are wool fragments, is that right?"

"That's so, my lord," the tubby forensic sorcerer replied, peering down to examine the fragments under a small but powerful glass that he took from his magical carpetbag. "But, considering that the room was not used for clothing or bedding storage, and that the missing cape is the only woolen garment of the Prince's that had been unpacked, I'd say there is a reasonable chance that most of these particles are from Prince Ixequatle's cape."

"It's certainly worth the experiment," Lord Darcy acknowledged. "Proceed, Master Sean."

Putting aside the glass, Master Sean deftly gathered up all the shreds of wool with his right thumb and forefinger and rolled them into a ball the size of a pea. "Now, you see, we have to shift our methods. The Law of Similarity has given us all the information we can squeeze out of it. We no longer concern ourselves with similarities, but with identities. Not, 'is this a fragment of wool?'

but, 'is this fragment of wool from Prince Ixequatle's mantle, and if so, where is that mantle now?' "

Master Sean took from his symbol-covered carpetbag a carved crystalline casque the size and shape of a pocket watch and unscrewed the clear, crystal top. Placing it carefully on the table, he gently dropped the pellet of wool inside and screwed down the top. "The Law of Synecdoche tells us that the whole and the sum of its parts are interchangeable. If an object has a unique and vigorous identity, then each of its parts shares in that identity. And those parts that are severed from the whole will seek to regain their position—their identity—as a part of the whole. When properly energized, that *seeking* will become active rather than dormant. Let us now see whether we can energize this pellet of wool to seek for its home in the mantle of Prince Ixequatle."

Master Sean relit the candle and placed it at the edge of the table about eight inches in front of the crystal case. Then he carefully decanted a measured amount of a fine silver-specked green powder onto a small mirror that he held between two fingers. Lord Darcy noticed that Lord John was watching the Irish Master Sorcerer closely, noting the exact position and relative motion of each gesture. The young Mechicain sorcerer moved his hands slightly in imitation of Master Sean's broad motions, to put the actions into his muscle memory. This sort of imitation, Lord Darcy thought, went beyond flattery. Lord John was, after all, a master in his own right now (or was it, with a magician or priest, 'master in his own *rite*'?). His action showed the depth of his belief that Sean O Lochlainn was truly a Master Sorcerer.

Master Sean measured the angle between the candle flame and the crystal container with his eye, and then, after murmuring the appropriate spell, with one puff he blew the powder through the flame toward the crystal.

There was a small, high-pitched explosion, and the area was filled with a green glow, and a myriad of bright sparks flashed at random, as though just for a moment ten thousand fireflies had darted through the room.

When the dazzle was gone and their eyes had readjusted, Lord Darcy saw that the crystal container was now glowing of itself with a soft green light that seemed to come from somewhere inside it.

Master Sean peered down at the crystal and turned it from side to side. "It appears to have worked, my lords," he said. "The ball of wool is now synecdochically attracted to whatever larger woolen object it was shed from. You see how it presses against the, ah, south side of the crystal casque, no matter how I turn it."

"Then the mantle—if it is the mantle—is somewhere to the south of us?" Lord Darcy asked. "I apologize for asking the obvious, but I have learned in matters magical to always state what I think is happening, because it so often is not what is actually the case at all."

"This time, my lord, you are right," Master Sean told him. "Although direction finding with the crystal casque is approximate until you get quite close to the, ah, object sought, I would say that the mantle is somewhere to our south."

"Well then, let us go in pursuit of our synecdochical reward," Lord Darcy said. "I will have a couple of guardsmen come with us, as there is no way of knowing what we will find at our destination, wherever that may be. But I tell you, Master Sean; I am going to be grievously disappointed if our search leads us to a meadow, and it turns out that the absent landlord kept a sheep in that room for purposes of his own."

"Little fear of that, my lord," Master Sean said. "These wool fragments have been washed, carded, and some of them were dyed red."

"Ah!" Lord Darcy said. "That is very reassuring. Let us be off, then, and 'follow this road where ere it leads us, though it be to the ends of the earth', as the poet said."

Lord Darcy pushed the door to the outer office open. "I hate to bother you, Chief Vincetti," he called, "but I must borrow a brace of your armsmen, if you don't mind. We're going to take a little trip."

"Of course not, my lord," the Plainclothes Chief Master at Arms called back. "I'll have two of the finest waiting for you when you come out. For how long will you need them, my lord?"

"I can't say at the moment," Lord Darcy replied. "Not very long, I trust. How far away do you suppose the end of the earth lies?"

"My lord?"

"Never mind, Chief Vincetti. I trust I shall not even keep your lads overnight. If it will be longer, I'll notify you."

"Oh, that's all right, my lord. I just wanted to know whether to tell them to bring a change of clothing."

"They will have to make do with the clothes they have," Lord

Darcy said. "We'll be ready to go in a few moments. And, Chief, see that the men are armed with pistols in addition to their shortswords."

"Very good, my lord."

Lord Darcy closed the door and turned back to his companions. There was a sparkle in his eye. "Are you packed up, Master Sean?" he asked. "Then let us be off. Somewhere to the south of us truth awaits!" He took his heavy cloak from the rack by the door and shrugged it over his shoulders.

"You think finding this mantle will prove important, my lord?" Lord John asked.

"Can you doubt it?" Lord Darcy replied. "Wherever we find it, and whatever we find with it, will increase our knowledge of the crime. So far we have been limited to discovering facts about the victim. I find myself drawn to the idea of the mantle's importance as a moth is to a flame—as Master Sean's crystal casque is to, we devoutly hope, the mantle itself."

They left the office and, with two men-at-arms quickstepping behind them, quit the Residence by the big front door and headed rapidly south along the Great Way. After about twenty minutes they were at the southern edge of town, just passing the Langert Street Ferry, which was pulling out as they went by. Fort St. Michael loomed ahead of them, growing steadily larger as they strode down the avenue.

When they were about a mile from the fortress, Lord Darcy suddenly stopped. "Is it true," he asked Master Sean, "that magic spells do not work over running water?"

"Aye," Master Sean said, stopping and looking up from his crystal casque.

"Even this one?"

"This one? Oh, I see what you mean. Well, my lord, this is a peculiar case. The *spell* won't work over water, my lord. But the spell is merely used to sensitize the wool ball. The action of the sensitized ball is what we call a sympathetic reaction. It is not strictly magic, and it will work over great distances. Of course the water distorts the effect slightly, and in a random fashion—which is why it can't be used in a device for communicating over water—but it doesn't diminish it."

"So the cape might not be on Saytchem Island at all?"

"That's right, my lord."

"I thought so," Lord Darcy said. He turned to Lord John. "I

believe that we are going to have to get a boat. But we must play this out to be sure. Will you go back to the docks and ready one of the Coast Guard cutters for us? We shall return for it as soon as I verify that we have run out of island and Master Sean's crystal is still pointing something approximating south."

"Of course, my lord," Lord John said. "Why don't I get the boat and have it swing around to the tip of the island to pick you up?"

"Excellent!" Lord Darcy agreed.

"Thank you, my lord," Lord John said, and he lit out at almost a dead run toward the Coast Guard dock behind him.

Lord Darcy and Master Sean continued on their way, following the urging of the woolen pill inside the crystal casque. They skirted Fort St. Michael, and were rewarded by seeing the little pellet still pressed up against the side of the casque, pushing firmly west of south, clearly pressing for a goal that was past the fortress, past the shoreline, and somewhere out into the great bay.

"Well, my lord, what do you think?" Master Sean enquired as they stood on the stone wall at the southern tip of Saytchem Island and stared out at the choppy water.

"I think the missing mantle is either on yon Pyramid Island, or on a boat heading toward the Southern Continent."

About twenty minutes later Lord John showed up in a New England Coast Guard steam launch under the command of his friend Lieutenant Assawatan. The boat pulled up gingerly to the breakwater, and Lord Darcy and Master Sean jumped carefully aboard, followed by the two men-at-arms. "Lord Darcy!" Lieutenant Assawatan called down to them from the craft's small bridge, "Master Sean! Welcome aboard. I am at your disposal, gentlemen. Where to?"

"Pyramid Island, I believe, if you'd be so good, Lieutenant Assawatan," Lord Darcy called back. "At least head that way until further notice."

"We'll be there in twelve minutes, my lord!" Lieutenant Assawatan called.

The craft billowed steam and swiveled around. With a mighty clanking of its engine and swirling of its two axially mounted paddle wheels, it churned into the bay, gathering speed as it went.

Lord Darcy went forward and stared at the approaching pyramid. It was as much a part of an alien culture, he realized, as if it had been made by giant ants, or people from another planet.

What made it so? The pyramid shape was not unique to the Azteques or Mayans, certainly, although the Egyptian versions didn't have stairs going up the sides, or temples at the top. But there was something about the squat and looming pile of stones in front of him that spoke of a consciousness which thought alien thoughts and sought alien goals. And indeed, Lord Darcy reflected, their goals were alien indeed. There was the game of *tlachtli*, for example; very much like football as played in the Angevin Empire, but played with a small, hard rubber ball that could easily cripple a player. Lord John Quetzal had described the championship games played in Tenochtitlan up until barely fifty years ago. The games were hard-fought, punishing exercises, with no quarter given and none asked. And, at the conclusion, the captain of the winning team would have his head ceremonially cut off and thrown down a well. The *winning* team.

Had it been the captain of the losing team, it would have seemed harsh, cruel and savage. But the winning team captain? There was something so grotesque and incomprehensible to Angevin thought in that action that it was upsetting to contemplate.

Lord Darcy gave Master Sean a questioning glance as they approached the island, and Master Sean nodded. The ensorcelled pellet was, indeed, pointed at or around the pyramid. Somewhere on that island was Prince Ixequatle's woolen mantle. Or what was left of it.

The steam launch, in a display of mechanical virtuosity, swung around in a wide arc at the last second and backed up to the pier at Pyramid Island. Chief Master-at-Arms Karlus was running onto the pier, fastening his sword belt around his waist as the launch pulled up. "Your Lordship," he said, drawing up to a position of attention and saluting sharply. "What an unexpected pleasure. I trust there's nothing wrong?"

Two sailors quickly fastened a boarding ramp in place, and Lord Darcy and his small contingent crossed onto the dock. "No problem, Chief," Lord Darcy said. "We have a little more investigating to do, that's all. Have there been any disturbances of any kind since last I was out here?"

Chief Karlus shook his head. "Nary a thing, Your Lordship," he said. "Not while I've been here, and none reported to me in my absences."

"You go back to New Borkum to sleep, do you?" Lord Darcy asked.

"No, my lord," Chief Karlus said. "We brought tents and bedrolls. A guard sloop brings hot meals once a day, and the men take two days off out of every ten, in rotation."

"I see," Lord Darcy said. "Very dedicated and very efficient of you." He looked around. "Where have you set up the tents?"

"Oh, not on the island itself," Chief Karlus said. "It didn't seem right, somehow. And, besides, some of the men said they could never sleep with that great thing looming over them. I sort of feel that way myself, if it comes down to it."

"Where then?"

Chief Karlus pointed to his right, over at the forested mainland. "Over there, my lord. It's a lot closer than New Borkum," he said. "No more than half a mile. We have a guard skiff, and there's another boat we found on the other bank, which we're using temporarily until the owner shows up to claim it. A small fisherman sort of rowboat. So, you might say, we have the makings of a fleet, my lord. There's a clearing right opposite, and a road. Not much of a road, more of a track, but good enough for a man or a horse. The men can use it to return to camp on the night—or morning—before they go back on duty. It is only about a half-hour walk to the West Bank of the Langert Street Ferry."

"It sounds like you have the situation well in hand, Chief Karlus," Lord Darcy said. "Keep up the good work. I trust it won't go on much longer."

Master Sean, his crystal casque held before him, climbed slowly up the pyramid steps, closely followed by Lord Darcy and Lord John. The two conscripted men-at-arms came behind.

Suddenly, quite close to the top, Master Sean stopped.

"We've passed it," he said.

"What do you mean?" Lord Darcy asked.

"It isn't above us, my lord," Master Sean explained. "It is now below us."

"Well, I'll be—" Lord Darcy stamped on the step. "It's in there! It's in the pyramid!"

"I would say so, my lord," Master Sean agreed.

"But I thought these things were solid," Lord Darcy said. He turned to Lord John. "Aren't these things solid?"

"Not exactly, my lord," Lord John replied.

Lord Darcy turned and sat on the pyramid steps. "Just what—exactly—are they, then, my lord?"

"As far as I know," Lord John said, "and I am far from an expert on these matters—"

"You're the closest thing to an expert we have available," Lord Darcy said.

"That's true, my lord. Well, the Azteque calendar runs in a fifty-two-year cycle—"

Lord Darcy leaned back on his elbows. Master Sean sat on a convenient stone ledge. They both prepared to listen. If Lord John wanted to start his explanation of the putative hollowness of the pyramid with a digression on the Azteque calendar, well, it would undoubtedly all tie in. "Go on, my lord," Lord Darcy said.

"The world, you see, is going to come to an end at the end of one of these cycles."

"Is it now, my lord?" Master Sean said.

"So the Azteque religion believes. The only problem is, they don't know which one. Earlier worlds, they believe, have ended at the completion of these cycles, and theirs is fated to as well. But it could be this cycle, or the next, or so on; they don't know when."

"That must be a problem," Lord Darcy said.

"Indeed. So, at the end of each fifty-two-year cycle, the Azteques prepare for the end of the world. To show their gods that they are ready, they destroy all personal and public property."

"A pyramid, I take it, is public property," Lord Darcy said.

"That is so."

"But this pyramid has been standing here for some five hundred years," Master Sean objected. "And I believe that many in Mechicoe are much older."

"That is certainly so, Master Sean," Lord John said. "And there are two explanations for that. Both based on the fact that it's quite difficult to *destroy* a pyramid."

"Aye, that's so," Master Sean said, looking around. "It would take quite a few tons of magically potentiated gunpowder to do this thing any major damage. And the Azteques do not have such things, praise the Lord. It must have taken them twenty years to build this, and it would take them another twenty to tear it down."

"It took closer to two hundred years to build this, I would imagine," Lord John said.

"How's that?" Lord Darcy asked.

"In spurts, of course, not continuously. You see, they would have started with a smaller pyramid, perhaps a fourth this size. Then, at the end of the cycle, they would have destroyed everything *inside* it—if it had an inner chamber— and anything in the temple atop it."

"To prepare for the End of the World," Lord Darcy said.

"That's right, my lord. And then, when they were sure that the new cycle was starting properly, and that the world hadn't ended, they would have filled up the old pyramid with rubble, and built a new one atop it, making the whole perhaps a third larger."

"I see," Lord Darcy said. "And then, at the end of the next cycle—"

"The whole thing would have been repeated. So, finally, after three or four cycles, they would have had a giant pyramid, like this one, filled with rubble, with a temple or two on top."

"Why filled with rubble?" Lord Darcy asked.

"Because the old rooms from the previous cycle were not to be reused. That would have meant that they hadn't *really* been prepared for the end of the world, you see, if they were planning to reuse anything from the last cycle."

"Ah!" Lord Darcy said.

"So, by tradition," Lord John said, "as this is at least a three-cycle pyramid, it should be packed tight with rubble inside, with the only usable space left in the temples on top."

"And if someone desired to violate this tradition and clear away enough of the interior rubble to make some sort of hidey-hole," Lord Darcy said, poking at the pyramid steps with his walking stick, "where would this person find access to accomplish this project?"

"That I do not know, my lord," Lord John said. "I believe that, traditionally, the entrance to the interior of the pyramid was concealed in the temple on top."

"Well, it's a starting place," Lord Darcy said, rising to his feet. "Come, let us investigate."

The temples looked as they had left them; indeed, they looked as though, were they left for another century, or a dozen centuries, they would not change. There was something eternal about their very emptiness; the deserted shells of the past, waiting for the future.

"Let us take Huitsilopochtli's former abode first," Lord Darcy suggested, rubbing his hands together as he examined the front doors of the two temples. "I rather fancy that if there is any mischief afoot, he is involved."

"The missing garment is definitely below us now," Master Sean said, manipulating the crystal case in his two hands. "Just a wee bit below us, I think."

Lord Darcy instructed the two men-at-arms to wait outside, prepared to come running if called, and not to be surprised at anything. Then he and the two master magicians entered the deserted temple of Huitsilopochtli and paused just inside the door. "The entrance is somewhere in the floor, I would imagine," Lord Darcy said. "Although the walls are thick enough."

"The altar stone?" Lord John suggested. "Mind you, that is only a guess. The people who built this might have been of my race, but they were not of my persuasion. I do not have much of a feel for their actions."

"I don't think we're going to find it very easily," Lord Darcy said. "After all, they've had centuries to figure out how to hide it." He looked around at the blank gray stone. "Is there any way we can 'magic' this room? Some sort of spell that would make the hidden reveal itself—if you see what I mean?"

Master Sean thought for a minute, staring into space, one hand on his hip and another to his lips, and then turned to Lord John. "Perhaps something could be done with the Law of First Causes. What say you?" he asked.

"Umm," Lord John said, taking a pose that unconsciously parodied Master Sean's. "Aye! It might work. It just might at that. It depends on how strongly the purpose is committed into the stone, of course, but it sounds possible."

"The question is, which permutation will do the job," Master Sean said, kneeling down and lightly running his fingers over the stone floor, as though to read with his fingertips the secrets hidden in the very texture of the stone.

Lord Darcy went over to the low shelf that ran the length of one wall and sat down on it, leaning back against the wall and willing himself to completely relax. Starting from his toes and working upward, he let a wave of relaxation sweep over his body. There was nothing better he could do now; his two magicians were working for him, and to hurry a magician was no more profitable than to hurry the tides.

"It needs be done in two parts, I would say, Master Sean," Lord

John said. "One, the vesting of the stones, and the next, the willing of the stones."

"Aye, that's the way to go. Only it is certain that with the first we must give imposition, and with the second, direction, else we will have merely inarticulate tremors in the stone."

"That's right, of course," Lord John agreed.

"Of course," Lord Darcy murmured, but not loudly.

"Do you remember that paper of Sir Percy Erdnase's?" Master Sean asked. "The one that appeared in, I believe, October last's *Journal of the Angevin Sorcerers' Guild*?"

"I must confess to being several months behind in my reading of the *Journal*," Lord John said. "But wait—I do know the one you mean. What was the name of it now? Oh, yes: "The First Cause Considered as a Double-Folded Matrix." A fascinating treatment, indeed."

"Aye. Indeed. Sir Percy is a brilliant theoretician, as well as being one of the finest practitioners of the Thaumaturgic Arts. But, lad, do you remember the math?"

"I think so," Lord John said. He reached into his blue leather symbol-covered magician's bag and pulled out a silver wand. Turning, he sketched some symbols on the empty air, with slender lines that etched a sharp blue light into the gloom of the temple. "Is that what you mean?"

Master Sean took his wand out and rapidly filled in the air around Lord John's symbols. His additions glowed purple, and were of a slightly thicker line than Lord John's. "You've basically got it," he said, "but you must fill in the terms on both sides in a matutinal progression. There—and there—and watch out for the dangling subscript here."

"Oh," Lord John said, "of course!"

"Of course," Lord Darcy agreed quietly, staring at the air in front of them, which was full of twisting, colored worms.

The two magicians worked out their formulas in the air for another ten minutes or so, and then, having agreed on the appropriate *modus thaumaturgi*, they opened their magical bags and began sorting out the required ingredients for their recipe. Slowly the glowing colored lines in the air faded out, and gloom once again was the prevailing color in the erstwhile temple of Huitsilopochtli.

"It will be another few minutes, my lord," Master Sean said, as he put three small bits of charcoal in his brass thurible and carefully opened a packet containing a finely divided powder that was the color of the patina on ancient bronze.

"Call me when you're ready," Lord Darcy said, deciding that it was time to stretch his legs. He stood up and wandered outside to where the two men-at-arms were standing. For all the time that this two-magician spell would take, physically tapping, pushing, pulling, and probing each stone in the floor and walls would take much longer. This wasn't some mansion with a false door concealed behind thin wooden paneling; each of those stones in the floor or the wall weighed upwards of a ton. Lord Darcy was a firm believer in letting scientific magic take the drudgery out of his life.

It was midafternoon, and a chill breeze had sprung up since morning. Lord Darcy pulled his cape around him and watched the whitecaps chasing each other across the bay. A trim-looking barque was heading out through the narrows, all sails set, ready to spend from two to three weeks as a small chip on a vast ocean, her crew completely cut off from the rest of humankind before she made port in either England or France.

It was probable, Lord Darcy reflected, that within the next twenty years, as the steam engine was perfected and better spells were developed to improve its efficiency and power, the day of the sailing ship would gradually draw to a close. And that, he thought, would be a loss. The steam packet was a fine ship, for its purpose—which was crossing the ocean in one-third the time taken by the average sailing ship. But they were noisy, dirty things, and they didn't make a man's heart leap to see one in the distance, as that three-masted barque did, with its white sails all puffed out by the pursuing wind.

Perhaps what the magicians should work on, Lord Darcy decided, was a method of controlling the wind, and not the ship. *Everybody always talks about the weather,* he thought, *but nobody uses it properly.*

"We're ready, my lord," Master Sean called. "I will not swear to you that anything is going to happen, but you may want to be in here in case it does."

"I wouldn't miss it," Lord Darcy declared, "for a royal wedding." He went back into the dingy temple, where Master Sean and Lord John had erected a square-cornered brazier, which was emitting pink and white smoke in alternate bursts. "I'll sit in the corner," he said, "where I'll be out of the way."

"Beg pardon, my lord," Master Sean said, "But I wouldn't sit anywhere, and I'd keep out of corners until we have finished this test. I mean, my lord, we don't know what's going to move, or shift, or open, when we do this. And we want to be sure that whatever it is, we can get out of its way while it does. If it does."

"I see your point, Master Sean," Lord Darcy said, stepping carefully to the center of the floor, where the two magicians were standing. "What is it that may happen?"

"Well, Your Lordship, the Law of First Causes states, in a general sort of way, that a first cause becomes primary, and can be reverted to with the lowest expenditure of energy. Now, what that means in this case is that when an object is used for something— something important—that use becomes its primary purpose. And therefore, when an object is magically induced to do *something*, what it will do first, and most easily, is its first cause."

"And how does that apply to this pile of stones, Master Sean?" Lord Darcy asked, waving his hand to encompass the surrounding temple.

"Well, you see, my lord, for most of these stones their First Cause is just lying there, being part of a temple. But if, as we assume, some of these stones have a second function—that of being a secret doorway to the underlying pyramid—then, over the past few centuries, when the temple has not been used as a temple, but these stones *have* been used as an entrance, that has become their first cause."

"Or so we hope, my lord," Lord John added.

"Do you see?" Master Sean asked.

"It is not as clear as it could be, Master Sean, but I fear it is as clear as it's going to get," Lord Darcy said. "You might as well get to it, and I'll see what I see."

"Very good, my lord. This should be interesting. I hope we don't have to put it under seal; I'd like to write it up for the *Journal* if we get any results." Master Sean stooped down and lifted the brazier by its long brass chain. "I'll take it around the area, Lord John, if you'd be good enough to hold the lines of power."

"I shall," the young Mechicain sorcerer said, looking serious and intent. He spread his legs wide, lifted his arms, clenched his fists, and concentrated. The muscles in his shoulders and arms tensed.

Master Sean went slowly around the room, waving the censer

up and across at every step. The smoke billowed out through the holes in the top, now pink and now white, as Master Sean mumbled the words of power that would activate the spell.

Life and the life processes are but an unimportant part of the whole that is the universe; intelligence and the designs of intelligence but a pattern drawn on sand. And yet that pattern which is life can pull into its weave much that is not of life, and give it a reason, a function, and a purpose that transcends the life that made it, in all physical measures of mass, distance, and duration.

So is entropy thwarted in some small measure, in random pockets throughout the universe.

The room rumbled as Master Sean moved. It seemed to be stirring itself, pulling itself together, assuming a purpose. Was it Lord Darcy's imagination, or were the corners more square, the walls straighter, the floor more even? And the altar—didn't it seem rounder, smoother; wasn't there now the impress of a supine body, its arms and legs spread as it awaited the knife?

The First Cause, Lord Darcy thought, staring at the waiting altar. *For centuries these stones have been nothing but the house of an evil god. And that is what they remember. But what does a stone know of good or evil?*

A deep murmur filled the room, and Lord Darcy had the eerie feeling that the stones were trying to talk. But none of those present knew the language of the stones, and whatever message they held remained locked in granite.

Having made two circuits of the temple room, Master Sean stopped censing and brought the thurible back to its tripod in the middle of the floor. Then, standing opposite Lord John, he assumed an identical position, arms and legs spread, head up and staring at the ceiling. His muscles tensed.

The rumbling of the stones of the temple sounded deeper and deeper until the sound was beyond human hearing, and Lord Darcy could feel it through the soles of his boots.

But one stone—one section—one part of the right-hand wall was going up in tone as the others were going down. It grew shriller and shriller until the sound was almost painful, and then all at once it stopped.

And the rumbling stopped.

And all was still.

Then, with an almost delicate, squeaking noise, the stone in the right-hand wall moved inward and swiveled in its own length, revealing a passage into the narrow alley between the two temples. For a moment there was a preternatural silence, and then, with a low grinding sound, one of the massive stones in the rear corner of the same wall pushed open in turn, disclosing a cut-out segment the size of two crouching men. The hole in the stone was framed with a heavy-looking iron hoop.

Master Sean put the solid cover on the thurible, cutting off the smoke.

Lord John stretched, and yawned, and shook his head from side to side to clear away the psychic strain. "We seem to have had a multiple reaction," he said.

Master Sean nodded. "I thought Sir Percy's equations were valid," he said. "A very interesting differentiation."

Lord Darcy looked from one of them to the other. "A very good job," he said. "One of our mysteries is now explained: That hole in the wall shows how whoever was using this temple got in without disturbing the seal, the lock, or the spell on the door. Very well placed, too; anyone sliding into that passage between the temples would be invisible from below. Now let us discover whence that turnbuckle stone in the corner leads." He went over to examine the stone. "Ingenious," he said. "Would we have found it without the aid of your magical test? Quite possibly not."

Master Sean and Lord John joined him in staring at the hole-in-a-stone. "The whole stone must be on a pivot," Lord John said. "And the balance must be perfect; a piece of granite this size must weigh over a ton, even with that hole carved out of it." He reached his hand out and pushed the stone slightly.

"Careful, my lord," Master Sean said. "There may be more to it than that."

Master Sean raised the silver ankh that hung from a heavy chain around his neck and held it before him in the stone cavity. The closed circle atop the *crux ansata* flickered slightly when held in one position.

"I suspected so," Master Sean said. "Wait a second." He looked around for his staff and then went to retrieve it from where he had left it by the door. "Watch this," he said, thrusting the staff into the cavity in the stone.

Nothing happened.

"Hmm," Master Sean said. "More subtle than I thought." He took a small, sharp knife from his pocket and, with a quick gesture, pricked his thumb, allowing a few drops of blood to fall on the head of his staff. Then he once again inserted the staff into the iron-rimmed cavity.

There was a sudden flash, and a sudden crash. A thin iron bar had whipped at waist-height across the cavity and smashed into the far side, just missing the staff. Instantly it retreated into the niche in the iron band that had concealed it.

Master Sean wrapped a bit of clean cotton gauze around his thumb and tied it in place. "Can't be too careful with an open cut, with some of the substances I use," he said.

Lord John examined the man-trap. "Tuned to human blood, do you suppose, Master Sean?"

"Aye," Master Sean replied. "With a very specific Word of Power to make it harmless. And that hoop, and its associated spell, are recent, too—and Angevin. They are neither ancient nor Azteque; I'll swear to that! Since we have not the hours to spend searching for the word, I think we'll just remove the spell. If you'd give me a moment of your time, and a modicum of your skill, my lord—"

"I am at your command, Master," Lord John said.

Together, with smoking thurible and waving wand, they went to work. Four minutes later Master Sean was capping his thurible and setting it aside. "As harmless now as a newborn babe," he said. "Thank you, my lord."

"So the hoop is an Angevin addition to the ancient Azteque stone, eh?" Lord Darcy said. "This case commences to increase in interest. Are there any more little tricks concealed in this stone, Master Sean?" he asked, looking with respect at the no-longer-concealed entrance to the interior of the pyramid.

"I think we'd best proceed with caution, my lord," the tubby sorcerer replied.

"Well then," Lord Darcy said, "we shall. Master Sean, you and I will enter this secret passage—I assume that this device leads to a secret passage—while you, Lord John, wait here in case of trouble."

Lord John Quetzal looked for a second as though he were going to argue, but it passed. Instead he said, "How will I know if you're in trouble? The stone walls will muffle any sound."

"True," Lord Darcy said.

Master Sean turned and rummaged through his carpetbag for a minute. "Here," he said, handing a small circular disk to Lord

John. "One of a pair of tuned disks. I will keep the other in my pocket. If we need help, I'll whistle into it, and you put yours to your ear when you hear the whistle."

"Ingenious, Master Sean," Lord John said, turning the small disk over in his hand. "A sort of portable teleson, is it? But it needs no wires."

"The same principle, with a few changes," Master Sean said. "Good for a few hundred yards without wires. It will work through anything, except, of course—like the teleson itself—running water."

"Clever," Lord Darcy said, looking at the device in Lord John's hand. "What will modern magic think of next?"

Master Sean smiled almost shyly. "It's my own design," he said.

"So I had assumed, my friend," Lord Darcy told him. "You should apply to the Patent Steward for a Royal Charter. It will prove to be a useful, as well as an ingenious, device. Well, shall we go onward?"

They had to crouch to enter the iron-rimmed cutout. Lord Darcy pushed against the right-hand wall, and slowly the huge rock swiveled to enclose them within the wall. "Ha!" Lord Darcy called. "There are steps here, under the stone. Careful, Master Sean! I will be descending in front of you. Here, wait a second—" Lord Darcy pulled from his pocket a device that was one of the secrets of the Angevin Secret Service.

A thin tube, containing a series of zinc-copper couples that provided a source of power which was still not fully understood, the device heated a steel wire to true white-heat; hot enough to vaporize the wire in an instant if it were not protected. But the wire was under the protection of a spell that passivated it, causing it to glow fiercely with its white light and yet not be consumed. Behind the wire, a parabolic reflector cast the light into a beam, making the device similar to—although brighter and much smaller and more convenient than—the familiar dark lantern. At the flick of Lord Darcy's thumb, and only *his* thumb—as the device was tuned to him—Lord Darcy had the light of hundreds of candles at his command.

He thumbed the button, and the beam of light sprang into existence. Pointing it down the steps, he went cautiously ahead, feeling his way carefully with each step, keeping a wary eye on the walls and ceiling of this narrow, extremely steep stone staircase. Master Sean stayed close behind him, ankh in hand, muttering protective spells as they descended.

The staircase turned after five yards, and then turned again, and again. At the end of the third turn, some thirty feet below the level of the temple, it opened into a large room.

Lord Darcy shined the light around the room. It was hard to tell the actual size, because large pillars spaced about every six feet broke the room up visually into many small areas. Oil lamps hung from supports on each of the pillars, and additional lamps were mounted every ten feet along the walls.

Lord Darcy took out his flint and steel, and Master Sean his fire-wand, and they went around the room, lighting the lamps.

"There is good ventilation in here," Lord Darcy commented, as another lamp flickered into light under his hand.

"My lord, I think you'd better come over here," Master Sean called. "I believe I have found the Prince's cloak."

Lord Darcy hurried over to where Master Sean stood. There, stretched between two pillars, lay the wool cloak. On it was resting the body of a man. The sides of his head were shaved, leaving a stripe of hair down the center. He was dressed in the painted leather winter leggings of the local native tribes. From the waist up he was bare. There was a gaping hole in his chest where his heart had been.

11

"A MOHAWK, I understand, Your Grace," Lord Darcy said. "Tentative identification, based on his hair and garments. We still don't know who he is, however. A messenger is being sent to the chief of the Mohawk tribe to have someone come down and identify him."

There were in His Grace of Arc's private audience room; Lord Darcy, Master Sean O Lochlainn, and Lord John Quetzal. Once again they were seated across the large desk from the Duke. His Grace was not pleased. "I trust this is not the start of an epidemic of ritual murders, my lord," he said to Lord Darcy. "Perhaps we had better make Pyramid Island out of bounds for everyone except the coming Azteque party. Although, come to think of it, it has been pretty much out of bounds for the past century. With that avoidance spell on the pyramid, nobody has gone near the island all these years. After all, there is nothing on the island but the pyramid."

"I am very much afraid," Lord Darcy said, "that ritual had nothing to do with it. It seems that, rather than being out-of-bounds, Pyramid Island is the center of what must be a large, and very secret, smuggling operation."

"Smuggling, my lord? Who would be smuggling what, and for what purpose?" Duke Charles looked puzzled and concerned.

"We can only conjecture, Your Grace," Lord Darcy said. "Master Sean's forensic report is on your desk. Would you like to go over it now?"

His Grace of Arc turned to the short Irish sorcerer. "Perhaps it would be just as well if you tell me your findings, Master Sean," he said. "That way I'll have you here to ask questions about what I don't understand."

"Very good, Your Grace," Master Sean said. "I'll start at the beginning, then, shall I?"

"The beginning of what? Not too far back, I trust," His Grace said, chuckling. "Start with the discovery of this new body, if you'll be so good."

Master Sean forbore telling the Duke that such had been his intention, and merely nodded. The term "beginning" obviously had a different connotation for the Duke; perhaps because he could trace his family tree back for eleven hundred years.

"Lord Darcy, Lord John Quetzal, and I discovered a secret passage in the erstwhile temple of Huitsilopochtli, atop the pyramid," Master Sean said, beginning at his beginning. "There is a secret door into the temple, concealed in the rubble between the two temples. Then a separate concealed entrance to the passage. It descends, via flights of stone stairs, to a concealed room inside the pyramid itself. This room, in the shape of a sixty-foot square, has eight-foot-high ceilings, which are held up by a grid of stone pillars about three feet wide. It had once been a temple atop the pyramid, when the pyramid was smaller. We have not yet ascertained to what god or goddess the temple was consecrated, except that it was not Huitsilopochtli or another of the grossly evil ones."

"How do you mean, Master Sean, the pyramid was 'smaller'?" Duke Charles asked. "Has it not always been the same size since its completion?"

Master Sean looked over at Lord John, who took up the explanation of this peculiarity of Azteque pyramid building.

"I understand," the Duke said after hearing Lord John's description. "Then, this temple must have been full of debris at one time?"

"Yes," Lord John agreed, "and subsequently cleared out. Probably quite recently."

"Master Sean's forensic tests, done with Lord John's assistance, indicate that the room was being used to store contraband goods," Lord Darcy said.

"What sort of contraband goods?" His Grace demanded. "And how recently?"

"Gunpowder," Master Sean said. "There were definite traces of gunpowder. And a sort of heavy grease that is used to ship iron and steel machinery, to protect it from rust. I would say the room was used for storing these things up until the time of the murder, two weeks ago."

His Grace leaned forward. "What sort of machinery?"

"I'd be guessing, Your Grace," Master Sean said. "But my guess, if you want it, would be—guns."

Duke Charles nodded. "My guess also," he said. "The tribes have been getting a small number of repeating arms from somewhere. So far, not enough to cause a serious problem, but we don't know what the critical point is. Or who is supplying the guns. Also there seems to be an attempt, by trickery and deceit, to turn the native tribes against us. That's what Major DePemmery is investigating now in FitzLeeber Land, although we're trying to keep that quiet. But how did the smugglers get to the pyramid itself, even to use a secret door? It had a protective spell on it, did it not?"

"Aye, Your Grace. And a peculiar sort of protective spell it was, according to Lord John."

"It had—holes—in it," Lord John said. "Master Sean called them 'windows,' and that's a good description. It was set so that anyone coming to Pyramid Island with a legitimate purpose could approach and mount the pyramid."

"I don't call smuggling a legitimate purpose, begad!" Duke Charles said firmly, slapping the desk top for emphasis.

"Aye, Your Grace, but, you see, the *smugglers* did," Master Sean explained. "And the engagement in the original spell must have been such as to permit that interpretation. Much magic is a matter of intent. And, in this spell, the intent was close to, but not quite what it should have been."

"We don't, at this time, know whether it was an unfortunate misspelling, which the smugglers took advantage of, or a connivance at treason," Lord Darcy said. "Father Adamsus is going to search the Cathedral records tomorrow, to track down for us the covenants of the original spell and each renewal. That may or may not be helpful; we shall see."

"And the murdered man?" his grace asked.

"Died at the same time as the Prince," Master Sean said. "The interesting thing is, Your Grace, that Prince Ixequatle was also killed in that room. There were clear traces of his blood there. But his body—and not the other—was taken upstairs to the temple. Although the other murdered man was found lying on Prince Ixequatle's woolen cloak."

"That is interesting," Duke Charles said. "It's sort of like a puzzle, isn't it, Lord Darcy? I can see how one can get tied up in solving these things. Why would the murderer leave one body in place and drag the other one up flights of stone stairs to the temple? I assume that they were both killed by the same person?"

"I think that's a safe assumption, Your Grace," Lord Darcy said. "And I think I know why the bodies were separated."

The Duke stared at him for a minute and then said: "Speak, Lord Darcy; we're all ears."

"The Prince was brought upstairs because the murderer knew that he would be missed and searched for. The other man was left downstairs because the murderer knew he wouldn't be."

"Go on," His Grace said.

"They needed time to clear out their warehouse—that room in the pyramid. There were several stones movable from the inside that opened a larger door on the south side, on the same level as the room. Ideal for moving their illicit goods, but it would still take time to clear out the room. If you had gone looking for the Prince, and discovered that he was last seen headed toward Pyramid Island, you might have found the secret room sooner. Someone might have looked for it—do you see?—the way we eventually did, looking for the Prince's cloak."

"And the murderer didn't bring the second body upstairs, either because he didn't have the time or because he didn't want to confuse us."

"Very thoughtful of him, I call it," Master Sean said.

"Very clever of him, certainly," Lord Darcy said. "It was meant to distract us, and distract us it did. Had it not been for the Prince's cloak, we never would have thought of looking for a concealed room in the pyramid. And I am supposed to think of that sort of thing."

"This murderer seems like a brilliant and dangerous antagonist," the Duke said, "if, indeed, his reasoning is as you suggest. A purpose behind every move."

"True," Lord Darcy agreed. "Which makes the puzzle all the more puzzling: Just *why* were the hearts torn from the chests of those two young men?"

"To further confuse us?" Duke Charles suggested. "The heavens know, *I'm* confused."

"It could not have been Azteques using the secret room," Lord John said. "They take their religion and beliefs very seriously. Reclaiming a room from a previous cycle would be sacrilegious. Besides, aside from the Prince's party, there were no Azteques here. Only fallen Azteques, a few of them. As a good Christian, and the son of a good Christian, I exempt myself from either category, you understand."

"Of course, Lord John," the Duke said.

"Azteques would neither pervert their ceremony, nor draw attention to themselves that way," Lord Darcy said. "No, there was a *reason* why those hearts were removed. I am sure of it as I am that the Pope is English."

"It had something to do with preserving the secret of that stone chamber, no doubt," His Grace said. "I am probably only striking at shadows when I say that this has the earmarks, to me, of a Polish plot."

Lord Darcy rose. "I have been thinking the same thing, Your Grace. It is in the small things that you shall know them, and the small things hint strongly of *Serka* plotting."

Lord John Quetzal looked from one to the other. "I thought we had left the *Serka* behind on the Old Continent," he said. "I grant that the world is round, as the philosophers say, but we are over six thousand miles from Polish territory, in any direction."

"The arm of the *Serka* is long," Duke Charles said, "and their capacity for troublemaking is unbounded by oceans or physical distance. King Casimir is not pleased that we have come so blithely to the Northern and Southern continents of the New World, and called the one 'New England,' and the other 'New France.' Why not, he must say to himself, a 'New Smolensk' or a 'New Lithuania?' Now, he cannot hope to bring this about tomorrow—"

"I should say not!" Master Sean interrupted indignantly.

"—but somewhere in his long-range plans I'm sure there is a timetable for the, ah, liberation of the New Continents," His

Grace went on. "And if, in the meantime, he can cause us any embarrassment or difficulty, I'm sure he will do it. And the *Serka* is his right arm."

"But if he arms the natives to drive us out," Lord John said, "then, when he does come, he'll have to face armed natives."

Duke Charles stirred. "'When he does come,' Lord John?"

"I speak for his thinking only, Your Grace," Lord John replied. "There is in my mind no possibility that he could succeed with such a venture. But it seems madness even to try."

"Aye, it is that; but madness can cause much trouble, nonetheless." The Duke sighed and rose to his feet. "Find out for me, Lord Darcy, Master Sean, Lord John; find out what's going on, and why. Two men with their hearts torn out is a mystery, but an association of native tribes up in arms against the Empire—and those arms gunpowder weapons—would be a tragedy for both sides."

"We will do our best, Your Grace," Lord Darcy said, bowing slightly from the waist as Duke Charles left the room.

The Duke turned back from the doorway. "If nothing calls this evening, my lords, Master Sean, I would have you attend the dinner in the Residence, and the fete afterward. It is Founding Day, marking the hundred-and-sixth anniversary of the founding of Nova Eboracum. There will be fireworks."

"Thank you, my lord," Lord Darcy said. "We shall attend."

"Lord John, I am sure, has received an invitation," the Duke said. "But it suddenly occurred to me that you two, Lord Darcy and Master Sean, are probably not on any of the invitation lists, for all that you are staying in suites in the Residence. Am I right?"

"I do not recall receiving an invitation," Lord Darcy said, "As far as I am aware, I have received no mail here save for a note from my, ah, cousin, suggesting that we dine. She confesses to an ulterior motive, having several young lady friends that she wishes to impress."

"You would be quite a catch, my lord," the Duke said. "For dinner, of course, I mean."

Lord Darcy smiled. "It is Master Sean that they are truly fascinated by," he said. "There is a certain air of—magic—about him that these young girls find irresistible, according to my cousin. The note was very specific about my bringing him along."

"I have given up eating dinner," the Master Magician said stoutly, "to prepare for Lent."

12

THE RESIDENCE IN Nova Eboracum was barely twenty years old, and parts of it, indeed, were much younger than that. And yet it carried itself with the sense of decorum that is usually acquired only with the patina of great age. Just as some women are dowagers at forty, with or without a dower, some buildings are institutions at birth.

In his design, the architect had eschewed all hint of the modern and gone for the heavy formality of the Queen Stephanie period. Back home a touch of the new, a hint that King John IV was on the throne—and had been for these past twenty-seven years—and that the world had progressed since one's grandfather's day, might not be amiss even in a public building. But here on the frontier, where the Angevin Empire held a tenuous grasp on a great continent, there was something solidly reassuring about a ducal residence that, at least in appearance, might have been firmly established in that spot for the past three hundred years instead of scarcely two decades.

The building was in the shape of a capital letter *E*, with the three tines facing the interior of the island, and the flat back paralleling the broad lawn that led down to the bank of the Arthur River. The central tine held the administrative offices, although they tended to spill out in both directions. The two outer tines were residential apartments for the Royal Governor (always a duke, and currently Charles of Arc), various essential seneschals, provincial officials, and guests.

The celebratory dinner, a stand-up buffet, was to be held in the Long Ballroom, which ran the length of the spine of the building. Large picture windows spaced along the outer wall opened to the great lawn, which gradually rolled down to the Arthur. The Long Ballroom was made up of the North Ballroom and the South Ballroom, each capable of seating three or four hundred people for a State banquet, and normally separated by an extension of the central hallway leading to a pair of large doors; the formal exit to the lawn. To create the Long Ballroom, several walls were removed and a section of ballroom flooring was inserted in place of the tile floor of the central hallway. It took a day and a half to ready the room for use, and another day and a half to disassemble it. But such a large room was not needed more than two or three times a year; on Founding Day, the King's Birthday, and perhaps for a really important wedding or a State funeral.

Lord Darcy tied the tie on his ruffled shirt with the easy grace of long practice, and slipped into the gray dress tunic with red piping that was the most formal garment he had brought with him. It was formal enough for most occasions, but it wasn't *court* formal—a style that was about three hundred years behind the times. Customs and dress at court changed with glacier speed.

Luckily, the Duke had assured him that there would be a wide variety of dress at the dinner. "There isn't enough court dress in this town to fill a cloakroom, much less the Long Ballroom," he had said. "We are very informal out here in the wilderness."

Lord Darcy inspected himself critically in the full-length mirror affixed to the inside of the armoire door. His ears, he thought for the thousandth time, were a trifle too large, and his nose was definitely too long for any standard of good looks. The best that could be said, he decided once again, was that he had an interesting face. The ornate Horry clock in his study struck seven, the high bell-like chimes reverberating through the apartment.

Lord Darcy was a fastidious dresser, but he was not usually overly concerned with that part of his appearance that he had been born with. That he would take up with his Maker at some appropriate time. And besides, it did not seem to scare off such women as he wished not to be scared off; and what more could a man want?

But once in a while, when staring at himself in a glass, he found himself making a critical appraisal of what he saw. It was no sort of vanity, but rather the inevitable reaction of a man who had made a habit of studying and analyzing everything in his view.

"Well, Mullion," he said, as his court-appointed valet came into the room, "what do you think?"

"About what, my lord?" Mullion asked, putting down the caffe tray Lord Darcy had sent for. "Your caffe, my lord."

"My appearance," Lord Darcy said, taking the cup from the tray and downing the satisfying beverage in one long swallow. "Am I fit to meet with New Borkum society this night?" he asked, wiping his lips with the provided napkin.

"Yes, my lord," Mullion said.

"Is it formal enough to wear my dress sword, do you think?" Lord Darcy asked. "Or should I leave that piece of ironmongery in the closet?"

"I couldn't say, my lord," Mullion replied.

"Are you coming to the festivities?" Lord Darcy asked, knowing that all, from the highest to the lowest in the Residence, were invited.

"I think not, my lord," Mullion said.

"You'll miss all the fun," Lord Darcy said, trying to provoke some sort of response.

"Fun, my lord?" Mullion managed to get into those few syllables the intonations of a man who has just been asked to eat worms.

Lord Darcy sighed. He had once again tried to make conversation, to get a positive response out of Mullion; and once again he had failed. Although that was an interesting negative: What sort of person reacts with distaste to the idea of "fun"? A religious fanatic, perhaps? Well, Lord Darcy had best not let it become a challenge. If the man didn't wish to talk; if he desired to do his job at the lowest possible level of compliance, despite the fact that he was clearly bright enough to do better, that was his affair. But it was curious.

If there was an ulterior motive for Mullion's behavior, Lord Darcy would soon know it. He had put the taciturn valet's name on the list of those to be checked. Not exactly a suspect, just an unanswered question. Which would soon be answered on flimsy white paper with a red line down the left hand margin.

"Thank you, Mullion," Lord Darcy said. He decided on the sword and buckled it on. A gentleman was not dressed without his sword. Giving one final tug on the corners of his tie, he left his apartment for the Long Ballroom.

It was still early, but the ballroom seemed to be about a quarter-full already. Which, Lord Darcy estimated, meant there were something over three hundred people in the room. And the dress was, as the Duke had said, informal. There was a smattering of court dress around; The Duke himself, several lesser lords and ladies attached to the court, various seneschals and the like, and all the working servants were attired in the garb of the fourth Richard. Lord Darcy walked slowly around the room, observing the other guests, who were costumed in a variety of interesting ways seldom seen in London.

There were townsmen dressed up in New Borkum finery; wide trowsers, high boots, lace-front shirts, and embroidered jackets that closed at the waist. There were frontiersmen in their fringed leather garments. There were natives from the local tribes in beaded leather jackets, leggings, and soft moccasins that looked very comfortable. Some of them wore feathered headdresses of various designs, which Lord Darcy took as a sign that they were chiefs or underchiefs of their tribes. The feathers came from hawk, eagle, or a large local bird called the gobbler. It was supposed to taste a lot like chicken, but Lord Darcy had observed that that was said of almost any unfamiliar food.

Military and naval uniforms were also in evidence, as were the dress jackets of the merchant navies of at least a dozen seafaring kingdoms around the world.

The women's dress was less varied in style, if more varied in the individual realization of that style. The Angevin ladies present were all in versions of the high-waisted, low-cut, heavily pleated, long-skirted dress popularized the previous year by Princess Ginjer du Lac, younger daughter of the King of the Scots, when she was presented at the Imperial Court. Even the poorest goodwife or demoiselle on New Borkum had managed to gown herself in a reasonable version of the princess' dress.

The few native women who were there were all substantial

ladies of matronly years ("We're not going to let any of the young virgins of *this* tribe go to that Angevin dance. The Great Spirit *knows* what sort of foreign foolishness goes on there!"). They wore bright, varicolored blouses with heavily beaded skirts.

An arm slipped under Lord Darcy's arm. "Good evening, Cousin," a mellifluous voice trilled, "I've been looking for you. See how thoughtful I am, even to distant relatives; I brought you a drink."

Lady Irene Eagleson, her blond hair done up in a fantasy hairdo of twists, turns, and flowing shapes, which strangely complemented the simplicity of her red dress, stood by his side, two glasses carefully balanced in her free hand. "I hope Robertia ouiskie and sparkling Belenzon is satisfactory, my lord," she said, offering him one of the glasses.

"It might well be," he said, taking the glass and holding it to the light. "A local brew, is it? I am unfamiliar with the ingredients, but if you chose it, Cousin dear, I'm sure it's delightful." He raised the drink to his nose, to see what hints its aroma would offer. It smelled of ouiskie. Lady Irene, Lord Darcy noted, had a scent that murmured of beauty and femininity; no doubt compounded of rare floral essences and unspeakable parts of musk deer, it made his senses ever so slightly reel, and made him think uncousinly thoughts toward this lovely young lady. No, let him be honest; it wasn't merely the scent. In the bottle, or on another wrist or neck or breast, it would not provoke this reaction. It was Lady Irene; a girl he was meeting only for the second time, despite their fiction of kinship.

I wonder, Lord Darcy thought, *whether I've suddenly reached that age they write about, when men suddenly lust after young girls. Or, perhaps, I'm truly attracted to her. If the latter, fine. If the former, I had better go take a cold shower and go to bed with an almanac tonight. But how to tell?*

Or perhaps he was being ensorcelled. Perhaps this was the result of a clever love-spell. No, Lord Darcy decided. That had happened to him before, in the course of duty, and it felt different—a blind, compelling, unreasoned urge that left a part of the brain standing back and knocking for attention and wondering what was going on and why. This was a more relaxed, more pleasant, and surely more honest feeling than the compulsion of a spell.

I will not worry about it, Lord Darcy thought. *Events will follow their course regardless.*

"The ouiskie," Lady Irene was saying, her large blue eyes staring up at him from under their long lashes, "is a local product, from the Duchy of Robertia, to the south. It is very highly regarded by those who are connoisseurs of such things."

"As is my pipe tobacco," Lord Darcy noted. "From Robertia, that is."

"The water is a naturally fizzy water from Belenzon Spring, to the north of here," Lady Irene told him. "They are supposed to be a pleasing combination. I find the water pleasant mixed with white wine, but I confess that ouiskie is a bit too strong on my tongue."

He sipped at the drink and found it surprisingly good. "Very pleasant, my lady," he agreed. "Very smooth and mild. I am surprised—" he searched for a word.

Lady Irene laughed. "Surprised to find something so civilized out here?" she suggested. "Expected to find a raw product, from the distillery to your lips?"

Lord Darcy smiled and nodded. "Something of that sort," he admitted.

"Well, we can certainly supply that, too," she said. "But this particular example of the distiller's art has been maturing in charred oak casks for twelve years." She smiled. "Almost as long as we've been apart, Cousin."

"It was remiss of me," Lord Darcy said, with a matching smile. "Horribly remiss. To have been out of touch for all this time. What was I thinking of?"

"Well," Lady Irene said, with a charming pout, "not of me, obviously."

"On the other hand," Lord Darcy said, as though suddenly realizing—"you never wrote!"

"Oh, I did, I did," Lady Irene assured him. "I was just too bashful to send the letters. You would have laughed at my schoolgirl crush."

"Ah," Lord Darcy said. "Would I?"

"I certainly hope so," she replied. "But I'm twenty-six now, and hardly a schoolgirl any more."

Lord Darcy looked down at her, but she had turned her head away. "My lord," she said, "let us talk over old times, and discuss family matters. How has Aunt Bertha been all these years? Does Cousin Edgar really enjoy walking on all fours and baying at the moon? Important business of that nature. Would you like to step outside onto the lawn with me? I believe it is not too cold as yet."

"Delighted," Lord Darcy replied.

Together they strolled out through one of the open windows, her hand lightly on his arm. When they were about ten yards away from the house, and Lord Darcy was wondering what he could say to this strange, and strangely appealing, girl, she turned to him. "We seem to be alone," she said. "There are a few things I have to report to you about, and this seemed a convenient time. I don't believe any of them are meaningful to your investigation, but that is for you to say."

"Report?" Lord Darcy asked. It seemed a strange choice of words.

"My friends call me 'Muffin.' Did you know that?" she said lightly, sharing a girlish confidence. "It's from some opera or other, I believe."

Lord Darcy stopped in midstride. He was seldom startled, but this young lady had managed to come close. "Muffin?"

"There, now I've done it," Lady Irene said. "I've upset you."

"Surprised, perhaps," Lord Darcy acknowledged, looking around casually to make sure they could not be overheard. "I wouldn't say 'upset'. So you are the local agent of the Most Secret Service?"

"One of them," she said. "I do hope you're not the sort of man who thinks I'm too small, too young, or too—er—female, for such a job."

"Neither too young nor too small," Lord Darcy assured her. "And I have never thought gender a bar to such service. But, how did you—"

She laughed quietly. "'How did a nice girl like me'—is that how that starts? I suppose I'm not fit for anything else."

"My lady?" Lord Darcy frowned. "Not fit?"

"When I was fifteen I was going with my mother to Alexandria," she said softly, staring off at something in the darkness across the river. "My father was in the diplomatic service there. Our ship didn't make it. We were captured by Barbary pirates. I spent six months in Mahdia being—trained—by a man named Effez before he sold me to the Sultan of Hafsid. He gave me as a gift to the Osmanli Sultan, who presented me to his eldest son, Mustafa, on his birthday. It was there I learned to sing."

Lord Darcy raised an eyebrow, but he said nothing.

Lady Irene went on: "For four years I was the favorite of Mustafa, until he tired of me. Which probably saved my life, since his mother had decided that I was dangerous, and was going to have me killed. I managed to smuggle myself on a ship bound for Venice by offering myself to a sailor. He tried keeping me on the ship when we had arrived, but I crawled through the porthole and swam ashore.

"I stayed in Venice for two years, while my family debated what to do with me. Finally they sent for me, and I returned to London. They had decided that I really couldn't be presented in court, everything considered,—so, after six months, they sent me here. In the meantime I had met the head of the Most Secret Service—without knowing who he was, of course—and he interrogated me about conditions in the Osmanli Empire. Then he offered me a job."

She stopped talking and turned to Lord Darcy, waiting for him to speak.

For a long moment he was silent.

"I didn't know you could sing," he said finally.

"Soprano," she said. "You'll have a chance to hear me shortly. I'm supposed to sing two numbers as part of the entertainment later." Then she shrugged a funny shrug and put her hands lightly on his chest. "That's it?" she asked. "After what I've just told you, that's your only question?"

He smiled and put his arm around her shoulder. "You're good, Lady Irene, you're really good," he told her. "I thought that the singing part of that story might be true. Was any of the rest of it?"

She looked at him with her mouth open in astonishment for a moment. Then she shrugged again, and smiled a twisted little smile. "A bit of it," she said, "but very little."

"It is an interesting fiction," Lord Darcy said. "I wonder whether the choice of details tells more about you or about the sort of person you usually have to tell it to."

Lady Irene pulled her hands away from Lord Darcy as though he had just bitten her. "I don't—" she said angrily, cutting herself off without finishing the thought. Then she shook her head slightly and slipped her arm back through Lord Darcy's. "Silly me," she said, "to get angry at someone I like because he caught me lying to him. Your question is interesting, my lord."

"And the answer?" Lord Darcy asked mildly.

She considered. "I'd say the honors are equal," she said. "The men to whom I usually must tell the story need to hear something of the sort, and I must confess I get some satisfaction out of telling it. They would think a pampered girl who lived a blameless life in and around a series of Angevin courts could not have the, let us say, toughness of mind to do some of the things required of her. And if they lacked trust in my ability, the mission would suffer. As the ladies in another, perhaps similar, profession might say, the story is good for the trade. I hope that catching me out hasn't made you think I'm hopelessly incompetent. I assure you it's not so, and most men enjoy that story. Tell me, how did you know it wasn't true?"

Lord Darcy smiled. "I didn't say I didn't enjoy it," he said. "I'll trade you. If you'll tell me the truth—because now I really *am* curious—I'll tell you how I knew."

"You ask a lot," she said," but all right. You start."

"I knew your story wasn't true," Lord Darcy told her, "because bits of the evidential detail were false. And that sort of story is either all true or not at all true."

"You're saying that I can't be a little bit pregnant," she said, "and I'll agree. Which bit of my description beggared belief?"

"Well, for one thing, the last recorded instance of Barbary pirates capturing a ship was in 1957; a couple of years before you were born."

"I thought—" she began.

"Yes, Lord Darcy interrupted, "most people do. Romance dies hard. Also, if you *had* been captured by pirates, they would have ransomed you, as they had been doing since the time of Julius Caesar. On the theory that your relatives would pay more for you than—ah—anyone with baser motives. They have many beautiful women of their own in North Africa, even if few of them are blond."

"That's it?" she asked.

"As I said, one weak point will destroy such a tale," Lord Darcy told her. "But there is the additional fact that Abd-ul Hamid's eldest son, whose name, incidentally, is Hasid, was at Oxford with me."

"Damn!" Lady Irene said with feeling.

"Your turn," Lord Darcy said. They had continued walking while they spoke, and they now stood on a bluff overlooking the river. Below them was the small pier at which Lord Darcy had arrived at the Residence. Across from them were the tall cliffs on the opposite shore, now cast in shadow like a row of brooding giants.

Lady Irene shrugged. "The truth is stranger, if less romantic," she said, matter-of-factly. "I would make up something else, except there is cause for you to know the truth, and I would like to tell you. I am part of a Polish plot to infiltrate New England."

Lord Darcy turned to look fully at this lovely lady in the dim light, peering at her as though to read the truth written in her eyes. "Stranger, indeed," he said. "If so, why are you telling me?"

"Because I am, indeed, a loyal subject of the Empire, and a faithful agent of His Majesty's Most Secret Service. It is the Poles I'm lying to. Of course you have to take my word for that, but, as you'll see, the burden of proof is with me. Luckily, the Poles cannot see the burden I carry."

"Tell me," Lord Darcy said.

"What part?" she asked.

"Start at the beginning."

"Five years ago," she said, "I fell in love. His name was Guiliam, and he was a Doubter. I was moving in a circle of Doubters, and was more or less one of them, spiritually if not philosophically. It seemed so exciting to have a cause, so *right*, so important. And when my parents and the other adults I knew told me what a fool I was being, why, it merely tested the armor of my righteousness. What could anyone over forty know about truth, or justice?"

"I remember the Doubters," Lord Darcy said. "A scruffy group that went around destroying what it did not understand. Was that only five years ago? It seems an age. But then fashion changes rapidly among the young, even in doubt."

"We doubted everything," she said, "the rightness of Imperialism, and divisions of society, and the social mores, and the sexual mores. *Especially*, I suppose, the sexual mores. And you're right; what we doubted we attacked. Usually physically. Guiliam was one of the leaders of the movement. He was very convincing. He wanted to strike at society, and I helped him. We broke into some Government offices to burn papers and destroy things. It was very satisfying, the feeling of destroying things for a good cause. Then I found out that Guiliam was stealing some of the papers I thought he was burning. He told me it was to give them to the newspapers. He was lying. He was, as it turned out, a Polish agent."

"Um," Lord Darcy said.

"I didn't know that at the time, of course. By the time I figured it out, he told me that I was in too deep to pull out. He said that he might be a spy, but I was a traitor. I had helped him steal secret papers."

"Many an older and more experienced person than you has been caught in such a trap," Lord Darcy said. "What did you do?"

"I cried for three days, and then I went to see Sir Kevin DeWitt and confessed everything. I might have been a fool, but I was no traitor."

"The Marshal of England?"

"It might have been an odd choice. I know he has to do with the courts and things, but doesn't investigate anything or arrest anybody. But he was the highest-ranking official whom I knew personally. He was an old friend of my father's."

"Yes?" Lord Darcy said.

"He listened to me carefully, and then suggested that I go see Lord Peter Whiss. Which advice I took."

"And what did Lord Peter say?"

"Well, he didn't arrest me. He said there was no law against being a dupe, and that I had behaved very courageously in coming to see him."

"So you had," Lord Darcy agreed.

She nodded. "I believe that was the single most courageous act I have done in my life. Since then, I have done things that would seem to require more bravery, but I was better trained and knew what I was getting into. When I went to see Lord Peter, I was frightened out of my mind. I thought they were going to take me to the Tower and cut off my head."

"And instead?"

"Lord Peter asked me if I'd pretend to go along with Guiliam; act as though I were too frightened to do otherwise. He wanted me to find out who Guiliam was working with, and what sort of information he was seeking. He said I didn't have to, and that there would be no punishment if I refused. I was frightened, but I thought that I should do this. You know?"

"I know," Lord Darcy assured her.

"And that's how it began," she told him. "I found that I have an affinity for this sort of work. I have an absolutely retentive memory, and I think fast. And I consider that what I am doing is more important than anything else I could be doing, so how can I stop?"

"How, indeed?" Lord Darcy said. He was familiar with the lure of the work, as he felt it himself. The challenge of pitting yourself, your intellect, against a player on the other side, the gratification of success, the danger in failure. It could be like a drug.

"Do you believe that story?" she asked.

"It has the ring of verisimilitude," Lord Darcy said. "Which, I suppose, should make me suspect it. But somehow I think it's at least substantially true."

She nodded. "It is the truth. And now, having worked my way up in the hierarchy, I am over here at the behest of the *Serka*, to pry Angevin secrets out of the Imperial Governor. They believe I've turned mercenary, and am doing this for the large sums of money they pay me. I also help them smuggle guns to the native tribes. In between time I do little errands for the Most Secret Service." She put her hand to her forehead in mock exhaustion. "Oh! The social whirl. I hardly have time to go to my dressmaker's."

Lord Darcy decided that he liked this girl. "How many of them are there?" he asked. "Did the *Serka* agents have anything to do with Prince Ixequatle's murder?"

"I don't know the answer to either of those questions," she said. "I know my immediate contact, and a few of their lesser agents. I don't think there are more than two dozen, possibly quite a few less. And they have some people working for them just for money; criminals who don't really know for whom they're working. Also I don't know for sure whether the *Serka* was involved in the Prince's murder, but I just discovered last night that they had been storing guns in the pyramid up until the night of the murder."

"How did you find out?" Lord Darcy asked.

"I was asked to pass a message on to the captain of the *Sibyl*, which just came into port, not to drop his smuggled arms at the pyramid, but to wait for instructions."

"Who is the chief *Serka* agent here?" Lord Darcy asked.

"I am trying to find out," she told him. "It is a man, that's all I'm sure of. I have only seen him at meetings, elaborately cloaked and masked. She paused, and then added, "If I had to guess about whether the *Serka* was involved in the Prince's killing, I'd say not."

"Why is that?"

"Because my superior, whoever he is, didn't ask me to get friendly with you, to try to find out what you're doing—how well you're doing—that sort of thing. If they were involved in the Prince's death, you'd think they would have."

"You'd almost think they would have, anyway," Lord Darcy said.

"I'm glad they didn't," she said. "It gives us a chance to get to know each other without anything complicating the issue."

Lord Darcy nodded. "So it does," he agreed. "What did you want to tell me?"

"Your query about Mullion was passed on to me," she said. "In case I could recognize him as a *Serka* agent."

"Well?" Lord Darcy asked.

"He isn't, as far as I know," she said. "But, as it happens, I know what he is. Your valet is a Paradoxical Materialist."

"What is that?" Lord Darcy asked.

"It's a sect that has been gaining in popularity, particularly here in the colonies for some reason. They believe that there are no mysteries, only paradoxes; and that if you don't know the answer to something, it is because you are asking the wrong questions. They feel that nothing should be taken on faith, but everything should be examined, probed, taken apart, and fully described; and only thusly can the universe be known."

"Oh, yes," Lord Darcy said. "One of the material science sects. Anything that can't be touched doesn't exist. Any answer that can't be reproduced is the wrong answer. They think magic is merely a manifestation of some mental power that we don't understand."

"That is a fair description of the group," Lady Irene agreed.

"I wonder what it is about these beliefs that makes them so abstracted from the world, so complaisant, and so morose," Lord Darcy said.

Slowly, arm in arm, they wandered back into the great ballroom. The buffet dinner was now being served, and they filled their plates. Lord Darcy tasted gobbler for the first time, and it did taste like chicken.

"Well, my lord, I trust you find our hospitality to your liking," Count de Maisvin said, appearing at their side out of the crush of people. He was, as usual, dressed all in black. But the silver-trimmed formal jacket, with its double row of buttons, gave him a striking look of foreign elegance. If anyone could bring black into fashion, Lord Darcy thought, it would be the Count. De Maisvin bowed to Lady Irene. "My lady. So charming, and so beautiful. I hope you are going to sing for us tonight."

"I have been asked to," she told him, "and it will be my pleasure."

"What will you sing?" he asked. "Something patriotic, no doubt, given the occasion."

"I'm singing the 'George'," she told him. "You can't get much more patriotic than that." She referred to the anthem based on the old Plantagenet battle cry: "God for Harry, England and St. George," which—with the name changed to that of the current monarch—had been sung at patriotic moments for the past five hundred years.

"My face will glow with an innocent courage, and my patriotic fervor will be revitalized from listening to your sweet voice," de Maisvin said, bowing again, and wandering off into the crowd.

She shook her head. "He talks like that," she told Lord Darcy. "Often."

A handsome young lad of about sixteen or seventeen, in elaborate court dress heavily into green and gold, walked by looking distressed. "Julian!" Lady Irene called. He turned.

"My lord, let me introduce you to Sir Julian Despaige, a ward of Duke Charles's," Lady Irene said. "Julian, this is Lord Darcy."

Julian's eyes grew big as he shook hands with Lord Darcy. "My lord," he said. "It is really an honor. I've been hoping to have the chance to meet you since you arrived."

"I could swear we have already met," Lord Darcy said, reaching back in his memory to try to place the thin-faced boy with the light brown hair. He snapped his fingers. "Winchester Palace," he said. "Several weeks ago."

"I've been here for two years, my lord," Sir Julian said.

"Hum," Lord Darcy said.

Sir Julian smiled—a wide, disarming smile. "It was my twin, James," he said. "Nobody can tell us apart."

"You're here, and your twin is in London?" Lord Darcy asked. "Well, praised be for small favors. I dislike the feeling that my memory is becoming undependable. It is a pleasure to meet you, Sir Julian."

"What were you looking so worried about when I called you?" Lady Irene asked the lad.

"Nothing important," he said, looking embarrassed. "Duke Charles has beguiled me into reciting a poem as part of the festivities."

"You are very good at reciting," Lady Irene told him. "Nothing to be nervous about."

"It is one thing to declaim a few stanzas in the presence of appreciative friends," Sir Julian said. "It is quite another to stand on a platform and recite Lord Dif to half the population of Nova Eboracum, most of whom couldn't care less."

"People like good, rousing verse," Lord Darcy said.

A small orchestra trotted onto the platform at one side of the ballroom, and the members began setting up their instruments. "I must be excused for a few minutes," Lady Irene said. "I believe I begin tonight's entertainment." She kissed Lord Darcy on the cheek and made her way toward the platform.

Sir Julian sighed. "Well, if she can do it, I guess I can also. I'd better find out when I am scheduled for. I hope I have a chance to speak to you later, my lord."

"We'll make a point of it," Lord Darcy said, and watched the lad hurry off toward the platform.

Lord Darcy wandered over to the buffet table and poured himself a cup of caffe, thinking speculative thoughts while the orchestra finished setting up. As he sipped the caffe he saw a familiar tubby figure in sorcerer's blue hurrying toward him.

"My lord, I've been looking for you," Master Sean said earnestly when he was close enough not to have a yell. "Have you heard the news?"

"Not a bit of it, Master Sean," Lord Darcy said.

"The Azteque treaty party has arrived," Master Sean announced. "They are camping on the other side of the river, as they refuse to cross running water after dark. Which means they'll be in New Borkum with the first ferry tomorrow morning."

"How exciting," Lord Darcy said calmly.

"I'll wager His Grace doesn't think so," Master Sean said. "He wanted this murder cleared up before the Azteques arrived. He will be very displeased."

"I hate to displease His Grace," Lord Darcy said, "but I fancy this is going to take a couple of days more to clear up. I'm sure they can appease the Azteque party for that long. That, thank heavens, is not my job."

"A couple of days more?" Master Sean said. "Does that mean that you know who did it?"

"I have a glimmer," Lord Darcy told him. "So far, it's just a glimmer, but it may brighten into a spotlight, with a little effort."

"I hope so, my lord," Master Sean said.

From the platform the prefatory bars of the Plantagenet anthem sounded, and all eyes in the room turned to the slim girl who was standing before them.

Lady Irene's voice rose in the centuries-old musical salute: "God for Joh-on—"

13

LORD DARCY WAS just emerging from the bath a little after six o'clock the next morning, when there was a discreet tapping at his bathroom door. "My lord," Mullion's lackluster voice sounded through the wooden panel, "Some gentlemen to see you, my lord."

"I don't want to see anyone at this hour," Lord Darcy called through the door. "Bid them come back after breakfast."

"They said it's important, my lord," Mullion said, sounding even more doleful. "I have put them in the den."

"Don't tell me who it is," Lord Darcy called in an annoyed voice, applying a towel to various parts of his anatomy, "let me guess."

"Yes, my lord," Mullion replied.

Lord Darcy sighed and, wrapping the towel about his middle, opened the bathroom door. "Who is it, Mullion," he asked, "and what do they want?"

"It is Major DePemmery, my lord," Mullion said, showing no curiosity as to why his master had decided not to guess, "and a native."

"A native?"

"Yes, my lord."

Lord Darcy silently resolved to give his man, Ciardi, a substantial raise when he returned to London. "Tell them I'll be along in fifteen minutes," he said, "and ask them if they'll join me for breakfast. If so, expand the breakfast to feed three and serve it in the dining room. Call me when it's ready."

"Yes, my lord," Mullion said, bowing and retreating.

Lord Darcy rapidly shaved and dressed, and went to meet his guests. Major Sir John DePemmery was a tall, lanky, clean-shaven man dressed in the fringed buckskins of the frontier. His face was stern, his eyes were sharp and intelligent, and his grip when he shook Lord Darcy's hand was firm and hard. "Pleasure," he said. "Been hoping to meet you someday. Sorry about the early hour. Just got back last night. When I heard you were here, when I heard what happened, I came right over. This here's Chief Chisolnadak of the Mulgawas. He traveled with me."

The Chief, a middle-aged, solid man in the painted and beaded winter dress of the northern tribes, had a battle-ax slung through his wide beaded belt, and a bow and quiver of arrows on his back. His face was daubed in a simple pattern with red and brown paint. "A pleasure, my lord," he said. "I believe that, if what Major DePemmery says is true, you can help me and my people."

"Chief," Lord Darcy said, shaking the large blocky hand. He thought he recognized the accent. "Brestlemere?" he asked.

"Quite right," Chief Chisolnadak told him. "Seven long years in an English boys' preparatory school, and then four at the University of Paris, to ready me to return to the forests of what you call New England. Life takes many strange twists and turns before it ends."

"Breakfast, my lord—gentlemen," Mullion announced from the study door.

"Come, messieurs," Lord Darcy said. "We will discuss our business over the breakfast table."

At the table Lord Darcy's two guests settled in to breakfast with a single-minded intentness, filling their plates with smoked fish and bacon and eggs and large hunks of the New England corn bread, and concentrating on eating their way from one side of the plate to the other. They had traveled through three hundred miles of forest in under three weeks, Major DePemmery told Lord Darcy between bites, and they had a bit of eating to catch up on.

"Reason I'm here," DePemmery said when he had pushed aside his plate and refilled his caffe cup, "Heard of the case you're on. Murder in the pyramid and all that. Went to see the Duke when I arrived, of course. Got His Lordship out of bed. Standing orders. Told him about my trip, and he told me all about Prince Ixequatle."

"I hope you don't think I've usurped your case," Lord Darcy said, looking curiously at the thin investigator, who obviously had not been to sleep at all that night.

"Nonsense!" DePemmery said. "The Duke appoints whom he likes. That's his business. Glad you're here. I'm no great shakes at fancy murder investigation anyway. Not trained to it, you know. Around here a murder is usually the result of a grudge. Someone shoots somebody, or hacks 'em up, and then flees into the woods. I track 'em and bring 'em back. Good at that."

"Damn good," Chief Chisolnadak agreed. "For an Angevin."

"What I wanted to talk to you about," DePemmery said, leaning back in his chair and fixing his hawklike gaze on Lord Darcy, "is gun smuggling."

"Yes?" Lord Darcy said.

"Someone is smuggling guns to the Western tribes," DePemmery said. "That much we've known for months. What we had to determine was how and why. Now I understand that you've pretty much discovered how."

"In a rudimentary sense," Lord Darcy told him. "The weapons were being brought in by ship and stored in a secret room in the pyramid. It was ideal for the purpose, because it had a spell on it that kept everyone away. The cleverest part of it was that, since there was *supposed* to be an avoidance spell on the pyramid, it caused no suspicions. However, as you can see, that raises several interesting questions."

"Like how long has the *Serka* been operating in New England, and who in the Duke's court is involved," Major DePemmery said.

"It would have to be someone in the administration, to fudge records and arrange to have the avoidance spell changed," Lord Darcy agreed.

"As far as the why," Major DePemmery said, "that was the purpose of my trip. To get the facts. There's been a lot of skullduggery going on to the West while we've been sitting here growing our crops and trading with the local tribes for fur and such. And not that far west, either."

"What sort of, ah, skullduggery?" Lord Darcy asked.

Major DePemmery swiveled in his chair to face Chief Chisolnadak, who cleared his throat. "Tell His Lordship the story, Chief," DePemmery said.

Chief Chisolnadak frowned. "There are men," he said, "traveling about the land of the Seneca, the land of the Iroquois, the land of the Mulgawas; men of much guile, who spread hatred and envy. They look like other Angevin trappers, hunters, that sort. But they are not. In private they call themselves Brothers of the Feather; they say they have come to free their redskin brothers from Angevin bondage. This is a bondage that our braves were not aware they suffered from until these Brothers came. But now they think they know. These men are turning tribe against tribe, and all against the Angevin Empire. For years, perhaps a decade, they have brought these wormtongue words; now they bring guns. Not many yet, but they promise many more—soon."

"Ha!" Lord Darcy said.

"Then, for the past four or five months, these Brothers have been trying to stir up the young braves to go on a crusade against the Azteques. They say an Azteque party is coming north to make a treaty with the Angevins. They say that the Azteques and the Angevins are going to divide the land between them, and murder the Seneca, the Iroquois, and the Mulgawas."

"How was this intelligence received by your braves?" Lord Darcy asked.

Chief Chisolnadak shrugged. "You know young people," he said. "They do not think with their brain, they think with the seat of their pants. They are excited. They want to go to war with everybody. And some on the Council of Elders are similarly affected. They say Azteques are ancient enemy. I tell them that none of them are that old, although some of them act like it. Now they won't talk to me."

As he discussed his tribal problems the cadence of Chief Chisolnadak's voice changed; the language was still Anglic, but the person speaking had dropped his Angevin schooling and spoke from deeper roots.

"They want to go to war with us?" Lord Darcy asked.

"No," the Chief told him. "Not this time. They want to destroy

Azteques. They want to wipe out the treaty party. And they have been promised the guns to do it."

"So they don't have the guns yet?"

"A few repeating rifles," the Chief said. "Samples. Not enough to fight a war. Maybe six or seven. With little ammunition. But they have been promised many more. Maybe two or three hundred. With many bullets."

"I see," Lord Darcy said. He leaned over his caffe cup. "What can I do?"

"Find the guns," Chief Chisolnadak said. "Keep them out of the hands of my braves."

"They were stored in the pyramid," Lord Darcy said. "They're not there any more."

"Finding out what happened to them," Chief Chisolnadak said slowly and distinctly, "is more important than finding the killer of an Azteque prince."

"If the braves of the inland tribes get these guns while the Azteque are here," Major DePemmery said, "we'll have a full-scale war on our hands. Makes no sense, but it is so."

"You should understand," Chief Chisolnadak continued, "that the guns are a symbol. My braves would go to war with the muskets we have, and with the bows we have used for centuries, with no hesitation if need arose. But these Brothers of the Feather have made promises along with their warnings. They have promised guns. If the guns arrive, then the warnings will be taken more seriously. And our braves will go on the warpath against the Azteque and the Angevin. That, as the Major says, makes little sense, but it is so."

"I believe that finding the guns, or at least who has them, and finding the killer of Prince Ixequatle are the same exercise," Lord Darcy said. "We are, even now, preparing to round up the *Serka* agents in Nova Eboracum. We are stopping and searching several suspected ships. But the guns are probably already removed. The agents in the field—your 'Brothers of the Feather'—will be harder to get in our net. You could help us, Chief, by arresting the ones that show up in your territory and sending them back here for trial."

"If you stop the guns, I will be able to do that," the Chief said. "If you cannot stop the guns, I will not be able to do that. If you cannot stop the guns, then I may no longer be Chief."

"Then I had better stop the guns," Lord Darcy said. He pushed himself away from the table and stood up. "The Azteque treaty party is arriving today, probably just about now. I want to take a look at it. Perhaps you two should get some sleep, and we will speak further this evening."

"Good idea," Major DePemmery said. "One can run indefinitely on three hours sleep a night, but thinking is another matter. And I believe some hard thinking might be in order about now. We'll be off. Speak to you later, my lord."

Lord Darcy saw his two guests out and then grabbed his cape and followed. The Sergeant of the Guard had a horse saddled and ready for him, and Lord Darcy swung up into the saddle and headed south along the Great Way.

It was a damp, foggy morning, and the horse showed the need of a little warming exercise, so Lord Darcy broke it into a trot, and then a gentle canter, until both horse and rider had worked off the chill of the early morning air. When they came into sight of the Langert Street Ferry, Lord Darcy slowed the horse back down to a walk, and watched the activities at the ferry with interest as he approached.

A company of the Duke's Household Guard foot soldiers, in spotless uniforms with gleaming metalwork, was drawn up in double rows on both sides of the street leading to the ferry. Between them a couple of platoons (or whatever the Azteques called them) of Azteque warriors had already arrived on the ferry and were standing motionless in a four-abreast column.

A large, ornate wooden platform was on the ferry now, as it pulled into its slip. In the center of the platform was a square structure that looked like a miniature temple, which Lord Darcy deduced was the traveling home of the Eternal Flame. It took a couple of minutes to tie the ferry securely to its moorings, after which twelve men, six on a side, hefted the platform to their shoulders and walked off with it.

Lord Darcy sat watching for the next hour, as the ferry made three more trips across the Arthur, and the Azteque Retinue d'Ambassade gathered itself on Saytchem Island. Several Legion officers also made the trip across; presumably from the company which had escorted the Azteques up from Mechicoe. When the Azteques were all assembled, they formed into a six-man-wide marching unit and, to the beat of a single, rather hollow-sounding drum, began to march into town. As the Azteques started up, Lord Darcy turned and rode back to the Residence.

"Ah, my lord," Master Sean said, catching up to him as he strode down the wide entrance hall. "I've been waiting here for you."

"What is it?" Lord Darcy asked, pausing in midstride. "Has something happened?"

"Not exactly, my lord. That is, not yet. His Grace the Duke wishes to see us right away."

"Ah!" Lord Darcy said. "You didn't want to face the—that is, His Grace—alone. Am I right?"

"I think that His Grace probably feels certain pressures right now, and he is going to pass the feeling on to us, his loyal servants," Master Sean said. "He did so badly want the murder of Prince Ixequatle solved before the Azteque treaty party arrived."

"Hmm," Lord Darcy said. "We'd best go speak with His Grace."

With the tubby Irish sorcerer trotting at his side, Lord Darcy strode down the corridors to the Duke's private chambers. "Tell His Grace that Lord Darcy and Master Sean are here, if you please," he told the Duke's secretary, who guarded the outer room.

Duke Charles did not look pleased to see them. From the expression on his face, it would have taken a lot to please him right then. Count de Maisvin stood by his side looking distinctly unhappy.

"Come in, my lord, Master Sean," the Duke said, waving them into the large room with the hand-painted wallpaper of hunting scenes that was his private study. "Well, the wheel has turned, time has marched along, and the Azteque Ambassade is arrived. In a little over three hours I am going to have an official meeting with a chap called Lord Chiklquetl, who is their Minister Plenipotentiary, as well as being their High Priest, and I think I know the first question he's going to ask."

"I'm sure, Your Grace—" de Maisvin began.

"He is going to ask me how it happens that a royal prince of the Azteques can get murdered here," His Grace continued firmly, "in Nova Eboracum, the site of government of New England, and we do nothing about it."

"We can't just catch a murderer to order, Your Grace," Lord Darcy said reasonably, "much as we might like to. We use logic, deduction, careful detective work, and the finest forensic magic anywhere; but we cannot perform miracles. Even Lord, um, Chiklquetl should see that."

"That is just what he will not see, my lord," the Duke said. "That is just what we do not want him to see. It is bad enough that the Prince got murdered on our territory, but I can get Lord Chiklquetl to accept that. One can't be guarded if one is going to refuse guards and go off into dark corners, no matter how efficient the guards are.

"But the Azteques do believe that we, the Angevins, perform miracles. It is that belief that enables us, with less than ten thousand people on this whole continent, to keep from being pushed back into the sea. If the million or so Azteques to the south of us did not think that we can perform miracles, we would be in severe trouble. For one thing, the Good Lord knows they'd never sign this treaty if they didn't think they had to."

"I see," Lord Darcy said. "If Your Grace would like to dismiss me from the case—"

"By God, Darcy, I didn't say that! Who would replace you? You're not going to run out on me that easily!"

"I didn't mean that, Your Grace," Lord Darcy said.

"No, no, of course you didn't." His Grace dropped into a chair. "Sit down, sit down, all of you," he said, waving his hand at them. "We've had enough of pacing about, and it doesn't seem to get us anywhere. Now let us have a bit of intelligent discussion about what we have done, and what we're going to do about all this."

Lord Darcy sat on one of the brocade-covered chairs that surrounded the central table. "We have actually made a lot of useful progress, Your Grace," he said. "I could not take my oath that it has gotten us any closer to the killer, but I believe it has. We have a mass of information, we seem to have inadvertently broken up a smuggling operation, and we're working on uncovering a nest of *Serka* agents here."

"Here?" His Grace said, looking surprised. "In Nova Eboracum? Or in the Residence itself?"

"Somewhere in the government of New England, at any rate," Lord Darcy said.

"I should pay closer attention to some of those reports I sign," the Duke said. "Count de Maisvin, what do you know about this? And why didn't you know it months ago?"

"We had some indication that something was going on," de

Maisvin said, "but until the murder—until we discovered that the pyramid was being used to store weapons—we had nothing solid to go on. Just rumors of the sort that caused Major DePemmery to go on his trip inland. It took Lord Darcy's brilliant discovery of the secret room in the pyramid for us to get some understanding of what had been going on."

"Master Sean's discovery, not mine." Lord Darcy said.

Duke Charles stared from one to the other. "The report I am going to have to write to His Majesty about this is going to make him wonder about his choice of administrators," he said. "That something like this has been going on under my very nose, and I remained unaware of it. Rumors of unrest in the interior. Rumors of modern weapons in the hands of natives. And I treated them like—rumors. A prince of the Azteques comes here, and I permit him to be murdered."

"Come now, Your Grace; there are ways of making the situation sound bad, and ways of making it sound good," de Maisvin said. "You are elucidating the negative. Looked at from the other side, there has not been a native uprising in the twelve years you've been here. Indeed, we are on good terms with most of the native tribes. Commerce has increased. The farmers are healthy, happy, and reasonably safe."

"One thing," Lord Darcy said, "the natives have not yet gotten the weapons, for some reason."

"They're probably hidden somewhere right here in New Borkum," Count de Maisvin said. "We'll have to put out double patrols, keep a close watch on all wagons out of town."

"Can we use magic?" the Duke asked, turning to Master Sean. "Some sort of divination to see where the guns are concealed?"

"Probably not, Your Grace," Master Sean replied. "Most homeowners have privacy spells put on their homes just for, ah, privacy, if you see what I mean. Of course most of them will be simple, inexpensive spells, put on by journeyman sorcerers, and I or another master could defeat such a spell with ease. But that would be unethical unless we had specific cause to suspect a given household. I would have to get an exemption from the Bishop to proceed. And, in any case, it would involve doing each of them one at a time."

"That would take far too long," His Grace said, "even if the Bishop would approve." He sighed. "Draw up a plan, de Maisvin. Put guardsmen at the ferry to check wagons crossing, and at the

Great Way bridge to the north. Notify the Coast Guard to keep Saytchem Island under watch around the clock. They may have to call up reserves to do it. Warrant the Legion to stop and search any suspicious cargos along the outer roads. Don't use Company B for that; they deserve some time off."

"Very good, Your Grace," de Maisvin said. He took out a small notebook, and made some notes. "Lord Darcy, there's a detail of men on Pyramid Island under your direct command. Do you still need them there? They would be useful elsewhere."

"A few more days," Lord Darcy said, "and then I'll release them. I want to go back to the island once again, before the Azteque dedication ceremony. That won't be for a couple of weeks, will it, Your Grace?"

"It might not be at all, if we can't come up with that young prince's killer," His Grace said.

"I shall do my best, Your Grace," Lord Darcy said.

"That has always been good enough before," Duke Charles said. "Let us hope it still is."

"Yes, Your Grace," Lord Darcy said.

14

THAT AFTERNOON LORD Darcy and Master Sean took mounts from
the guardhouse stables and rode down to the Langert Street Ferry.
"One last look inside that temple," Lord Darcy told Master Sean
as they waited by the gate for the ferry to pull in. "I have a feeling
that we have overlooked something; and I have learned to never
ignore such a feeling."

"Aye, my lord," Master Sean agreed. "We should all learn to
pay close attention to such feelings. Many's the person who has
just a touch of one of the rare Talents: clairvoyance, or clair-
audience, or precognition, or such; and it appears just often
enough to give you little hints about what's going to happen, or
what did happen, and that mostly in moments of stress. Or so it
seems."

"What you're saying, Master Sean, is that when a little voice
inside of you tells you to duck, you should duck first, and then
worry about where the voice is coming from," Lord Darcy said.

"Aye, my lord," Master Sean agreed.

The motive power for the cable that drove and guided the ferry
came from four patient oxen, huge beasts that spent their days
walking around a massive capstan in the ferry building. Lord

Darcy watched the animals walking around and around as the ferry pulled into its slip. They seemed healthy, well-fed, and content with their life. Perhaps going around in a large circle all day, pulling a wooden pole, was not boring for an ox. Lord Darcy asked the ox-driver.

"They only work half a day, you see," the ox-driver, an old, gnarled, totally bald man told Lord Darcy. "Then they go out to pasture and the other team moves in. It being real hard work, even for four oxen, turning this great machine, we can't work them more than half a day." The man spit into the straw that was spread out beneath the animals' feet. "I, contrariwise, work the whole blasted day myself, with only two half-hours off when the boy takes over for me."

"I see," Lord Darcy said.

"You can't drive an ox too far," the man said, "It don't pay. Some of them will just stop when they've had enough, and you can't cajole, or beat them into going any further. Some of them will suddenly stop in their tracks, and when you try to move them, they sort of slowly fall over. They've died, you see, with no warning. They just decided that they've had enough of this world, and want to see if the next is any better."

The man spit again. "Now, you can't tell one kind of ox from the other," he said, "and it really doesn't matter anyhow. In either case, it isn't smart to drive an ox past where it should be driven. So they only work half a day."

"Fascinating," Lord Darcy said.

"Now, a man," the man said, "he isn't smart enough to stop nor stubborn enough to die when he's had enough. So I work a full day. From six in the morning to eight at night. Sometimes ten."

"Thank you, goodman," Lord Darcy said.

"I think they eat better than I do, too," the man finished, and then turned back to his animals.

Lord Darcy looked over at Master Sean and saw that the tubby sorcerer was holding on to his saddle horn and trying not to laugh. "If I thought that my life was no better than that of the ox I was driving," Master Sean said, "I believe I might stop driving the ox."

"Don't suggest it to the driver," Lord Darcy said, smiling. "At least not until we return this evening. The oxen will have been changed, but he'll still be here."

"Aye, my lord," Master Sean agreed.

The gate came up, and the ferry unloaded the passengers it had brought across.

"You'll have to dismount, gentlemen, and lead your animals on board," the ferryman told them, swinging over to the little stand from which he collected the fares. "That'll be a quarter-bit from each of you—a sixth-bit for yourselves, and a twelfth-bit for your mount."

Lord Darcy took a silver half-sovereign from his purse and tossed it to the man. Then he swung down from his palfrey and led the beast on board.

The three-quarter-mile trip across the Arthur took slightly over a quarter-hour. On the other side they remounted and started south along the wagon road that paralleled the river. After ten minutes or so the road turned inland, and they had to continue along what was no more than a well-worn trail into the marshy land along the river bank. It was twenty minutes later before they reached the clearing that was directly opposite Pyramid Island.

There was a ring of tents around the clearing, and a stone fireplace had been built at the inland end. Some few strands of early grass grew around most of the area, but the center, which domed up slightly, was bald and bare. A circle of young, first-growth trees surrounded the area, showing that there had been a fairly severe fire within living memory.

A Corporal of the guard and three guardsmen were in the temporary camp when Lord Darcy and Master Sean arrived. They were doing housekeeping chores, awaiting the arrival of the cutter that would bring their evening meals. Alerted by the sound of approaching hoofbeats, they greeted the riders, with rifles at the ready. As soon as they recognized the investigator and his tubby assistant, they lowered their weapons.

"My lord, Master," the Corporal said, grounding his rifle and saluting. "Sorry for that greeting, but we didn't expect you."

"Just paying an informal visit to the pyramid, Corporal," Lord Darcy said, "and I thought I'd come the back way. Didn't mean to surprise you. Has anything happened to make you so, ah, cautious?"

"Nothing you can rightly put your finger on, my lord," the Corporal said. "Some of the men thought they heard noises at night—but it could have been bear, or raccoon, or overly active imaginations. But Chief Karlus said there was no point in taking

chances, whatever it is, so he has issued us these rifles and twenty
rounds each for the rest of our stay."

"Quite right, Corporal," Lord Darcy agreed. "Would you have
one of your men row us out to the island? Master Sean and I wish
to go pyramid-climbing again."

"Very good, my lord," the Corporal said.

The back side of the pyramid, Lord Darcy noted as they were
rowed across, looked, if anything, more foreboding than the front.
There was nothing of human scale from this view; the temples on
top were meaningless boxes, the stairs were on the other side, and
the steps of the pyramid itself, each over three feet high and under
six inches deep, were not meant to be negotiated by any earthly
creature.

After landing at the makeshift dock, Lord Darcy and Master
Sean walked around the massive pyramid to the front. They began
slowly climbing the stone stairway, pausing every few feet for
Lord Darcy to look around and prod at the quiescent stones.
Occasionally he would bend over and closely examine one bit of
rock, or put his ear to the stone and listen for a few seconds.

"You think it's going to talk to you, my lord?" Master Sean
asked, watching Lord Darcy's curious behavior.

"Not at all, Master Sean," Lord Darcy replied. "I think this
pyramid has done all its talking for quite a while; your ingenious
magical techniques have drawn it out far more than it intended to
be drawn. I am merely, to speak metaphorically, listening for such
incidental noises as I might hear."

"And have you heard any?" Master Sean asked. In a world
where magic works, metaphor is taken quite seriously. Sometimes
the analogue represents the object in a very physical way.

"Not a sound," Lord Darcy admitted. They continued up to the
top of the pyramid.

Lord Darcy stood in front of the temple of Huitsilopochtli and
stared out at the great bay before him. "Look," he said, pointing
at a two-masted barque anchored in midbay. "There's the *Siby*
Still waiting for the command to discharge her illicit cargo."

Master Sean peered out at the ship. "It hasn't unloaded yet?"

"We think not," Lord Darcy said. "It moved away from its pier
shortly after Lady Irene brought it the message, and moored where
you see it. The captain must be awaiting instructions to unload
but they haven't come yet."

"Why don't you apprehend him?" Master Sean asked.

"We're keeping him under observation instead," Lord Darcy said. "Powerful telescopes are watching at all times. We want to see who goes aboard. If no one makes contact by tomorrow night, the Coast Guard will bring it in."

Lord Darcy turned away from the view and focused his attention on the work at hand. Rather than going into either temple, he slowly worked his way around the outside of the two and the narrow space between them, part of the time on his hands and knees, part of the time flat on his stomach, examining every inch of the stone surface.

Master Sean stood with his arms folded and watched Lord Darcy crawling about. The sight satisfied him and made him feel good. Lord Darcy was working as though he had hold of something; Master Sean could recognize the signs. And when Lord Darcy had hold of something, however tenuous, he could usually squeeze it into revealing the elusive truth.

"Come here, Master Sean," Lord Darcy called about twenty minutes later. He was now at the back of the pyramid, about three stones down from the top.

"Yes, my lord?" Master Sean asked, peering over the edge at him.

"There's a small stain on the corner of this stone," Lord Darcy said. "Would you give it a similarity test, if you can manage it."

"Certainly, my lord," Master Sean said, pulling open his symbol-decorated carpetbag. "What shall I test for, my lord—blood?"

"Possibly," Lord Darcy said. "But much more probably the same oil that we found in the hidden room—the oil the weapons were packed in."

"Aye, my lord," Master Sean said. "I have saved a small sample of it for testing purposes. It will take me but a minute."

Master Sean prepared himself for the test and then, standing at the edge of the platform and keeping his body straight, slowly leaned forward. His body went through an arc of a hundred and thirty degrees before he ended up, upside down, facing the suspected spot. He went to work.

"It is the same sort of oil, my lord," he said, swinging back to an upright position.

"Good," Lord Darcy said. "I assumed it was, but one cannot construct a logical chain on assumptions. Now the chain is complete."

"You know who the murderer is?" Master Sean asked.

"For some time I have known who the murderer is," Lord Darcy said. "The difficulty was in proving it. Now I believe I can do that."

"Through that spot of oil?"

"No. That was merely confirmation. Come, let us return to the Residence. I think we are going to have a busy day tomorrow."

15

"YOU CAN GO now, Mullion," Lord Darcy said, sitting at his desk in the study after dinner, "I'll look after myself for the rest of the evening."

"Yes, Your Lordship," said the incurious Mullion.

Ten minutes later Mullion appeared at the study door. "Good night, Your Lordship. I've left the dishes stacked."

"Good night, Mullion. Of course you have." Lord Darcy heard the front door open and close, and he got up to make sure that his temporary man had gone in the direction he seemed to take. Not that he suspected Mullion, but a possibility eliminated is a risk not taken.

After assuring himself that he was indeed alone in the apartment, Lord Darcy returned to his desk and the reports he had been going over.

Three hours later the doorbell tinkled. Lord Darcy glanced at the clock and saw that it was almost eleven, which was earlier than he expected his appointment. He rose and went to the door.

Lady Irene pushed by him into the apartment. "I trust I'm not disturbing you, my lord. I must apologize for springing myself upon you so late," she said.

"Don't apologize," Lord Darcy said, closing the door behind him and showing her into the study., "I'm going over details I have gone over a dozen times before, like a carpenter measuring and remeasuring the same piece of wood. Come, Cousin Irene, distract me. Tell me funny stories of our aunt Bertha." He took her hand. "May I offer you some wine?"

"No, nothing, thank you." She closed the study door behind her.

"I must speak with you," she whispered. "Is this room safe?"

"Safe?"

"Can we be overheard?"

"Not possibly," Lord Darcy said, noting that the girl was trembling slightly. "The room has been checked and secured by Master Sean. It is part of our routine when we are, ah, away from home. And, curiously, he went over it again earlier today. But just to be sure—" Lord Darcy went to the table and raised the lid of a small egg-shaped case that rested on a gold quadripod. The crystal egg inside glowed with an undisturbed green light. "We are alone," he said, "And unobserved."

"Good," she said, but she did not raise her voice. "Come sit with me on the couch.. Do not let go of my hand."

Lord Darcy allowed himself to be pulled to a seat on the couch. "What is it?" he asked. "What can I do?"

"I'm to take you to bed tonight," Lady Irene told him softly, staring intently into his eyes.

"I'm complimented," Lord Darcy said carefully. "I could even say I'm delighted. But that's an odd way for you to phrase it."

"Yes," she said. "I have been instructed to make love to you."

"Instructed?"

"And then to kill you," she finished.

Lord Darcy nodded without changing his expression. "I see," he said. "Somehow the suggestion sounds a trifle less appealing than it did a moment ago. The *Serka*?"

"I received the order a few hours ago," she said. "I don't know what to do!"

"How did the order come?" Lord Darcy asked. "And how are you to do the job?"

"In an envelope under my door," she said. "On a sheet of read-once paper, which disintegrated as I finished reading it. There was also—this." She took from her purse a small paper twist, barely large enough to hold a caffe bean. "I am to put the powder inside in your drink before we retire to the bedroom. You will then die of exertion, or so it will seem, during the course of our, um, endeavors."

"Good God!" Lord Darcy said. "What a horrible thing for you. Have you ever been called to perform such a service before?"

"I imagine it is even more horrible for the victim," Lady Irene said. "No, no—so far, I have never been involved in a like act, although I understand it is a common method of assassination in the *Serka*, when they can manage it."

"I can see why," Lord Darcy said. "In some ways, it is almost perfect. It is the sort of accident that is almost always hushed up. Although several rumors involving the demise of well-known men come to mind. I think some careful checking of a few natural-death cases is in order."

"My problem," Lady Irene said in an earnest murmur, "is that if I fail to kill you, the *Serka* will, most assuredly, kill me. You are a wise and clever man; help me find a way out of this dilemma."

"I see what you mean," Lord Darcy said. "The interesting question is: Why would they suddenly decide to kill me?"

"The note didn't say," Lady Irene told him. "I don't think I like this game much anymore."

"And why do they think that we are so attracted to each other that I would not find it striking unusual for you to show up in my bedroom?"

"I imagine that someone observed us together at the anniversary fete and made a not-unnatural conclusion from the way we were looking at each other."

"Not unnatural, eh?" Lord Darcy said, smiling.

"Not at all unnatural," Lady Irene assured him.

"I'm glad of that. Now, let us think our way out of this perplexity. How can you kill me without my suffering any ill effects from the deed?"

"Or how can I not kill you without *my* suffering any ill effects from the deed?" Lady Irene suggested.

"No," Lord Darcy said thoughtfully. "What with one thing and another, I think it would probably be best if you killed me."

"My lord?"

"There is one reason why the need to do away with me might have just arisen. If so, I can respond best by allowing myself to be killed."

Lady Irene put her hand against his shoulder. "But my lord Darcy—"

Lord Darcy took the hand into his own. "Oh, I intend to die in name only, I assure you," he said "Come now, this should be quite interesting. Let me see—"

The doorbell sounded again, and Lord Darcy excused himself and went to answer it. When he returned to the study he was accompanied by a handsome, rugged-looking officer of the Imperial Legion. "Lady Irene Eagleson," Lord Darcy said, "allow me to present Colonel Ivor Hesparsyn of the Duke's Own. He has just returned from escorting the Azteque treaty party from Mechicoe."

The two politely acknowledged each other, but each of them flashed Lord Darcy a strange look. His Lordship laughed. "You each think me insane," he said. "Each of you has come to see me on most secret business, and is wondering why I would welcome the other at a time like this. Well, my friends, we are going to help each other."

"Whatever you say, my lord," Colonel Hesparsyn said, but it was clear he was merely being polite. Lord Darcy returned to the couch with Lady Irene, and the Colonel lowered himself into a straight-back chair opposite them.

"Colonel, I requested your aid in the coming events because, as you and your men have been gone for the past three months, you couldn't possibly be involved in some of the events that have happened since you left," Lord Darcy said. "And, looking at your record, I see that you're trustworthy, intelligent, loyal, and competent to handle any job that comes up. Well, take my word for it, Lady Irene is, as well. And she has just provided the last link in the chain of evidence."

"I have?" Lady Irene asked.

"Indeed," Lord Darcy said. "Tell Colonel Hesparsyn why you came to my room tonight."

Lady Irene blushed, a fact which surprised her as much as it did Lord Darcy. Then she complied, telling clearly and concisely who she was, and what she had been ordered to do.

"Well I'll be damned!" the Colonel said when she finished. "Excuse the profanity, my lady."

"People fight their wars in different ways," Lord Darcy remarked.

"That's a fact," Colonel Hesparsyn said. "I think you're a very brave young lady. But what are you going to do about this? We could take Lady Irene away someplace where she would be safe. If I put my men to guarding her, I think we can keep her safe regardless of who this villain is."

"I don't think we have to do that, Colonel," Lord Darcy said.

"But thank you very much for the offer," Lady Irene told the Colonel. "I may take you up on it sometime. The thing is, Lord Darcy has decided that the best thing would be for him to die."

"He—you—my lord?" Colonel Hesparsyn was at a loss for words.

"I assure you I expect to live through my death," Lord Darcy said. "But the chief of the local *Serka* wants me dead for a reason. I think I know what that reason is, and it would be best to allow it to go forward."

"I'm willing to be convinced," the Colonel said. "Besides, as Lord Guiliam Rottsler, the nineteenth-century philosopher, wrote: 'Is not each man's death strictly his own affair?' "

"Did he?" Lord Darcy asked. "It's an affair that many of us would as soon never consummate. But I go gladly to mine—this time. Lady Irene, would you sneak through the corridors and bring Master Sean back, please? Tell him to use the Tarnhelm Effect in returning, and come invisibly to these chambers. In the meantime, Colonel Hesparsyn and I have a bit of strategy to discuss."

"I will, my lord," Lady Irene said. "But I hope you know what you're doing."

"So do I," Lord Darcy said.

Master Sean O Lochlainn looked down at the body of his friend and chief, Lord Darcy, and sighed. "A difficult job at best," he said. "But this should suffice." He folded the arms across the chest.

Lord Darcy lay on his own bed, dressed in a bathrobe and slippers, his eyes closed, his breathing stopped, his heart stopped. The only difference between the magically induced cataleptic state he was in and true death was that, for the next twelve hours or so, Master Sean could bring him back to life. If anyone but Master Sean tried, or if Master Sean waited longer then twelve hours, Lord Darcy's chances of being restored were vanishingly slim.

"I think I'd better go," Colonel Hesparsyn said. "I have no explainable reason to be here." He shook Master Sean's hand. "If

I hadn't seen it— I don't think I'll believe it until I see Lord Darcy up again."

Master Sean looked down at the body. "Truthfully," he said, "neither will I. This is going to be a very long day for me." He turned to Lady Irene. "I, also, will leave, my lady. Wait about half an hour, and then come find me and tell me you just realized His Lordship is dead. *Me*, you understand. Nobody else. If anyone interrupts you, make sure you get to me before anyone else has a chance to reach the body. It's very important."

"I understand that, Master Sean," Lady Irene said.

"You sure you can do it? Staying here for that half hour, I mean."

"I'll have to," she said. "It won't be pleasant." She also took Master Sean's hand. "Take care of yourself," she said. "Don't let anything happen to you today."

Father Adamsus walked slowly out of Lord Darcy's bedroom looking faintly disturbed. He kissed the heavy gold cross he carried and put it back into its black leather case. As though seeking the answer to a puzzling question, he went down the hall and turned into the parlor, where the New England friends of Lord Darcy were gathering as word spread of his untimely death.

"Can we go in now, Father?" Duke Charles asked, rising from the dark wood chair with the red velvet cushion on which he had been waiting. The whole room was done in dark woods and red velvet, which was why Lord Darcy had not used it; he found the combination depressing.

"What?" Father Adamsus said, startled out of his preoccupation by the question.

"I asked if we could go in now," the Duke repeated patiently.

"Yes, certainly," Father Adamsus said. "I've done everything I can for him."

As Duke Charles and Count de Maisvin left for the bedroom to pay their last respects, Father Adamsus sought out Master Sean where he sat quietly in a corner. "Did you notice, Master Sean," he said in a low voice, "there is a strange—feel—to that room, to that body. It doesn't feel right, somehow."

"Ah, yes, Father Adamsus," Master Sean said. "You, being a sensitive, would notice that sort of thing. Yes, Father, I was aware of it. As a matter of fact, it's the result of one of the spells I used on the body. I'll explain it all to you in the near future, if you like."

"Ah?" the good Father said. "You relieve my mind. If it's something you've done, then I'm sure it's for the best. Although this is still an incredible shock. I think I'd best go and sit with Lady Irene and see if I can comfort her. The psychic shock to her must be severe if, ah, Lord Darcy's death was as I have heard it."

"I think she could indeed use some comforting, Father," Master Sean agreed.

16

THE NIGHT WAS cold and dark, and the sliver of moon that was visible did little to light the land below. The squat lugger, sailing without running lights, rounded the corner of Pyramid Island and cautiously approached the beach on the mainland to the south. It anchored a few yards offshore, in water no more than a few feet deep, and a dozen barefoot men carrying folding spades dropped off the side and crept silently ashore. Ahead of them was the clearing where Chief Karlus and his men had camped until they were called away that afternoon.

The men reached the edge of the clearing and waited, feeling strongly that they should not go on. As they had been instructed to wait at that spot, the feeling mattered little. A minute later another man dressed all in black and with, even in that darkness, a black mask covering his face, walked into the clearing and put down a small bundle he carried. An occasional dull light flickered in front of him as he worked a spell over the bare ground, and the slight breeze carried the murmur of his words back to the waiting men.

The feeling that they should not enter the clearing dissipated and the man in black beckoned them on. They followed his gestured commands to dig *here* and *here*, and busied themselves efficiently and silently moving earth.

A foot under the hard-packed earth, the diggers came to wooden hatches that pulled off to reveal two large underground rooms filled with crates of Dumberly-FitzHugh repeating rifles and boxes of ammunition. They dropped their spades and began hefting the heavy crates to the surface.

Suddenly it was light. In a split second the night vanished, the protective dark was gone, and in its place the blazing light of a magical sun lit up the clearing and its secret diggers.

"Stand where you are!" a powerful, commanding voice ordered from within the surrounding brush. "You are completely surrounded. Anyone offering resistance will be shot where he stands!"

The men gazed around in astonishment. From the surrounding woods appeared a line of Imperial Legionnaires, each carrying at the ready one of the O'Sullivan multiple-fire shotguns that the Legion used for close work.

Some of the men glanced back toward the bay, but when they did, they saw that an Imperial Coast Guard cutter had somehow pulled alongside the lugger, and the men left aboard were standing on the foredeck with their arms raised very high.

The men in the clearing stood up slowly and raised their hands. There was nothing else they could do. The fighting seemed to be over before it had begun.

"Watch it now—there he goes! Don't let him get away!" Master Sean O Lochlainn stepped out from between the line of Legionnaires, star-tipped wand at the ready, and gestured toward the beach. "He's under a cloak of invisibility!" he yelled. "Their master—the man in black. A squad of you head for the beach while I neutralize the spell!"

Master Sean's star-tipped wand traced an intricate pattern in the air, and his voice, unexpectedly deep and sonorous, boomed across the clearing. A black-clad man popped into view, racing toward the bay. The man turned and gestured, and disappeared again, as a crack of lightning marked the clash of the two powerful spells.

Lord John Quetzal strode into view from the far end of the beach. Arms upraised, he wielded a serpent-headed wand in his left hand and a thin, silver-bladed sword in his right. He spat out two sharp words, and the beach turned dark, as though the magical light had gone out just there and nowhere else. But in the dark, the invisible man suddenly became visible, glowing with an eerie light as he raced toward the water.

The man in black stopped his flight and turned, pulling from his cloak a stubby wand tipped with a two-headed hawk. He raised it and gestured toward Lord John.

A great quiet fell over the earth, and it felt, to those who were watching, as though the two antagonists were far larger than they were, as though they somehow took up half of the night sky, and their shadows covered the world. The man in black became a huge hawk, who soared into the sky and turned to come screaming down on the giant figure that was Master Lord John Quetzal. Lord John raised his silver sword and held it ready as the hawk swooped.

What the men frozen in place watching this battle saw—a giant hawk glowing with unnatural light, a giant man gleaming in silver like his sword—was the visual symbol for the magical reality of the battle. Master Sean, watching from the edge of the forest, saw it as quite something else. He was powerless to interfere, since any spells he cast now would endanger Lord John as much as the magician in black. But he wove his spells carefully as he watched, to ensure that if Lord John faltered, he could take over and defeat this powerful adversary.

But he knew that if Lord John faltered, Master Sean's spells would do his courageous student no good. In that second he would be dead. Master Sean could avenge but not save the young Mechicain magician.

The hawk reached Lord John, and man and bird met with a shattering blow that sounded like a mighty peal of thunder and shook the surrounding earth. In Nova Eboracum, four miles away, people awakened and peered out their windows and wondered at the noise.

The two figures separated, and the bird fluttered to the ground some distance from Lord John. It could be seen now that the silver sword in Lord John's right hand was broken. He flung it away.

Master Sean knew that because of the weave of power, Lord John could not change hands with his serpent wand, and was now forced to wield it with his left hand—as the giant hawk leapt across the short distance between them to renew the attack.

The serpent wand enlarged, and became the serpent, which rose to meet the attack and wrapped itself in mighty coils around the bird.

With beak and talon, the bird ripped at the enveloping snake, but it was slowly beaten down—choked—strangled—enveloped in the constricting coils of the serpent; and it fell to the ground—

—as Master Sean remembered that Lord John Quetzal was *left-handed*!

The perspective changed: The snake and the bird receded into the depths of whatever dimension they had emerged from, and the vision became that of two men, each sitting on the beach, about ten yards apart, breathing heavily and glaring at each other.

Each of the two fighters, a powerful magician, was a match for the other, and the furious psychic battle that had just been waged left them both exhausted and neither a winner.

But Master Sean quickly stepped into the breach, and muttered the words of power that would compel his own spells into being.

The man in black threw up a previously prepared warding spell as Master Sean's magic began its weave about him. The spell could not last more than a few seconds, but in that short time—

—the man in black drew a .40 caliber MacGregor pistol from beneath his cloak and blew his brains out.

"Well, I'll be—" Master Sean said.

Lord Darcy stepped up to him. "You did what you could, Master Sean," he said. "Nobody could have prevented this. And perhaps it is better this way. You'd better go see to Lord John; the lad may need your help."

"Nay, he's fine," Master Sean said. "And a fine job he just did, too." But nonetheless he hurried down to the beach, as the Legionnaires began rounding up the surviving henchmen of the man in black.

17

"I HAVE HAD many shocks in my lifetime," Duke Charles said, "But I'll match the past few days against any of them. First, Lord Darcy dies, and then he comes back to life; and now this!" He turned to the investigator. "You are going to have to explain, Lord Darcy. I shall have to file a report to His Majesty, and I can't put in 'and Lord Darcy waved his hand, and all was light.' I must have some idea of where the light came from."

It was the next evening, and Duke Charles had waited patiently all day, while the principals of last night's action had gotten a few hours sleep—at his insistence—before reporting to him. But he was not prepared to wait any longer.

They were gathered around the great table in the Duke's private dining room, all who were intimately involved in the affair: Lord Darcy, Master Sean, Lord John, Father Adamsus, Lady Irene, and the Duke himself.

"The power of the *Serka* is broken in New England, at least for now," Duke Charles said. "And I assure you that I'll see that it has no chance to rebuild. We have rounded up everyone of importance, based on the evidence you collected and the information from Lady Irene. Those who were not caught at the gun cache were arrested quietly in their homes. We will be some time questioning them. By the time we're finished, with the aid of a few arcane spells that our inquisitor uses, we'll know as much about the *Serka*'s New England operations as they do. I fear I have been lax, but I shall not be so again."

"Don't blame yourself," Lord Darcy said. "It has been building for years, and it was most cleverly done."

"But why were those two poor lads murdered in the temple?" Father Adamsus asked, "and why were their hearts ripped out?"

"I think we must assume," Lord Darcy said, "that the second victim, the one found in the secret room, was an Azteque agent. He had discovered something about the hidden guns, and brought the Prince out to see it for himself. That's the only reason I can think of that an Azteque prince would be in a secret room with an apparent Mohawk. We can get that verified by Lord Lloriquhali, who should recognize him. But, at any rate, somehow they discovered the secret room, and they were murdered for it."

"But why was the body of the Prince put in the temple, if he was murdered below?" Father Adamsus asked.

"Well, Father," Lord Darcy said, "it was to achieve just what was achieved: Nobody looked for a secret room. The killer couldn't know that the Prince had told no one of his impending trip to the pyramid. If he had disappeared while supposedly at the pyramid, then a search would have been conducted for him, which would have included a magical investigation of the pyramid itself—which probably would have uncovered the secret room before the smugglers had a chance to clear it out. Therefore they couldn't leave the Prince's body in the room, and they couldn't dispose of it in any way, because a search would still uncover the secret room, even if it failed to turn up the body. But leaving it on the altar certainly diverted everybody's attention from a possible secret room within the pyramid."

"That's so," the Duke agreed.

"And if anyone missed the other victim, why all the better; it would leave the clear implication that *he* had killed the Prince, and then fled from his crime."

"Then the ripping of the victim's heart out was just to add verisimilitude to our finding the Prince's body on the altar?" Duke Charles asked.

"On the contrary, Your Grace," Lord Darcy said. "The removal of the victim's heart was the only truly essential act aside from the murder itself. Had I understood that, I would have solved the case much earlier."

"It was essential?" Lord John asked, sounding puzzled. "The killer *had* to do it?"

"That is so," Lord Darcy said. "To understand the crime, you must understand that."

"If you wish us to understand, my lord," the Duke said crossly, "then you must explain."

"Of course, Your Grace," Lord Darcy said. "Picture the scene. The murderer is in the secret room. He is startled by the sound of footsteps coming down the staircase. Prince Ixequatle's companion must have observed the opening of the concealed door, and learned how to do it. Perhaps he was in hiding. Perhaps he was undercover, as one of them; we may never know."

"The missing hearts, my lord," the Duke reminded him.

"Of course. The murderer is confronted by the Azteque prince, who recognizes him. His identity and his secret are at risk all at once. Even though he is a master magician—as events turn out—he has no self-protection spells ready. Besides, using magic would leave traces that another master could detect. So he pulls his sidearm and puts a bullet into the chest of the Prince and his companion. He is an expert shot, and they each die instantly."

"And then?" It was Lady Irene.

"And then he takes an obsidian-bladed knife—probably from the Prince's belt—and cuts his victims' hearts out. He has to; since the Prince's body must be found, he has no choice."

"Aye, my lord, of course!" Master Sean said, smacking his right fist into his left palm, "The MacGregor!"

"That's it exactly, Master Sean," Lord Darcy agreed. "Our killer, the secret head of the *Serka* in New England, the secret master magician, the brilliant Count Maximilian de Maisvin, confidant of the Duke, is a holder of the King's MacGregor. He could not allow those bullets to be found. He carried what was most probably the only .40 caliber handgun in all of New England—the King's own presentation weapon. When the chirurgeon removed the bullet, he would instantly be found out."

"Well, I'll be—" the Duke said. "He *had* to cut out the hearts! Indeed he did! Why, it's obvious, now that you've pointed it out."

"He must have been a double agent, planted many years ago," Lord Darcy said. "He clearly received his magical education and

is training in espionage in Poland before he came here. We will
ave to find out where the title 'Count de Maisvin' came from, but
is almost certainly not his original name."

"He took the Oath of Loyalty," the Duke said, "He must have
sed one of his magical tricks to evade it."

"I don't think so, Your Grace," Lord Darcy said. "He used his
agical abilities to alter the spells protecting the pyramid, but I
on't think he could affect the loyalty oath."

"He could not, my lord," Master Sean stated positively.

"Then—"

"It was the wording of the oath that protected him," Lord Darcy
id. "Remember, de Maisvin was a spy, not a traitor. When he
vore loyalty to his sovereign, he meant it. His sovereign was
asimir the Ninth. If I were you, I would redo the oath, and be a
t more specific."

"I see," His Grace said thoughtfully.

"When did you suspect him?" Lady Irene asked.

"My attention was drawn to him early. He seemed too involved
the investigation for someone who was not an investigator."

"He said he wanted to help—" His Grace said.

"I'm sure he did, Your Grace," Lord Darcy agreed.

"But he was with us when we discovered the body," Father
lamsus said. "How could he—"

"The killing happened that morning," Lord Darcy said,
everal hours before you arrived. De Maisvin was probably
eing to the removal of the last of the weapons. The Prince and
s companion arrived, and were killed. De Maisvin cut out their
arts, placed the Prince on the altar stone, and then he and his
nfedcrates rowed back to the mainland with the last of the
uggled weapons. While his minions concealed the weapons in
e clearing, de Maisvin rode to the Langert Street Ferry and
ossed just in time to meet you at the cutter and head back to the
and for the exorcism ceremony."

Father Adamsus shook his head. "It certainly was fortuitous
t you came to New England at this time," he said. "The
rkings of the Lord are mysterious."

"They are," Lord Darcy agreed. "Lady Irene gave me the two
es that made me look most closely at the idea of de Maisvin
ng the killer."

"I did?" Lady Irene asked.

"Just so," Lord Darcy said. "The first was when you told me

that the head of the *Serka* had not asked you to find out how th
investigation was going, despite the fact that your, ah, cousin, wa
heading it. That could only be because he had a very good sourc
of information himself; and very few men answered that descrip
tion. The second was when you were ordered to kill me."

"What did that tell you?" the Duke asked. "That you wer
getting too close?"

"No," Lord Darcy said. "As far as de Maisvin knew, I wasn
close at all. It was because I wouldn't withdraw the guards fro
the temple, and incidentally the clearing where they wer
camping—right over forty cases of smuggled automatic rifles. A
de Maisvin had asked me to do earlier that day. And as de Maisvi
could do on his own authority once I was dead. I had a hint of th
when I visited the area and noticed that the guards had set up the
tents all around the perimeter of the clearing, and had left th
center clear. There was a mild avoidance spell on the center of th
clearing, beneath which the guns were concealed. De Maisvin ha
to get those guns out and to his restless natives before the Aztequ
Retinue left for home."

Lady Irene stood up. "This has all been very interesting," sh
said. "I believe there is an ancient Chinese curse: 'May you liv
in interesting times.'" She turned to Lord Darcy. "I'm please
my lord, that you are still alive," she said. "Very pleased–
Cousin. Let us speak of it later."

"I shall look forward to it, my lady," Lord Darcy told her.

"Well, Lord Darcy, I, for one, am glad that you and Mast
Sean happened to visit us when you did," Duke Charles said. "
it wasn't for the two of you, His Majesty's New England Territo
would have been endangered. The King shall read of my hig
regard for each of you, in my report."

"Thank you, Your Grace," Lord Darcy said.

"Only did my job, Your Grace," Master Sean said, looki
embarrassed.

18

"WE ARE GLAD you are back with Us, my lord," King John said, in the small, private interview chamber on the fifth floor of the private quarter of Winchester Palace. "It causes unrest among the criminal population of England and France when they know you're away, and forces Our constabulary to work long hours to prove that crimes can still be detected and solved in your absence."

Lord Darcy chuckled. "Thank you, Your Majesty," he said. "I was a bit slow on that one, but de Maisvin had me fooled for a while. A very likable man."

"He had us all fooled," the King said. "To think that he was one of the sixty-four men who carry the MacGregor .40 caliber. For exemplary service in the Germanys. We'll have to have someone go over those records and see just how he was serving then, and how successful he was at it."

"Incidentally, Your Majesty, the Gemini Secret—"

"Yes?" The King said.

"Your Majesty should tell Lord Peter to be more subtle. When I meet a lad at the Residence in Nova Eboracum who has a twin brother here at the Palace, and I remember the natural telepathic affinity of identical twins; really, Your Majesty— Gemini?"

"We see your point," the King said. "Let Us hope, my lord, that few others are as perceptive. Now, is there anything We can do for you, my lord, in return for the inconvenience and haste with which you were thrust into this? And as a reward for your further service to the Empire?"

Lord Darcy thought for a minute. "Not for me, Your Majesty," he said finally. "But, there is something."

"Yes? Don't make Us fish it out of you, my lord. What is it? As long as it doesn't dig too deeply into the privy purse, it's yours."

"Not mine, Your Majesty," Lord Darcy said. "I was just thinking—isn't it about time that Master Sean received some tangible recognition for his services to the Crown?"

"We should say so, my lord," the King agreed. "What did you have in mind, a purse of gold? A small cottage? What could a magician use?"

"I was thinking, Your Majesty, of a knighthood."

"Well!" the King said. "A good idea, my lord. He shall be on the next honors list. We shall make him a Knight—no, a Knight-Commander of the Golden Leopard. Master Sir Sean O Lochlainn, K.C.G.L. It rolls off the tongue, doesn't it? We like it, my lord. We like it!"

"So do I, Your Majesty," Lord Darcy said. "So do I."